LAST FERRY HOME

KENT HARRINGTON

The following is a work of fiction. Names, characters, places, events and incidents are either the product of the author's imagination or used in an entirely fictitious manner. Any resemblance to actual persons, living or dead, is entirely coincidental.

Cover and jacket design by Mimi Bark

Hardcover ISBN: 978-1-947993-09-9
Trade paperback ISBN: 978-1-943818-86-0
eISBN: 978-1-947993-12-9
Library of Congress Catalog Number: 2018932925

First hardcover and trade paperback publication:
March 2018 by Polis Books LLC
1201 Hudson Street
Hoboken, NJ 07030
www.PolisBooks.com

LAST FERRY HOME

Also by Kent Harrington

Dia de los Muertos
The Rat Machine
Dark Ride
The Tattooed Muse
The American Boys
The Good Physician
Red Jungle

"Might I suggest you prepare for a difficult journey?"
-The Piano

COUNTY OF SAN FRANCISCO – SFPD
HOMICIDE DIVISION SUPPLEMENTAL REPORT

DATE: APRIL 22, 2015 FILE NO: 999-05137-4251-011
CRIME:
MURDER - 187 P.C.

ACTION:
ACTIVE INVESTIGATION CONDUCTED/SCENE
PROCESSED AND DOCUMENTED/EVIDENCE HELD
FOLLOW UP INVESTIGATION
POST MORTEM EXAMINATIONS

C.C. #3006-05119

VICTIMS:
RISHI CHAUNDHRY
BHARTI KUMAR

DAY: (TIME OF DISCOVERY)
04-18-2015 (WEDNESDAY)
19:20 HOUR

LOCATION:
2800 BLOCK BROADWAY
SAN FRANCISCO CALIFORNIA XXXXX

SUSPECT: UNKNOWN
EVIDENCE HELD – INVESTIGATION ONGOING

CHAPTER 1

Five Month before the Murders

October. He could smell her perfume as he passed her in the doorway. She was an attractive, petite woman with keen expressions, still slightly girlish. He'd thought when they first met that she looked bookish but sexy, the kind of young woman the young professor would fall for in a movie. The detective liked her, but with reservations, a hallmark of their Facebook generation. He was only a few years older than she, but felt much older.

It was just past noon when he walked into Dr. Maya Schneider's office in San Francisco, ten minutes late for his appointment.

"Doctor," Detective Michael O'Higgins said, pensive and slightly agitated. He'd been forced to hurry, driving from San Rafael in the fast lane, having decided to make his appointment at the very last moment. The detective wanted to sound normal, even bright. He was aiming for his psychiatrist to refill his Valium proscription, and didn't want to set off any false alarms.

Dr. Schneider opened the door to her inner office, her sanctum sanctorum, smiling as she always did, signaling a professional affability that he thought she genuinely felt. She was wearing black pants and a simple white blouse, her usual attire. She was attractive: Sephardic-looking, almost exotic, her eyes brown with a searching quality he liked.

When he got to his appointments early, he would sit in Schneider's small waiting room. Without meaning to, he could eavesdrop on her calls on the other side of the door. They were calls to pharmacies or to colleagues. He learnt, overhearing her telephone conversations, she was teaching psychiatry at UCSF, which had impressed him. Once he'd heard her talking to someone he suspected was her boyfriend, because her tone was entirely different: coquettish.

The doctor wore no wedding ring and was not more than thirty years old, if that. Because they were so close in age, they had their generation's key bonds: cell phones, dating sites, Facebook selfies, thongs, Bezos drones, and the war in Iraq — where O'Higgins had served in the Marine Corps, having survived the battle of Fallujah.

On a few occasions a patient would leave her office and pass him in the waiting room, but not often. He'd guessed her practice was just starting, and she had only a few patients. The patients he did see were mostly up-and-coming young women, much like the doctor herself.

She was sitting now directly across from him. The doctor gave him an obvious look of appraisal: Is the patient unkempt? Is the patient sullen? Are his shoelaces tied? Are his eyes red from drugs? She glanced at her notebook, then back to him. Her notebook was similar to the one he'd kept in Iraq. His had included the names of the dead and the maimed he'd commanded.

She broke the ice. "How are you today, Michael?"

"I almost didn't make it," he said. "Tell me doctor, why do fools fall in love? Tell me why . . . sorry, I heard the song on the way here. But it's a good question, right?"

"Because that's what people do, Michael," she said, and smiled. "You're here, and not at the Giants' game. That's a start." She had a sense of fun. He liked that about her. Self-assured, but not uptight. She is a good person.

"Yes." He looked around the room, not wanting to engage, not feeling like it. His eyes landed on a block print of geese flying in winter. He liked the print. He'd liked to hunt when he was younger, before he'd shot at real live people in Iraq and seen them fall into the dirt gasping in pain, afraid.

His father used to take him duck hunting. Sitting in the ice cold, rain-wet blind out in the Central Valley had been fun, exciting. The moment they saw the ducks above them was always exhilarating and cathartic. The steam/fog rose from ponds that reflected the fall's blue-sky enormity. The ducks flying at speed. The sound of shotguns when they went off in the distance from other blinds. Boom-boom! The decoys roped together, tethered wooden flocks sitting dumb in the silver-skin water—waiting for falling death.

"Some geese mate for life," he said, trying to make conversation. "And some fools fall in love." He doubted he could shoot anything now, unless it was shooting at him.

"Yes," she said. "I've heard that, too." She turned on her searchlight gaze and pointed it at him, wondering what the trippy—what his teenage daughter would call random—conversation was really about.

"I didn't know what kind," he said, and looked at her. She was pretty, her expression intent hunting for answers. He wondered if she had ever experienced anything damaging or even truly disruptive — outside of a bad grade in med school. He studied her face and saw that Fate had left no marks yet: no war, no loss, not even a hapless love affair it seemed — not much, maybe a great orgasm that she catalogued under "that guy can fuck." He liked her, though. Something about her reassured him, something that wouldn't stop investigating. As a detective, he appreciated that dogged thing she seemed to have, her keen Jewish eye. He — his psyche — was the bone she was chewing on. God knew he wanted help. He wanted to be fixed, but didn't have a clue how to do that. If ever a man was adrift…

"I was wondering if it isn't time we talked about that day," she said. "What do you think, Michael? This is our seventh session. You've been avoiding the subject that brought you here. That day — the day it all happened. You've talked about the war, but not that day."

"Combat was easy compared to these last months," he said not answering her question. He knew exactly which day she meant.

"Michael, we have to go there. I wanted to wait —"

"Why?" he said. "Why do we have to go there?"

"Because you're here to get better. And now we know each other. You trust me — I think," she said.

"I'm here because it's noon on Friday," he said, crossing his leg, a sudden mean tone in his voice — his war voice. He rubbed his face. He'd not shaved. His face felt a little greasy. His running shoes were dirty and worn-looking.

"I've asked to be let back to work. My partner wants me back. He's confident I can do the job," he said. "You'd like him. He looks like Sam Cooke. Women love him."

"Are you ready for that kind of pressure? Being a homicide detective again?"

"I haven't a clue. Maybe? Maybe not. I want to help him.

Marvin is part of my old life. It's strange, when I'm with Marvin, it's as if nothing happened. I mean I can pretend that Jen — I can pretend — and I do pretend. Why shouldn't I pretend?" he said. "Is that wrong? Delusional?

"We had lunch, Marvin and I. And I pretended that it was before. He won't talk about the accident, so it's not hard. But when I walked in the door of my place, afterwards, I knew of course it wasn't like before, and I panicked. I ran for the new pistol I bought — Marvin had come and taken my Glock the day after it happened — and I pulled back the hammer on my backup, and stared at the barrel. It's an old-school .38. I was pointing at my face. I don't know how long, an hour maybe? I was this close to pulling the trigger. It's got a five-pound trigger pull, so it takes some pulling." He held his fingers up to show just how close he'd come.

It was all true. He'd even begun to squeeze the trigger. It had been close. Very close. Nirvana, an instant away. Only simple mechanical parts and friction had stood between him and death.

"But you didn't," she said, a startled look on her face. She leaned forward. He'd frightened her. Finally. Nothing he'd said about combat had seemed to faze her. She'd not understood that kind of death, that man's world. The women who had entered it in Iraq had to play by men's rules.

"No, of course not." He sounded mean again. "I wouldn't be here. Would I?"

"Why not?" she asked. "Why didn't you?" She was watching him as if he might explode. The six-foot-four-man bomb who usually came on time, and stared at her.

"I don't have a fucking clue. I wanted to pull the trigger, but I'm not man enough. Maybe because it was Monday and not

Sunday. Or because of my daughter."

"I don't think that's it," she said. "What do you mean, it was Monday?"

"Too long a story. A Chinese girl's suicide note, a jumper — she left a note on her refrigerator. That's what she'd written, something about it being Sunday and not Monday. She might not have done it if it had been Monday, she wrote," he said. "Okay, doc, what is it then —keeping me alive?" He called her "doc" when he was angry or upset, and she knew it. Their language had become intimate without their intending it.

"I think you don't want to hurt anyone. Not your daughter, not your partner, or your sister. Your brother? Your wife's family. I think you know that you would be passing something on," the doctor said, "something painful, and you won't do it. Suicide is an aggressive act."

She was right, of course. As soon as he heard it, he knew she was right. He'd not thought it. But he knew it was true. It was always the person who would find him that he cared about. What would they think? What would they suffer, discovering his dead body? If he could only just disappear, leave nothing behind. Zero out. He'd found lots of suicides as a patrol officer. Each one had taken something out of him.

He'd thought about going up to the Marble Mountains and just disappearing, walking into the wilderness. It was appealing, that idea: hiking into the wilderness and not coming out. Was death the ultimate dark wilderness? He was keeping that idea like a gambler keeps an ace, tucked away. He kept a topo map of the Marble Mountains open on his kitchen table, to remind him that his ace was in the deck. He could pull that card if he needed to. He just had to get in the car and drive off. Sayonara, fools.

"Maybe. Okay. I see. So I'm just holding it over myself. A threat."

"We should move on, don't you think?" she said. "I think so. It's time. You're not going to kill yourself. So let's do the work we need to do. And stop the pity party —"

"Pity party?"

He looked carefully at her and suddenly smiled back, the sting of the phrase passing. He wanted to hate her, as he did so many who wanted to discuss that day of the accident, but he couldn't. She was the investigator. He saw the look. She was the soul-detective, and she was going to get the perpetrator who was driving him crazy. Before, he hoped, the perpetrator killed him. His head was the scene of the crime. He was lying there for her to measure, photograph, map, and dust for prints. His psychology the corpus delicti. Who done it?

"You remind me of myself, sometimes," he said. "When I was working."

She smiled, enjoying the idea.

"What if I tell you I don't want to?" he said. "What are you going to do, lock me up? Charge me with being crazy — 5150? That's the police radio sign for nuts."

"5150?" she said.

"Loco in la cabeza." He made the international sign for crazy: pointing at his head and circling his ear with his index finger. "Look, doctor, I only came today to see if you'd sign off on my going back to work. And to refill my Valium prescription."

"Okay, I will — if that's what you want," she said. "You're not crazy."

"What about the Valium?"

"What about it? You're abusing it."

It was the first time she'd suggested that she might cut him off, and it scared him. Nighttime without Valium was a nightmare, worse: it was a Hieronymus Bosch painting come to life. Before he had the Valium prescription, he couldn't sleep. He would lie in bed and feel a physical pain, from the grief. It was as if someone was grinding his heart into small pieces every night and then feeding them back to him, one jagged piece of glass at a time. Sometimes he just wanted to scream. He'd experienced actual physical pain in his chest.

It was then that he'd taken to going for walks in the middle of the night, driving into San Francisco and going down by the Marina Green, thinking that being near the water would somehow cure him of the agoraphobia he'd developed. The police often stopped and questioned him. He would flash his badge and move on toward Fort Ross, sweating like a speed freak. Walking helped. He had whole days when he didn't sleep at all, and didn't even bother trying. Instead he stared at infomercials for "Butt Blasters" or get-rich schemes shouted at morons who didn't know enough to go to bed.

"I can't sleep without it," he said. "Without the medication."

"Have you heard of the therapeutic alliance?" she asked.

"No. Is that a new Obama thing? Israeli? German? English? I was part of the Iraq Freedom Alliance. The Iraq —"

"It's this. What we do here. The doctor-patient relationship. You trust me to help you. We work together to get to the bottom of what's troubling you. We work at it together. We're partners. You have to trust me, Michael."

He stood up, suddenly angry—white hot anger exploding. "Have you ever seen someone shot in the face? What the bullet does to their face? The way it smashes the bones? They don't look the same afterwards. I can tell you that!"

He was clenching his fists and yelling. She looked frightened, and he was glad. He was tired of her schoolgirl looks, the earnest-young-doctor looks, the straight-A-student-who'd-gone-to-medical-school looks. The unflappable-rich-girl looks. All of it. He was tired of the leather chairs, the geese on the fucking walls, and most of all her just-coined Authority that gave her the right to ask him anything.

"You want to know what's wrong with me, you silly bitch? My wife is dead! She's gone. How is us, working together, in some bullshit alliance, going to change that? Tell me. I'd like to know. And it was my fault —"

"Michael," she said. "Sit down."

And he did.

She wasn't afraid of him. Her tone was motherly, despite his calling her a bitch. He looked across to the print of the geese on the wall and shut his eyes. He wanted to throw up. He was as embarrassed as if he'd shit in his pants in public.

"Jesus, I'm sorry," he said. "Really — the fuse is getting shorter and shorter. Maybe I shouldn't be going back to work. Maybe I should quit altogether. I just called you a bitch." He felt ridiculous, all the anger out of his voice.

"What would you do?" she said. "If you didn't go back to the police force?"

"Camp in the woods," he said.

"What's that mean?"

"Camp. Eat s'mores. Sleep in our tent. I still have it, the one we used when our daughter was born."

"Why don't you tell me what happened that day."

He looked at her a long time. He didn't know how long he

stared at her; it seemed like an hour, or a century—a stolen eternity, like in war when panic sets in and ammunition is running low, metal boxes turned over, empty. Men yelling. Time standing around stupid and dangerous and waiting for Death to make up its mind.

"I can't. I'm afraid if I start, I'll go mad by the end," he said. "Do you understand? It's too hard. I won't live through it, Detective. I didn't do it, Detective. I swear to you, I'm not guilty. I didn't see who did do it! I was around the corner and only heard the shot, Detective! Fuck it."

"Tell me what happened that day," she said. "I believe it will help."

"You want me to go crazy? Is that it? Is that what you want? I thought we had an alliance."

"I want to help you, for God's sake. I don't want to lose you. Do you understand? You're my very first patient since I started this practice. Okay? Does that make you feel like you're in control? If I lose you, if you kill yourself, then what good am I? Give me a break, Michael," she said. "I am new at this. All right? Give me a fucking break."

This was a complete breakdown of the doctor-patient protocol, and she knew it. She'd crossed the line, but it had gotten through to him, like seeing someone cry in combat. The sheer honesty of it. It was like some trooper saying he didn't want to go back out on patrol. Who the fuck did want to go back out there? Only crazy people.

The two looked at each other, more like drowning people than like doctor and patient. She moved back in her chair, trying to take back her authority, reload the doctor program. He heard her snap her pen closed.

"It was foggy," he said. "I didn't believe the fog would come back, you see ..." he drifted into silence.

Their eyes remained locked.

"It was around noon . . ." he said. "I don't think I can do this."

She said nothing, but kept looking at him. The room was completely silent. In the distance he could hear a siren wailing, an ambulance heading down California Street far below them.

Before he could really start, their hour was up. He got only to the point of their sailing under the Golden Gate, passing its north tower. He was relieved. He got up and left.

Schneider realized for the first time that the traditional hour limit was more about the medical business than it was about medicine. Now it was she who was angry like a hunter who'd missed a clear shot. The bird had passed over her head. She called in his Valium prescription.

CHAPTER 2

Day of the murders

Every spring, two massive eucalyptus trees behind Detective O'Higgins' house became home to a flock of crows. The crows had to fight off red-tailed hawks that targeted the crows' eggs. The battles took place across a sleepy blue and radiant Marin County sky all summer long, violent and graceful fits of high-speed flight that often ended in a shapeless, plummeting death. The crows died defending what was theirs, torn apart in mid-air by the bigger, more powerful hawks. But the crows always came back the following May.

But it was March now and the sky outside his place in San Rafael was bleak, grey, and without depth. The crows were gone, and would not be back for months. He missed them. He had something crow-like about him, he'd thought, since the accident, in his battle to remain sane and upright. The madness-hawk wanted him dead. It would attack without warning, hoping to knock him out of the sky.

A rain storm made an intense roof-thumping, at times becoming so loud O'Higgins stopped what he was doing. The intense pounding reminded him of the cacophony of combat: gunfire and shouted orders. He saw platoons of dirty Marines shaping up, their black-plastic knee pads covered in a fine white dust, their young faces shaded by helmets. The troopers looking at a toppled Fallujah, full of "the enemy." The chaotic sound of the storm became the sound of helicopters and the screams of wounded, mostly civilians, being treated by twenty-year old medics who were out of their depth, their rubber-gloved hands gut-stained. Behind them depleted uranium rounds penetrated concrete flats, block after block pulverized, hunks bitten off by Marine artillery and contaminated for generations to come. They were, of course, "winning." The generals in the Pentagon could go play golf at US taxpayer expense.

Most of his men had never read a real book or seen the inside of a museum. They'd been moved on, grade by grade, through a system that handed out a vending-machine education and didn't care about them. Mothers who worked for minimum wage and couldn't afford childcare left them in front of SpongeBob SquarePants, brown and black and white mothers who had no idea where Iraq was. Their young sons were hapless, though singularly brave at times, punching above their weight, trying to be what their officers expected—brave Marines. O'Higgins knew they were pawns in a great game run by the super-rich for the benefit of the über-rich, who were living in unimaginable wealth and privilege.

They'd been Hell's Guards. But to what end? Guarding what, and for whom?

Some of his men were vaporized, and disappeared altogether—as if they'd never existed, their young lives folded into nothingness and back to where life came from, our shared universe of nothingness. It was a revolving, impossible-to-comprehend continuum from conscious life to oblivious death, oscillating on the battlefield and in a mother's silent womb.

Lost in that noisy past, O'Higgins realized the chaotic house-pounding was just the storm that had come in late that morning, and not the other thing. He went back to paying bills, knowing exactly where he was again. He regretted that he was not back at war, where things would be simple to understand, and his life evaded, or ended if he were lucky.

The once-sterling personal qualities that had made him so formidable and successful as a homicide detective, and before that as a Marine combat officer, had vanished on a Sunday afternoon due west of the Golden Gate Bridge, on a 40-foot all-wood sailboat that had sunk eight months before, killing his wife. He blamed himself. The facts were horrifically simple yet profound, like life itself.

His iPhone rang at almost exactly 6:00 p.m. This was the day he was back from leave and on call, whether or not he was fit for duty, or ready to go back to work as a homicide detective.

The sergeant on the line gave him the quick facts: two bodies had been found in a mansion on Broadway, in San Francisco's exclusive Pacific Heights neighborhood. Patrol had cleared the house. A women had been taken to the hospital. No details beyond that. O'Higgins listened carefully to each word, weighing it. It's official, he told himself as soon as he ended the call. I've caught a murder case and am back to work. And it's a double.

He set his phone down on the cluttered kitchen table: piles of unopened mail; unread Wired magazines, his wife's subscription; delinquent notices from the IRS, along with a raft of unpaid bills alongside that morning's dirty breakfast dishes.

He finished making out the check he'd been writing to his daughter's dance school in Sacramento, where she'd gone to live with his sister: $150 dollars. It was important he get that paid, he told himself. He finished filling it out, then signed it.

He found a book of stamps in his makeshift office and put the check in an envelope. He walked outside, not bothering to put on a jacket, to drop the envelope in the mailbox. The driving rain felt good as it pelted his shoulders. He put the mailbox's flag up. His partner, Detective Marvin Lee, called. The air around him smelled strongly of eucalyptus and rain. He spoke standing in the pelting downpour.

"That you, white boy?"

In their practiced shorthand, the detectives agreed to meet at the scene.

O'Higgins went back into the house in his soaking t-shirt. He got ready to go to work for the first time in months, walking through an empty and frightening house of sweet memories. Dusk dragged daylight's dream down Mount Tam and began to shutter San Rafael, leaving randomly gleaming strings of twinkling storefronts along Fourth Street. Humanity's throbbing pulse pushed through a dim winter twilight. Murder or no murder, life goes on.

All dispatch had told them was that a well-known businessman and a young woman, perhaps the man's wife, had been found murdered at the address on Broadway. The tony address signaled to the detectives that they would very likely be dealing with extremely wealthy people, perhaps even celebrities of one kind or another — investment bankers, or even Hollywood types.

Celebrities, or at least very rich people, the detectives knew from experience, meant the crime scene could be chaotic. Top-notch lawyers would be called immediately. The press would show up and bear down on the police in search of something, anything, they could sell as news. The District Attorney herself would be involved from the start, as rich people meant she had to appear large and in charge.

It seemed like a bad way to start over. But he'd caught a double in Pacific Heights, and that was life. He'd laid in his funk hole since the accident. It was time to get up and face the enemy again, like it or not.

CHAPTER 3

O'Higgins slowed his Ford and rolled down the window, identifying himself to an older patrol officer he recognized, who was keeping traffic off the 2000 block of Broadway. Patrol had created a cordon sanitaire around the scene, closing off both ends of the block, letting in only cars belonging to residents who had driver's licenses proving they lived on the street.

He pulled his car over and turned off his headlights but left his parking lights on, parking just down from the scene. He picked up his phone and noted the time for his report: 7:08 p.m. It would mark the time of his officially taking over the crime scene. Everyone now — patrolmen, criminalists, coroner's investigators, all the crime scene's players, even the body handlers from the mortuary — would acknowledge his authority, in some cases grudgingly. He and his partner were the generals in Homicide's well-ordered hierarchy.

As usual, he sat for a moment at the wheel of his car and took the scene in before being deluged by an infinite number of details. He didn't want to overlook what the killer, or killers, had seen when they came and when they left the scene. And he wanted to postpone, if for only a moment, the heavy responsibility that was waiting for him.

He rubbed his nose with the back of his hand as he had when

heading out on a sortie — everyone getting ready to man up, pretending not to be afraid but afraid nonetheless, smacking weapons and hoping for the best. There was luck in warfare, as in everything else.

The fog, blowing in from the west, was obscuring whole sections of the street. He looked directly above him at the street light and saw ineluctable specters ripped apart by the wind, turning fog into smoke-like tendrils crawling over roofs, slipping under the yellowish street light as they moved east. Are they Death's flag? The scene reminded him of the accident, his daughter's cry for help when it happened. It was fog that had worked against him that horrible afternoon. It was the enemy no bullet could kill.

He glanced in the rearview mirror and saw the wet street painted by a patrol car's blue and white flashing lights, the sidewalk where neighbors were gathering in nattering groups, their well-to-do white faces yellow under the streetlight. He turned back and faced the three-story mansion where the murders had taken place, perhaps only an hour or two before. Three uniformed patrol officers were chatting at the foot of the mansion's stairs. One of the officers, a young woman, turned and walked his way. She was wearing a yellow rain slicker made wet by the fog, which seemed to reflect all the strange light on the street.

O'Higgins noticed how well lit the block was. All the street lights worked. So different from the Mission District or Hunter's Point, where the street lights might be shot out by gangsters who preferred to have streets dark. Not here, baby. Here it's all lit up. This is big money, he thought, taking in the fabulous homes around him: Tudor, a huge Cape Cod on the corner, Art Deco, and a Craftsman-inspired mansion where the murders had taken place. These were fabulous places of the über rich. The houses, even at night, looked immaculate. Many were several stories, their front yards starchy, manicured by gardeners and signaling extreme wealth. Their latticed-and-box-hedged landscaping spoke of lifelong privilege, big-time universities and the rest of it. The untouchables.

He looked for his partner's car, but didn't see it.

He saw a lone metal For Sale sign swinging on its chains down the street. Pedestrians on the sidewalk directly across from the scene were showing the cold's effects, their faces partially hidden by coat collars and luxe scarfs. He didn't want to get out of the car and go to work. Didn't want to assume the dreadful responsibility that would be thrust at him as soon as he stepped out onto the street and took charge.

The female patrol officer walked toward him, trying to keep the crime scene's log book's pages from blowing up off her clipboard. The sheets flapped, and she clutched them against her fog-wet yellow rain slicker.

A patrol car's lights, at the west end of the street, danced across the faces of cops standing in front of the scene. He could see the patrolmen looking his way, anxious to speak with him. They had been in charge of the crime scene since the discovery of the bodies. It was a double murder, and would be double the work for him and his partner. Was he up to it? All eyes on you now.

Shit! Why couldn't I have caught a suicide? Suicides were easy as you could get in the homicide business, as the victim and the suspect were all in the room together. No pressure there. Over his career he'd had lots of those. If they jumped from the SF side of the Golden Gate, SFPD sent out homicide detectives. He'd called families all over the country and the world to explain that their loved ones had jumped from the Golden Gate. He'd thought of it himself. Maybe he too would have taken "the down elevator," as his first partner called it when they watched a 20-year-old Chinese girl bob in the bay, the Coast Guard trying to fish her tiny body out of the ugly dark water with a hooked steel pole.

He remembered her hair, which was very long. The dead girl's boyfriend had left her, they learned from her suicide note, which she'd carefully taped to her refrigerator. O'Higgins had read it standing in her quiet apartment, with just the sounds of Muni bus brakes as a kind of funeral music. The first line of her handwritten note said:

It's Sunday. I know I shouldn't do this, Mom and Dad … Maybe if it were Monday, but it's Sunday and I'm alone. So alone now.

He'd told his partner he would handle it, the call to the girl's family. He postponed it for a long fifteen minutes while he stared at the note on the refrigerator. The word Sunday had been underlined. What was it about Sunday, he'd wondered? His daughter had been born in the wee hours of a Sunday morning. It had been a joyous day.

He'd taken out his cell phone and made the call to Los Angeles. The girl had left her parents' phone number and address on a separate Post-It note, knowing they should be notified. It was a hard call to make. He'd made others over the years, but that young girl, her apartment so clean and tidy, stuck with him, as if they'd been friends.

Why hadn't someone, just one person, made a difference that Sunday? If someone had smiled at her on the way to the bridge. Just one person might have made a difference. But that was life.

People fell through the cracks.

The patrol officer, log-book in hand, knocked on his window.

O'Higgins rolled it down and signed in, noting the time in the logbook: 7:10 p.m. "What we got?" he said gruffly.

"Two dead inside the house. One in the elevator on the main floor. A second body on the third floor in the shower stall. A young female. She was stabbed repeatedly. It looks like the guy in the elevator had his throat cut, and he bled out."

"Okay," O'Higgins said. "My partner, Detective Lee, should be here soon."

"Yes, sir," the officer said. She looked very young, only twenty-two or three at most. Fresh-faced white girl. He got out of the car, reached into the backseat for his coat and slipped it on. It was cold outside.

The wind whipped around them. The patrol officer wasn't wearing a wedding ring. She did have a tattoo of some kind on her ring finger, he'd noticed.

"The father of one of the victims called 911, dispatch said. But he wasn't here when we arrived. The wife came home as we were clearing the house. She says she'd run down to the Safeway on Marina Boulevard and was only out of the house for half an hour or less. She was hysterical. We called an ambulance. She was that bad off. They took her to Mount Zion. She's there now. It seems the woman's two small girls are missing from the home. It looks like the Jane Doe in the bathroom was the nanny. The woman's husband is the other victim."

"So, two bodies," he said, looking at the house. "No others?"

"The husband and the nanny. That's all we found," the woman said. "I'm Officer Madrone."

"Thank you, Madrone. Who caught the handle?"

"My partner and I. I found both victims. My partner stayed with the wife after she arrived. I finished clearing the house with another officer who arrived to back us up. It was — the wife was pretty bad off, sir, screaming. It was difficult to get much from her."

"Anything I should know walking in? Anything I should be careful about not disturbing?"

"Bloody footprints in the hallways. The wife stepped in the elevator and tried to resuscitate her husband, and she made a mess. The husband is lying in the elevator on the first floor. I turned power off to the elevator. I had to open the elevator door to check and make sure there was a body in there. That's what the first call told us, nothing was mentioned about a second body. I used the emergency off button so it couldn't be called to another floor. The wife said their name is Chaundhry. They're from India." She looked at him. "That's about it." She was short and thin but stood ramrod straight, and seemed to have some mettle. He wondered how someone like her, so physically unimposing, chose to become a cop.

"Okay, I'll get to it," he said. "Anyone else step in the elevator, compromise the scene in any way?"

"No. Neither one of us did, anyway. The girl is lying in the shower stall. Looks like she was stabbed in the shower. I turned off the water. It was still running when I found her. I don't know why I did — but I did turn off the water, sir."

He nodded. He recognized a military bearing in the officer. Perhaps it was the way she'd said "sir;" she seemed used to delivering it.

"I'll go up and take a look. Be sure to have my partner sign in. The criminalists too, they're on their way. No one else goes in. So if the victim was the nanny, where are the kids?"

"Not clear. The wife said something about her daughters being at a neighbor's. She went crazy. Really crazy. She was looking for them hysterically in the house, afraid they'd been harmed. We didn't find her girls. I looked everywhere. I thought maybe they'd hidden somewhere, if they'd been there at all. They could be in the house still, I guess, but I didn't find them. I'm not sure the wife understands the nanny was killed too. She found her husband just as we arrived. We stopped her from going upstairs. She was screaming for the nanny to come help her."

O'Higgins looked at the officer. She was upset. He could tell she was trying to be professional, but her expression was betraying her. He'd seen the same tipped-over expression in Iraq. A set of headlights came up the street from the east, and he hoped it was his partner.

He glanced at his watch. The fog felt almost like rain against his face as he walked toward the scene, following Madrone. Dispatch hadn't mentioned any missing girls. It was worse than he'd thought, he realized. There might be more victims in the house, and they might be children.

He handed Madrone his card with his cell number. He told her to start questioning the immediate neighbors about anything they might have seen that would help, and to note who had security cameras. If she found the children with a neighbor, he said, she should call him.

O'Higgins opened the elevator door and stepped back in surprise. He recognized the dead man who was lying face up, his knees buckled, his throat showing a small gash almost like a tear.

O'Higgins had met him casually a week before, waiting for the ferry to Angel Island. No one else would know that except the victim's wife, who might or might not remember him. Either way, it would not keep him from being the lead detective, he decided. The victim's face had a terrified expression. Had the man realized he'd been mortally wounded before he died? Probably.

The man he'd been introduced to as "Rishi" that day on the ferry had bled out on the floor of the elevator. A bloody shoe track led from the elevator in a confused, dragged-around-and-stopped pattern toward the kitchen, fading out halfway down the hallway.

He closed the elevator door and studied the bloody shoe prints in the hallway. It looked like just one set, as Madrone had suggested.

The victim was the man he'd met, he was sure of that. He'd met the wife, too. He couldn't recall her name, but he remembered her. She'd been quite beautiful. Their two little daughters had been with them.

Marvin Lee walked up to the house's huge double glass front doors and came into the foyer. All they were missing were the criminalists O'Higgins had called, a photographer and a blood specialist.

"That's him, Mr. Rishi Chaundhry?" Marvin Lee said, coming down the wide and brightly lit hallway toward the elevator.

O'Higgins, crouching, turned from the shoe prints and looked up at his partner.

"Yes."

Lee was black, tall and handsome. He wore a teal green suit and a starched white shirt and a grey tie. Natty, as usual.

Marvin touched O'Higgins' shoulder in a sign of welcome. That was all Marvin would do to mark their reuniting. It was reassuring nonetheless, and O'Higgins appreciated it.

The light was on in the elevator. The dead man's white dress shirt was blood-soaked, the entire front. Both detectives were silent for a moment, running the scene in their heads — how it must have come down inside the elevator in those last seconds.

"So the victim is riding in the elevator and the assailant stabs him in the throat? The killer has got to be splattered with the victim's blood when he walks out of the elevator . . . he had to be close enough to stab him ... No, not necessarily," Marvin said, answering his own question. "Could have confronted the victim as he stepped out of the elevator. You've got to hold the door open? It's self-closing."

"No arterial blood anywhere out here on the wall or floor," O'Higgins said. The hardwood floors were clean other than the shoe prints. Blood on the white walls or floor would have been easy to see. "Maybe on those stairs?" he asked, pointing to a staircase with an oriental runner that led up to the second floor.

O'Higgins walked toward the stairs looking at the hallway, but saw nothing, not even the one set of shoe prints he'd seen going toward the kitchen. The floor on this side of the elevator was clean.

"No. Nothing."

"So the killer catches him in the elevator," Marvin said. He leaned in, keeping his feet in the hallway. He could see that the victim's blood had run off the elevator's floor and out via the slight half-inch gap between the elevator and the hallway.

They saw no obvious defensive wounds on the dead man's hands. Marvin shone his light on the elevator's elegant wood-paneled walls, revealing nothing obvious. They saw no sign of a struggle. He looked at the bottom of the victim's shoes, which were both stained with blood.

"Stepped on his own blood?" O'Higgins said from behind him.

"Yeah. He's not going to have zeroed out, blood pressure-wise, for a minute or so. They struggled in there before he collapsed, right?" Marvin said. "Long enough for the blood to pool. Maybe the asshole who killed him kept the door shut — you know. Till the guy died."

"Blood on the killer?" O'Higgins said. "From that wound. It's going to shoot out of that kind of wound."

"Lots, you'd think. Like a fire hydrant in summer," Marvin said. "Why isn't there blood on the walls?"

"And no obvious cast-off from the weapon," Michael said. Weapons left their own blood signature, a cast-off pattern that was easily distinguished from other bleeding-event patterns.

"Let's go eyeball the other victim," Marvin said. "Poor fucker, slipping around in his own blood. Jesus!"

They took the stairs up to the third floor. On the way up the stairs Michael told Marvin, who was moving up the carpeted stairs ahead of him, that he had met the victim and his wife casually on the way to Angel Island just the week before.

"So what. Won't matter," Marvin said tersely as they walked down the third floor hallway. They were both looking for blood on the hardwood floor or painted-white walls, but saw none. Michael glanced ahead and noticed that the ceiling heights were ten feet or higher. The walls were freshly painted everywhere, stark eggshell white.

"So someone kills her first? He would have left something on the carpet after all that blood downstairs, if someone had killed her after the husband."

Michael's cell phone rang. "O'Higgins."

"Sir, it's Officer Madrone."

He put the call on speaker so Marvin could hear. "Yes?"

"Sir, someone from the Indian Consulate is here. They want to come in and speak to you."

"Well, don't let them in," O'Higgins said.

"Yes, sir."

He ended the call.

"What the fuck? Indian Consulate?" Marvin said, his face twisting with annoyance.

"High profile, double homicide in Pacific Heights," Michael said. "That's what the fuck it is."

"Hey, what did you expect your first time back, a jumper? Shiiiit. And I know this family, too," Marvin said. "There was an article in last Sunday's paper about them. Society people. Billionaire. Sunday magazine, SF Gate. You can expect the press here very soon, my man. Educated White People in vans searching for the truth between commercials."

They made their way down the long hallway. Marvin opened doors, making sure there were no more bodies. They got to the master bedroom; it was empty, the bed made. The room was beautiful. Modern Indian art hung on the walls—oil paintings. The sparkling rich-people room was huge and looked like it could have been in Architectural Digest.

"Everything perfect like a movie set," Marvin said, admiring all the touches. He'd grown up poor in West Oakland, without a mother, and had a real respect for money and what it bought. He was the first to admit it.

They found the second victim, a young Indian woman, maybe twenty or even younger, in the bathroom at the opposite end of the hall from the master bedroom and across from another bedroom. She'd obviously been taking a shower when she was attacked. She had been stabbed repeatedly six or more times, on her left side alone. The stab wounds had been washed clean by the shower. Steam had created a thin red film that clung to the bright white subway-tiled walls of the shower stall, a grisly red mist. The girl was naked and had fallen with her two legs under her, supine, her back arched, her head partially turned toward them. She had a strange expression on her face — not quite a smile, but almost. O'Higgins had seen it on the face of countless other murder victims. A grim half smile left by Death's passing.

"So our guy cuts a throat downstairs. He or she then walks up here covered in blood, which they don't seem to get on anything. Not the floor, not the carpet, not the white walls—nothing. So — it's the other way around. She's killed first," Marvin said.

O'Higgins looked around the bathroom. Marvin's voice had a certain tone, one he seemed to take on at murder scenes, as if he'd been running and was slightly out of breath. It was his way of coping with the stress of seeing someone so vulnerable, so brutally put down.

The dead girl's jeans, sweater and panties were neatly folded on the end of the bedroom's queen-sized bed. The room was neat, with Indian art on the walls as well. He could see the girl's laid-out folded clothes through the open bathroom doorway. The killer must have seen them, too. Perhaps they'd signaled to him that the victim was in the bathroom?

The bathroom was orderly, no struggle. Whoever killed her had walked in and attacked her while she was showering, O'Higgins thought. He noticed a small bruise on the girl's cheek, the size of a fifty-cent piece and perfectly round.

"So someone opens the shower door and bam," Marvin said.

"Psycho time. Just like the movie."

"Yes. Maybe she knows them," Michael said. He looked at the stab wounds. They were all equal in width, washed very clean and all on her left side. No more than an inch wide, he thought.

"She turns toward the attacker when she's stabbed — where was the wife?" Marvin asked.

"At the grocery store, she told patrol," O'Higgins said.

"So is the husband screwing the nanny? She pops her nanny, then does Dad up close and personal? No sign of forced entry, patrol told me," Marvin said.

"No, I don't think so," O'Higgins said. "I doubt it was that simple."

Marvin looked at him, his handsome face quizzical. They lived by Occam's-razor logic, namely that the obvious explanation was usually the explanation, which in turn would point to an obvious suspect. But an attractive live-in nanny spoke for itself.

"Why not?" Marvin said. "Look at her. She's beautiful, man."

"I met the wife, that day on the ferry. I don't think she's a killer. Not the woman I met," O'Higgins said.

Marvin looked at him as if he'd heard him say that Martians were responsible for the murders and they could go home now.

Before the accident that so changed him, he would not have excluded the wife without first assuming she had an obvious motive—jealousy and opportunity. Most people were killed by someone they knew. But something had grown in him since the accident, something he couldn't quite put his finger on, a kind of second sense. He was sure, in his gut, that the young wife and mother he'd met on the ferry was not a cold-blooded killer. It surprised him that he would allow himself to think that. He knew it was unreasonable to harbor prejudice of that kind, especially for a homicide detective. But he did.

"Yeah, okay. The wife is pretty. That's really what you mean," was all Marvin said before they headed back downstairs. O'Higgins knew he'd shocked him. It was unprofessional, even absurd.

CHAPTER 4

One week before the murders

There was a super high tide that morning. O'Higgins could hear the bay splashing against the pilings beneath the hoary dock while he was waiting for the 11:00 a.m. ferry that would take him to Angel Island. The slapping sound of water: euphonic, the analog of a Japanese flute, hauntingly austere.

He'd been concentrating on the water's sound in hopes that the strange music would soothe his fear of riding the ferry. It wasn't working. He was getting anxious, and he couldn't even see the ferry yet. It was quite possible, he realized, that he might not be able to board, much less take the short ride across Raccoon Strait to Angel Island as his psychiatrist had suggested.

Dr. Schneider said he had to begin facing his irrational fear of open water in order to deal with it, especially since he was going back to work soon. He was psychologically adrift and knew it. He'd not shot himself, but he had gotten into a fist fight over a parking space. A hulking college kid had said, "Go fuck yourself," and O'Higgins enjoyed the beating he dished out between parked cars. Each punch was a relief as the kid's face slowly turned to hamburger under his blows. The kid's nose split first. Blood splattered the kid's new chrome rims. O'Higgins had jumped in his car and escaped the parking lot before the police arrived, but barely.

***

The day of the accident, the fog, so heavy in the early hours, had cleared by ten in the morning, but only for about an hour, in time for them to see the Farallon Islands miles away. The City and the Golden Gate Bridge were behind them and getting smaller.

He'd thought the islands beautiful: artillery-grey, stark, dangerous, their waters full of great white sharks. He'd always been attracted to the Farallons, to the island's great masses of birds that called the rocky islands home. Had he been attracted to the Farallons' well-known dangers, too? Their savage quality. Had something savage lurked in him since coming home? Something from Iraq that had gone dormant while his wife was alive — but now?

They'd had lunch, sandwiches his wife had made the night before: raisin bread with peanut butter and honey, his favorite. She'd sent him out to the Whole Foods to buy cookies for their lunch. It was almost noon when they ate. The air felt cool, the boat was running well. They were relaxing, heading due west. Everything seemed fine. He noticed the fog pouring over the Marin headlands at Muir Beach, but for the most part it would stay north of Tomales Bay in July.

He'd been wrong. By 12:30 the fog was pushing south, blue-white, primitive looking. In a short time it closed around them, unexpectedly. The Farallons disappeared. He felt uneasy. Visibility dropped to 10 feet and the wind, which had brought the fog, had also brought unexpected swells.

They'd decided to turn back because the swells had grown from practically nothing to five feet, and both his wife and his daughter were getting seasick. Even he, who never got seasick, started to feel queasy.

It was 1:07 p.m. when the tiller broke, the principal bolt that held the shaft. A clanging buoy sounded far in the distance. He remembered that sound. It haunted him now—its ugly clanking bell, somewhere in the grey mist. For several agonizing minutes he'd done everything he could to fix the useless tiller as the boat spun rudderless. His queasy feeling turned to panic. It was the same kind of panic he'd felt in Fallujah after a direct hit vaporized several of his men, leaving their positions vulnerable to being overrun.

To his horror, as soon as the tiller broke, the boat had turned broadside into the grey waves. He'd been going for the radio, to call for help — the radio just out of reach in the boat's tiny cabin — when they were hit broadside by a wave.

He'd heard the sickening sound of down-flooding, an unmistakable sucking noise the ocean makes as water swamped the boat's small cabin, pouring in as they went over, the deck listing horribly now and sending gear sliding into the ocean. Water snuffed out the little Cumming's engine. It was a sound he would never forget, that coughing death of his engine.

A second wave slammed into the boat violently knocking it down into a deep trough, the boat's port side deck completely submerged. The violence of the blow tore the lead-weighted keel off their hull in the bargain, insuring the sailboat would not right itself, and would sink from the torn gash in the hull—quickly.

Jennifer had been standing near him as the second wave, a ten-footer, crashed down on them. He'd grabbed her arm and pulled her toward him. They'd landed in the rough water together.

***

He spotted the Angel Island Ferry approaching, tumbling forward, pushing across Raccoon Strait, its gleaming white steel hull looking stark and clean and powerful. He felt something hopeful in the way the ferry progressed. Everything is a progression. The whole world turning toward day or night, love or hate, war or peace, lovers turning to lovers, sheets, breasts, awkward wanting love. Aching love. The moment of separation and the moment of complete unity. Nothing is dialed in; it's all chaos, an anthill of dreams and delusions; human beings always on the march toward what? Toward ... Death? Is that it, then? All of this means what? And what was he now, if he could not be a father and husband? He'd failed at the most important task a man is ever given: keeping his family safe.

He forced himself to stare out onto Raccoon Strait until he had to turn away. Was he really going to go out on the open water? Shit. Could he possibly stand the overwhelming, mouth-twisting fear? He would break out in a sweat. He would even stutter, something added to the growing constellation of psychosomatic maladies that were attaching to him like barnacles on a ship's hull, immobilizing him, sapping the life force that had once been so strong.

He sat with the fear dancing wildly, daring him to do something about it: get up and run away, perhaps? Back to his car? He sat ignoring the dare, listening to the slapping sound of the tide while sitting on a new plastic bench, his palms pressed into its slick, brand-new-feeling plastic slats. What kind of world made plastic benches, he wondered, suddenly angry. Where were the green benches of his childhood? Green wood benches that were marked by carvings: "Love Ronny" "I was here"— rough and human-friendly. Was everything going to be plastic? Was everything to be drained of life's touch? Death too had a plastic feeling, the faces of the dead plastic-looking and dirty. Fallujah stuck with him, its senseless slaughter. And after all that suffering, it belonged to the "enemy" again, he'd read.

"Is this the queue for the ferry to Angel Island?" a man asked him. He was well-dressed, about forty, dark-skinned, standing in line next to him. His English had a sing-song quality. O'Higgins guessed the man was an Indian, and probably on holiday. He'd been surrounded by tourists waiting for the ferry: American day-trippers, poor whites from Virginia, lacking confidence; blue-eyed, sturdy German families, kitted out with expensive dusty day-packs and the latest hiking shoes, ready to take on the world. Angel Island was next to be stormed.

A gang of overly tattooed young lesbians had brought their mountain bikes and their weirdo partially-shaved-head haircuts. Some wore short-short cutoff jeans that showed off brightly colored tattoos. A few strait-laced older people were dressed in Dockers and Players Club jackets. The Indian family seemed the most elegant, as if they'd decided, at the very last moment, to head for San Francisco, having left their home in India with just the clothes on their back. An innocence and joy about them had caught his attention and made him stare. It was what he thought his family had once: simple joy.

A seagull came down to the quay and attacked a strip of carefully peeled, still-intact orange peel. The gull made un-bird-like noises as it headed skyward, its wings at full span, still hungry and disappointed perhaps, despite his dangling peel-prize.

"I say, is this the line to the ferry?" the Indian asked him again.

O'Higgins nodded. The well-dressed, casually chic Indian

nodded back quickly, an obvious intelligence to him. His eyes sparked. The man had a handsome face with an affable expression that seemed to go perfectly with his lilting voice and striking blue eyes, a gift from the English who had ruled his country for 200 years.

O'Higgins had noticed the family when they'd arrived on the dock. It was hard not to, as the little girls were twins and very pretty, like their mother. The mother was slender, petite and spoke Hindi to the girls. He'd guessed the mother to be in her late twenties. She was very attractive, wore expensive looking clothes that made her stand out. The two girls were dressed in jeans, and had been running up and down the bird-shit splattered quay chasing each other. Their mother had given up trying to get them to slow down or stay in line. The little girls seemed happy, as if they hadn't a care in the world. We had been like that, he thought.

It was that kind of day. Perfect for children, he thought, watching the girls, enjoying their gaiety and the sound of their excited voices. Their pretty brown faces shone. He wanted to ask their names, but that was out of the question. He couldn't speak correctly when he was fighting this fear of open water. The strangled noises he made in sight of water were horrible, and the little girls would be frightened by the stuttering of a six foot-four Elephant Man-type weirdo.

People were shocked by his malady, and slightly afraid of him when he showed symptoms: sweating, stuttering, a dazed look as if he were a modern-day Frankenstein. Because he was a policeman, even if on leave, he knew his attention might be misunderstood. He'd kept an eagle-eye out for perverts himself, when out in public with his daughter. He ran across them every day in his line of work. They were like sharks, deep in the water until they attacked, leaving mangled bodies and mangled lives.

And like the sharks, they had all kinds of rights. Once caught, they could lie to his face. They could make fun of the victim's weakness. Worst, they could explain what they enjoyed about killing people, in agonizing detail. And he could do nothing.

Once he'd slammed a suspect into a wall. The man had murdered an 18-year-old mother after raping her in her apartment. The man had no reason to kill her, but he had, simply for sport. An anonymous female clerk happened to be walking by the interrogation room, and reported O'Higgins' act of violence. He'd been reprimanded, and the event duly recorded in his work record. His partner and others had lied for him, but it had done no good; the clerk stuck to her story. Later the suspect he'd "terrorized" confessed to killing sixteen women; he wasn't sure of the exact number, as he'd been doing it for twenty years. No one laid a hand on him again, afraid for their jobs.

"Thank you. Would you mind holding our place in line?" the father asked him.

O'Higgins nodded.

"You speak English? Yes?"

"Ye — ye — yes," O'Higgins said. He tried to get the word off his tongue. It was such a simple word, he thought, but it would not come out.

The man looked at him and instead of being afraid of him, as most were, he touched O'Higgins' arm kindly and nodded, perhaps thinking him simple. O'Higgins would never forget the touch. It had soothed his stuttering. He would remember that simple kindness the rest of his life. It might have been the beginning of his recovery. Point Zero. There had to be a first step on all long journeys. It was something about the reaching out to him, a stranger, and touching him. As if to say, "Don't worry, I am listening."

"It's — coming — now," Michael said, forcing himself to turn and look out on the bay. "See." He pointed toward Angel Island and the lovely white ferry on the water.

"Can you hold our place? Be right back. Children have gone off—again." Their father smiled at him and took off down the long line of queued people in search of his wife and kids.

O'Higgins noticed he was carrying an iPad in a smart-looking blue-leather case. He smiled at the man and nodded. It was something that had been impossible for him to do, until that morning—smile. He liked the man. He liked his easy manner. He liked his white pants with a white jacket, which seemed so out of place among the crowds of serious hikers, the jean-clad majority waiting for the ferry, everyone very earnest—the gang of thumping lesbians in the lead, ready to storm the island with their German allies and make it theirs.

His doctor said he should try to smile. It was difficult, but he was trying. It was partially on his psychiatrist's advice that he was here at all. The doctor suggested he stop going out only at night. She called it a cop-out; if he was truly interested in getting well, he had to "do normal things."

She wanted him to start going out and sitting by the water, for starters. She was a bright woman, but sometimes he wanted to yell at her for being so certain of herself and her prescriptions. She'd never been to war. She'd never seen the remains of a serial killer's work. She'd never worried about money. (He'd Googled her; she came from a wealthy family from the South Bay, and had gone to Stanford. Her grandfather had been an early investor in

HP and made a fortune.) He wanted to dislike her, but he didn't.

The fact was he liked talking to her. She was intelligent, and he admired that. She said he was to breathe deeply and try to face his fear. His psychiatrist was part of a new school of doctors who were rejecting the use of psychoactive drugs, based on data that said they didn't really cure patients. Rather, the theory said, the drugs just masked their symptoms, making them dependent prisoners. Only the heaviest of doses would address phobias or repetitive syndromes, turning patients into semi-adjusted, emotionally dead zombies who had stopped washing their hands every five minutes, but could no longer feel joy or hate.

His sister was the one who suggested he get therapy. She'd stopped by the house one morning and rang the bell while he'd been asleep. He was dreaming about the day of the accident, as he did every time he slept. The dream was always the same, with little variation, but in the dreamscape he was always unaware of what was to come. That was the irony. That was why he liked to sleep and dream. It was only then that he felt normal.

During the day, he felt great tension and fear: fear that he would kill himself, and fear that he would live another minute more. It was fear of both. Life was a torture of minutes and recollections and long, empty days of driving or walking. He'd become a "Meanderthal," a word he'd coined to describe the desire to peregrinate aimlessly on foot, another symptom of his mental turmoil.

He'd come to the front door in his sweatpants and a torn t-shirt, unshaven. His steps sounded heavy across the empty, untidy living room. He was a big man. He noticed how dirty the living room transom windows were. It had probably rained while he'd been in bed for the last twenty hours; the dirty windows were streaked by the rain and solemn-looking.

"I think you should see someone, Michael. It's been months," his sister said. She handed him a card with a doctor's name, a psychiatrist. "She said I can't make the appointment for you. You have to do that. You can get over this."

His sister, the baby of their family, turned and headed down his front stairs without saying another world. "They'll want you back at work soon," she reminded him. He'd not answered her. He had nothing to say. It was not anger, certainly not with his sister, who had stayed with him and his daughter those first few days after it happened. She had known he was not sane, and might try and harm himself.

He'd remembered a painting he'd seen once, of a black man drifting on a wrecked and tiny sailboat in the ocean. He dreamt he was on that boat at night, drifting with no land in sight. There were swells and sharks in the water. He'd woke up screaming so loudly that he'd hurt his voice. The next morning he'd made the appointment with the psychiatrist. It was either that or drive to the bridge—it was live or die, talk or end it.

The ferry had been crowded. As luck would have it he'd sat up on the aft deck, on a bench facing the Marin hills, along with the pretty Indian family. They were getting up and taking pictures of everything with their iPad, their gaiety infectious. He'd been silent. A few times the girls' father had looked at him and smiled about his children's hyperactivity, and for the first time since the accident O'Higgins found himself smiling back, unafraid of showing himself as he used to be.

It was those simple human exchanges that he would tell his doctor about later. It had shocked him, the profundity of the man's simple kindness that morning on the way to Angel Island.

It was a slight and meager smile, but it had happened, and without him thinking about it. It was a start.

And perhaps he'd fallen in a kind of love with the man's wife. He had to admit it to himself, no matter how painful or shocking. He was attracted to the wife in the most profound way. She seemed like a goddess, the goddess of Gentleness and Beauty. He made the trip, his fear subsiding by the time they got to Angel Island. The woman's smile, he thought, had the power to heal a man.

SFPD called that afternoon. He was to come back to work. His job as a San Francisco homicide detective was waiting for him, if he still wanted it.

CHAPTER 5

The Chaundhry mansion in Pacific Heights had an office suite on the first floor with spectacular views of the San Francisco Bay. O'Higgins was drawn to the opulent office's bank of windows, lined up behind a huge and cluttered "power desk."

From the office windows he could see Alcatraz, grey and forlorn, and beyond the Rock, Berkeley and parts of the East Bay. It seemed a wonderland of big-city lights. The city of his birth had always comforted him, like the face of a beloved person. San Francisco was his ultimate touchstone, its pulse his pulse, since his conception in the Mission District.

Marvin was outside speaking to the press, who had gathered outside on the street and were busy filing their first stories on the killings. They'd been expected. The two detectives had long ago decided to let Marvin speak to the press, as he was good at saying nothing in a forthcoming and affable manner the TV reporters especially appreciated. It was important in a high profile case to get the TV reporters on your side from the start, and professional affability was the key. Marvin, handsome, always made for good TV.

Things had moved quickly from a rather typical crime scene to an extraordinary one. The TV reporters, whose producers monitored the police band, had heard the first dispatch calls, which would have included a call sign for homicide, sending a patrol car to the address. The TV people had put two and two together, linking the house with the wealthy Chaundhry family. Three of the city's major TV stations had sent satellite trucks to the scene. Their trucks parked in a line along the street with their satellite dishes extended, looking like metallic mantises.

Michael turned and surveyed the antique desk, where a large computer screen glowed. The computer had been left on. He tapped the space key with his iPhone, staying away from the edge of the space bar. A spread sheet popped with multiple rows. The rows were titled in a foreign language; Hindi, he guessed. He sat down and wondered what the time stamp on the file might show. He was working. Someone came to the front door? Did he open the door to his killer? Or did the wife kill them both, and then concoct a story about being out of the house?

He stood up, making sure he didn't disturb the welter of papers around the keyboard. He looked carefully at the hulking Regency-style desk and began to pick through the piles of documents stacked on it.

Indian newspapers, printed out emails, several yellow legal pads were stacked around the computer's screen. A recent copy of the Chaundhry SA annual report to stockholders had a glossy cover showing an assembly line and computer motherboards being manufactured in a pristine factory. It was the desk of a man who seemed to be buried alive by his work.

He flipped through some of the paper documents, most of which were in Hindi. There was something from a law firm in the Channel Islands in English. He looked about for the husband's cell phone, hoping to find it on the desk, but didn't see it. No secretary? Maybe during the day. He would have to ask the wife.

A reference book showed a picture of a Blackberry on the cover. The writing was in English and seemed to have an official Indian government seal of some kind. He found an envelope from Lockheed Martin, the American aerospace company, and opened it. It held half a dozen plastic wafers, clear and very thin. He took one out and tried to bend it, but it wouldn't bend. Still looking for Chaundhry's cell phone, he dropped the clear wafer back in the envelope and put it aside. He noticed that the wafer was extremely sharp, nicking his finger.

He couldn't touch the body and search for the victim's cell phone—a Blackberry, he suspected. Only the coroner's investigators were allowed to go through the dead-man's pockets, or allowed to touch a victim's body at all. He'd always thought it a great irony that a homicide detective was prohibited from looking through a victim's clothing immediately, but they were. Often they would have to spend precious time identifying the victim when their purse or wallet was lying on the body, and right in front of them. But I know who this victim is … billionaire industrialist name of Rishi Chaundhry. Mr. Chaundhry had his life taken … by someone.

A family photo stood to the right of the computer in a wide and expensive-looking silver frame. It showed the four of them. The mother — Asha, he finally remembered — was looking at her husband lovingly. It was a professionally done portrait, no doubt, with a telltale staged quality. Everything perfect. The two little girls wore beautiful matching yellow saris.

He walked to the bookcase across the room. The latest Michael Connelly novel had a bookmark in it. O'Higgins had read the novel and liked it; he was a fan. Rows of shelves held books in Hindi and English, a whole row of business titles, some new, others leather-bound and obviously only for show, bought by the pound.

More photos showed what looked like extended family, back in India, judging from the exotic backgrounds. There was a sculpture in bronze of an elephant, some kind of Indian god he'd seen before. Ganesh. He turned and saw a safe, a large one, in a closet. The closet door had been left wide open. The safe was sitting in plain sight and looked brand new.

He walked to the closet, where a light was on. Inside was a metal rack for clothing, but nothing was hung on it. There was nothing else in the closet but the safe and an old-school telephone book, also brand new, lying on the hardwood floor and still wrapped in plastic, unopened.

O'Higgins squatted and examined the front of the safe. It had no marks on it at all. The safe's door had a logo of a bulldog. He looked again for obvious marks along the safe's door, but saw none.

God damn it …. It wasn't looking good for the wife, he realized. The girl upstairs was beautiful, everything about her. Any man might be tempted. It was a cliché, but that didn't make it any less possible. But the wife was a beauty herself. He remembered looking at her on the bow of the ferry. He'd been ashamed of himself. It was the first time since the accident that he'd noticed a woman in that way, felt her sexual pull.

He stood up and walked out of the closet. No one had broken in. The house had a state-of-the-art security system, and they had no report of an alarm going off. He went back to the computer, struck a key and tabbed through to the desktop. He saw an Xfinity.com icon. He clicked through, and the screen split into multiple views: the front door, monitored by a video camera trained on the foyer.

On the computer screen, he saw Marvin come up the stairs to the front door and enter the house. A second camera picked up Marvin moving through the huge foyer. The husband had had a preview of who was at the front door. The nanny had been upstairs. Had someone come to the door, forced their way in and killed the two? It seemed unlikely, as no alarms had been triggered. Was it someone Chaundhry knew, someone he simply let in?

A sign in the front garden notified everyone that the home was protected by a well-known security-system company. O'Higgins had checked the house's perimeter doors—the ones facing the backyard were all double French doors. They were undisturbed and double locked from the inside. They'd seen no obvious sign of a break-in anywhere on the ground floor.

His cell phone rang.

It was Marvin. "Where are you?"

"First floor, in the office, to the left of the stairs."

Marvin stepped into the office through the open door.

"Fuck. You won't believe this, but the Assistant District Attorney just called me and said he wants to visit the scene," Marvin said.

"What?"

"That's right. He will be here in less than an hour," Marvin said.

It was unprecedented. The District Attorney's office never involved themselves with a case at this stage, unless it was political in some way. The case was barely three hours old.

"This guy Chaundhry is a somebody," Marvin said. "And I got a guy in a turban downstairs from the Indian Consulate saying he wants to come up and secure some items of 'national importance' to the state of India. He's on the phone with the State Department right now."

"We've stepped into it," O'Higgins said.

"You think? This guy is one of the richest men in India. Case comes complete with batteries and a butt plug," Marvin said.

"What did you tell him? The Consulate guy."

"I told him no. No one comes in except Homicide or criminalists. Period. He didn't like it. Guy's got a turban on, man — really, a turban. Shit. And he's about six four. Big motherfucker."

"Sikh?" Michael said.

"Whatever, he's an asshole. Turban-wearing asshole."

O'Higgins could see his partner was rattled. Marvin had grown up in the projects, and was uncomfortable away from where he knew the streets. The wealthy had an effect on him regardless of their color, as if he were trying to imagine another dimension. He was keyed up. They were in strange deep waters where careers ran aground, and they knew it. They had no doubt of it now.

Billionaire. Fuck. DA. Consulate, O'Higgins thought.

"There's a safe." O'Higgins pointed toward the closet. "Untouched. Brand new, by the looks of it. Not even a scratch."

Marvin turned and looked at it.

"I think he was here working at his desk. He had a view of the front door and foyer from his computer's security camera hook-up, if he wanted it. So he would have seen who was at the door? Maybe I'm wrong, and we have to look at the wife." It was a stupid thing to have said, he realized, because of course she was a suspect.

"Did you find his goddamn phone yet?" Marvin said, nodding. "We need that phone, man."

"No. My guess is that it's in his pocket if it's not here on his desk. Back pants pocket, maybe? That's what I do with mine at home. The nanny's phone must be in her room. We'll find it. I'll go up and look again. She had to have one, too."

"They'll blame us if we miss one fucking thing. Fuck up one thing," Marvin said, talking to himself.

"Yeah," O'Higgins said. They looked at each other.

"Welcome back to work," Marvin said. "How is it feel so far? Enjoying it?"

"Rene is here," O'Higgins said. "She's getting her stuff out of her car, she just called. She said Woo is on her way too. Let's have her shoot the bathroom first. Then we'll do the elevator and the hallway. The elevator is going to be tricky. So the killer came through the front door?"

"Looks that way. The garage door is locked from the inside. You need an electronic key to get in, or a control," Marvin said. "I just walked down and checked from the driveway. They have security cameras across the street by the way. I saw them. Pointed this way. "

The desk phone rang, a land line. They let it ring; they couldn't hear who was calling, or if they even left a message.

"We should have patrol canvass the neighborhood right away see if anyone saw anything unusual, or has video of the street," Marvin said.

"I've already told patrol to check," Michael said.

"Rich people will have some high-end security," Marvin said. "The guy with the turban has our names, by the way. He knew who I was."

"How did he get our names already?" O'Higgins glanced at

his watch. They'd been at the scene for less than three hours.

"How the hell should I know? I'll go see where blood from the victim in the elevator may have gone. It looked like a lot had to have gone down the elevator shaft," Marvin said.

They both saw Rene Fields, SFPD's criminalist, come through the front door lugging her gear on Chaundhry's computer screen.

CHAPTER 6

In her dream Asha Chaundhry was standing in the grand foyer of her family's new home. The street outside was chaotic and appeared to be a street in Mumbai, not San Francisco's

Pacific Heights. It was an addled dreamscape. The street scene looked like a piece of color 70s-era stock film footage of Mumbai with its fantastic pulse: teeming humanity-filled streets punctuated by wandering white Brahman bulls, scruffy scooters with whole families on board, father intently leaning, a sari-clad young wife holding on, everything from marigold sellers to white-gloved policeman directing chaotic traffic.

Asha danced into the foyer, whirling, sitar music playing. She wore heavy Indian-style bracelets on her ankles. She was barefoot in a diaphanous red sari, naked under it. She stopped dancing and looked at the Piazzoni landscape painting. She stood in front of it, squaring off, as if to challenge its existence. Her pretty face showed an I-dare-you expression. She whirled provocatively in front of it, calling on it to produce the Painter-God who'd created it. She called to Rishi to come admire the painting with her in a loud voice. But he didn't answer.

She realized she was panting from her dance, the room airless and warm. She touched her flat midriff, slick with sweat; it felt as if it were a hundred degrees inside the house. She glanced around her. Everything seemed to be in its place, yet everything seemed queer and wrong, slightly askew. The loud Indian music, a morning raga, stopped.

"Rishi? Rishi, answer me!"

She wanted to confess that she was in love with the painter and explain to her husband why. She ran in a panic. The sitar music, with a wild tabla accompaniment, started up again and was very loud. She ran down the long hallway toward Rishi's office, the heavy brass ankle bracelets clanging rhythmically. Ting-ring … ting-ring… ting.

Would Rishi understand? Could he forgive her for her immoral, lascivious thoughts? She remembered that she was going to be a mother again, and the idea frightened her. Why? What had changed? Something had changed. Rishi's office door was locked. She tried frantically to open it.

Asha had found the large landscape painting online in a gallery in New York, and her husband had bought it for her without blinking. He was that kind of husband, and she loved him for it. He'd not hesitated when hearing the price, either: seventy-five-thousand dollars. It was shipped from New York the day she found it. She'd hung it in the foyer on Broadway.

This Piazzoni was even more dramatic and enthralling than one she had originally thought of buying at the Thomas Gallery. This landscape, by the famous California painter, was of Bolinas's Duxbury Reef during a storm. It was a large painting and commanded the entire foyer. You couldn't miss it.

All their guests had remarked on it when they walked into the house. You could tell people loved its raucousness and its depth of expression, its feeling of the crashing sea. The stirring, moody seascape had set the tone for the rest of the magnificent house. They had decided on a mix of Western and Indian art, all chosen by Asha and Rishi. And it worked, the blending of two cultures representing their generation's place and time. New Indian and 19th Century America, ironic and effective. It was them: tradition in love with modernity.

Because the landscape was seen as "old school," as one young Indian woman called it at a party Asha had given for the Indian ambassador's wife, it felt even more impressive and substantial. It "spoke" to people, who said how wonderful it was.

Some guests, especially the very young American tech executives, found the painting queer, even off-putting because it wasn't abstract, cynical or child-like. It was lost on young tech types, completely. Asha realized they had no method for seeing it. Their eyes were blind to nature's beauty, to nature itself, and their ears were deaf to everything it might say to them. They hated the painting and the emotional honesty it stood for. She'd overheard their silly remarks. Their reaction was unexpected and even frightening to her. She wasn't surprised when one of the young men told her very seriously that "eating was a waste of time," and that he drank most of his meals for the sake of efficiency. People at the party were flocking to hear about how he'd managed this breakthrough.

Asha woke with a start, snapping out of her drug-induced sleep. Her first instinct was to get up and find Rishi as if she were still at home. The bizarre dream had upset her. Cheating on her husband was impossible for her even to contemplate. In the dream, though, she had cheated, if only emotionally.

She upset the hospital tray in front of her. She pushed it aside and sat up in the bed, trying to get her bearings. Where am I? Where is Rishi? Where are the girls?

They had sedated her shortly after she'd arrived at Mont Zion's ER. She'd been more than just loudly hysterical when she arrived at the emergency room. She was on the point of harming herself. The young ER doctor, watching two security guards struggle with her, decided that she would have to be sedated. Her screaming was disruptive, even unbearable to those around her. She was given a powerful tranquilizer, in the Diazepam family, without her permission. It put her to sleep for seven dream-filled hours. The doctors moved her to a private room after they learned from the ambulance drivers what had happened to her husband. Everyone working in the ER felt badly for her, but they were equally glad that her hysteria had been "closed down."

Awake, she took stock of her surroundings, realizing she was in the hospital but not sure why. Have I been in a car accident?

The awful image of her husband's body lying so grotesquely on the floor of the elevator came back to her. She had managed to block it out. She screamed. Her ululation was piercing and horrible. Doctors and patients on the hospital's sixth floor heard it and were startled. It was truly blood-freezing in its intensity. It was one long cry for help.

A Filipino nurse rushed into Asha's room. Unable to get Asha to stop screaming, she slapped her across the face. The slap, shockingly unprofessional, had been instinctual. It worked. Asha stopped screaming. Another nurse, a young African-American, came into the room right after the slap. The first nurse left, realizing what she'd done. If reported, she could lose her job.

"Where am I?" Asha asked, her cheek red from the slap.

"In the hospital, Mount Zion," the young nurse said, realizing what had happened to her.

"Where's my husband? Where's Rishi? Where are my girls?"

She'd not accepted, even standing in the hallway and looking down at the body, that her husband was really dead. She'd seen a body, but it couldn't be Rishi. Her husband was fine. She'd just spoken to him, less than an hour before. It was impossible. It had to be some impostor, trying to terrify her. A horrible prank, she'd thought while staring into the elevator, holding its door open, looking at what could not be real.

"Can I get you anything?" the young nurse asked. Asha had not realized that she'd been slapped, not really.

"I want to see my husband," Asha said, trying to sound calm.

The nurse didn't answer her. Instead she nervously tidied up the hospital tray with its uneaten meal. An un-touched red Jell-O cup was turned on its side, and the nurse righted it. She could see the mark of the other nurse's hand on Asha's cheek, and it unnerved her. Angry, she decided she would report it.

"The police are coming at one o'clock to speak to you. A detective — O'Higgins, I believe his name is. He was here earlier, but he didn't want to wake you. You were asleep," the nurse said.

"Where are my daughters?" Asha asked again. Her tone was frightened, as if she knew the answer. "Where are my girls? I demand to know where they are." She'd raised her voice again, pushing the sheet away. She realized she was wearing a hospital gown, and could feel the cold on her naked back.

"I don't know," the nurse said. "The detective said he would be able to answer a lot of your questions. I'm sorry." The nurse wanted to retreat, but felt she couldn't.

Asha stared at the young woman and began to cry. The tears slid down her cheeks one after the other and fell onto her starchy hospital gown. The nurse watched her cry. She took Asha's hand and held it, not knowing what else to do.

"Rishi is dead?" Asha said. "Oh my God. Rishi is dead, isn't he?"

She'd gone to the Safeway on Marina Boulevard to pick up some things she'd forgotten. She was making Indian food for dinner, an eggplant dish Rishi loved. He'd been on his computer, working on some dreadful-looking spreadsheet in his office. The twins had a play date and were across the street at the neighbor's—the Gilberts, who had a daughter the twins' age—until dinner.

Bharti, the nanny Asha's mother-in-law had found for them when the twins were born, was tidying up the children's playroom. Bharti Kumar had been with them since she was fifteen, and Asha considered the girl to be like another daughter.

She went down the hall from the kitchen into her husband's office and explained that she was going to run to the market and would be right back. He hadn't spoken a word, but nodded in his gentle way signaling that he was busy.

"I love you," she'd said. "You over-worked man."

"I told you we should have brought our cook, Asha," Rishi said, without looking up from the computer screen. It was the last time she would see her husband alive.

***

Det. Marvin Lee stepped into Asha's hospital room and stood behind O'Higgins. They'd brought Asha's password-locked iPhone to the hospital with them, having found it in her purse in the kitchen.

"You're the policeman — the man from the ferry?" Asha said, looking at O'Higgins.

She was oddly relieved, as she was hoping she was dreaming, that this was all a nightmare — from the moment she parked her car in the driveway, snatched her handbag up off the passenger seat of her new black Land Rover, then walked up the steps to her front door with her sack of groceries.

The front door had a large panel of obscured glass that kept you from seeing inside. She'd punched in the code to the front door's high-tech electronic lock and stepped inside, trying to keep her iPhone from falling out of her hand, and went straight into the kitchen with the groceries she'd bought. Her pregnancy, only a few weeks old, had given her a sense of profound well-being. She felt it then, walking toward the kitchen and thinking about preparing dinner. She'd refused the army of servants they had in India because she wanted to be a "real" American-style mother and wife.

"Where are my girls? You must bring them to me, immediately. And my nanny? Where is Bharti?"

"We want to ask you a few questions," O'Higgins said.

"You are the policeman? The one we met on the ferry? The policeman?" Asha asked again.

"Yes. We met on the ferry to Angel Island," O'Higgins said.

"I'm dreaming, then," Asha said and smiled. It was a smile of relief. "I'm dreaming. Thank God!"

O'Higgins got closer to the bed. Chaundhry looked fragile. Her eye make-up was smeared and gave her a slightly crazed look. He realized he was looking at himself, in a way. He wanted to turn away and leave the room, but he steeled himself.

"This is my partner, Detective Marvin Lee," O'Higgins said as gently as he could. He felt the walls of the hospital room start to close in on him. He saw a white board with the words: "keep comfortable and informed" written in blue marker directly across from Asha's bed.

His own miserable pain had welled up bit-by-bit while

the criminalists, Rene Fields and Amy Woo, did their jobs: sorting through items that would be taken in to evidence, mapping the murder scene, taking photos, dusting for prints, taking Touch DNA samples from the elevator and the bathroom. They'd left Fields and Woo at the scene.

Both victims had bled out. Bharti Kumar had that startled look he'd seen on countless murder victim's faces.

O'Higgins looked at the wife. Their eyes met. He remembered Asha as she'd been on the ferry only a week before, so carefree and lovely, the epitome of the young mother. He was going to spoil that forever by telling her about Kumar. He began to stammer in an awful way, unable to come out with it.

"I … I … I need to …"

"Mrs. Chaundhry," Marvin said, stepping up. "We have some bad news. I'm sorry, but your daughters were taken from your home. It's not clear who has the girls right now. Your neighbors, the Gilberts, told officers that your father-in-law came and got the girls around 5:00 p.m. and left in what they thought was an Uber taxi. But we have not been able to speak to your father-in-law to confirm."

Asha looked at Marvin as if he were speaking a foreign language.

"We have your cell phone. We would like to keep it for the time being, if we could. Your husband's cell phone is missing. We think that whoever did this took it with them, but we're not sure. Do you know where your husband's cell phone might be? It's critical we find it," Marvin said.

"It's impossible. Bharti would never permit it," Asha said finally. "You're lying."

Marvin heard the door open and realized that O'Higgins had

walked out of the room. "We need your phone's password. Can you give it to me?" Marvin said.

"It's our address, 2845," Asha said. "Bharti knows it. Why didn't she give it to you? Where is she? Where is Bharti? She would know if Nirad has the girls."

"I'm sorry to tell you that Bharti Kumar is dead," Marvin said. "We found her body in a bathroom on the third floor of your home. She's gone. She was killed by whoever killed your husband."

O'Higgins, who had slipped out of the room while Marvin had told her the news, came back into the room with an old white-haired doctor who looked annoyed and tired of the commotion coming from Asha's room.

"I told you not to upset her, damn it!" the doctor said peevishly. Asha was crying hysterically.

The old doctor left the room and came back almost immediately with an injectable sedative. O'Higgins watched Asha go under. She tried to fight off two nurses and the old doctor who gave her the injection. He hoped to God he would never be treated like a wild animal, the way the doctor was treating Chaundhry. He almost said something, but stopped himself.

"I want to speak to Rishi," Asha said as she nodded off. "Tell him to get the girls." The drug seem to pull her violently down into the bed and into unconsciousness.

O'Higgins stood there watching until she stopped muttering. She woke up almost two hours later.

"It's you … the man on the boat."

"Yes," he said.

"Where are my girls?"

"We're looking for them," O'Higgins said. "I promise you."

He had Asha's iPhone in his hand. He was hoping that whoever had taken the girls would call Asha Chaundhry's phone.

Marvin had gone back to the scene on Broadway. They'd decided to keep the Chaundhrys' house closed down for another twenty-four hours. O'Higgins had no one to go home to as he might have done in the past, to catch a meal and explain to his wife what the case was about. Instead he'd decided to stay at the hospital and sat in the room waiting for Asha to wake up. He'd had time to look at Asha's texts and to take a call that had come in from one of Asha's girlfriends, who told him Nirad Chaundhry had been living with the couple for the last few weeks.

"I'm terribly thirsty," Asha said from the bed.

O'Higgins stood up and brought the short plastic water glass and helped her drink from its straw. The second sedative they'd used on her had enervated her completely. Her eyes were glassy and bloodshot.

While he'd sat there, waiting, he'd gone through her phone. It was a picture of a woman of her age: Photos, dozens, of her twin girls, of Rishi, and of the girls' school. Some of her husband and an older man who looked like her husband. O'Higgins guessed that was her father-in-law. There was a photo of a Hindu god, of some kind, as her phone's desktop. She had a WeChat account, but all the messages on WeChat were in Hindi.

Someone had sent Asha an Instagram photo while he'd been poking around—a selfie taken at what looked like some kind of university, as there were university-age students in the background. The girl in the Instagram photo looked like Asha and may have been a younger sister, or niece, he guessed.

He looked for anything in the text messages—there were more than 200. But they seemed to be mostly innocuous. Contractors of one kind or another, asking to be let into the house at a certain time, or Asha's girlfriends chatting about random subjects. He saw a picture of an Indian temple and noted it because it seemed to be in the Bay Area.

He finally noticed a text from someone, writing in English, who kept asking the same question but received no reply: Coffee? He counted over a dozen texts from the same person, Robert Thomas.

There were emails in both Hindi and English. New ones were coming in from immediate family members, wondering why they'd not head back from her. Asha's mother—in English— had left several voice messages, each one had sounded progressively more concerned and agitated. Then they'd stopped altogether. He wondered why Asha's mother wasn't still trying to reach her daughter. Had she heard the news about her son-in-law?

"My husband is dead?"

"Yes."

"Bharti too? You're sure?"

"Yes. I'm afraid so," O'Higgins said standing next to her.

"Why?"

"We don't know. Your girls are with your father-in-law, it seems. He picked them up at the Gilberts. It was an Uber car that picked them up. They were taken to the Indian Consulate and dropped off. We checked. So we've ruled out kidnapping. I've found your father-in-law's cell number and left a message for him. But he's not called back yet."

She stared at him. "Nirad has the girls? Why? I don't understand."

"We don't know. We're trying to contact him. Have you noticed anything strange in the neighborhood? Perhaps strange people canvassing?"

"No. Nothing." The hospital was quiet. It was a dramatic change from the morning, when it had been so hectic and noisy.

"Did your husband mention anything at all that might help us? Anyone who came to the house who might have done this?"

"No. Where is he? His body, where is it?"

"The coroner's office will take both bodies to the morgue."

"I have to call his parents," Asha said.

"Your father-in-law was at the house when you left to go to the store?"

"Yes. No. He may have been. I don't know exactly. He was due home for dinner. He'd called at lunch — I didn't see Nirad when I arrived. The girls were across the street at the Gilberts'. A play date."

"But your father-in-law was staying there at the house with you?"

"Yes. Yes. Give me my phone," she said. He handed her back her cell phone. "I would like some privacy, please — Detective," she said.

"Yes, of course." He made for the door and stopped. He thought of asking her permission to have the technical staff at Battery Street clone her phone's memory, but didn't bother. He could ask her later.

He looked at his watch. It was 5:00 a.m. He'd not slept for more than twenty-four hours, and was exhausted.

Asha Chaundhry was speaking in a low tone of voice in Hindi on her phone. O'Higgins walked out of the room and down the ward's empty, well-lit hallway. A nurse passed him and smiled; the nurses all seemed to know he was a San Francisco police detective. He nodded back.

He was glad that the two little girls were probably safe. The idea that they might have been kidnapped had horrified him. He went home to shower, lay down, and fell into a deep sleep. It was the first time he'd been able to sleep without taking a Valium. He woke three hours later, his phone ringing on the bed beside him.

CHAPTER 7

Four months before the murders

"Mother, please tell them both hello," Asha said.

She had two English girlfriends who had both been up at Cambridge with her. The two were staying a week with her parents while visiting India. It was Asha who suggested it. She tried to stay in touch with her English girlfriends since she'd married, but the circumstances of her marriage had made her Western girlfriends uncomfortable.

The two English women staying at her parents' house were typical of all her English and American friends who would never understand Indian culture, or accept her being happy in an arranged marriage, which she was. Although she understood their attitudes about arranged marriage — they loathed the idea, primarily because they were besotted with the idea of "romance" — she'd ignored their dire warnings, taken the plunge and married Rishi. She had not regretted it for a moment.

She hung up her iPhone after allowing her mother, a well-known concert pianist, to explain in great detail why she hoped Asha's father-in-law, Nirad Chaundhry, would not succeed in his bid for Prime Minister. There would be a general election in three months. The Indian press was full of speculation that Nirad would head the next government of India, bringing his Hindu

Nationalist Party, the BJP, back to power.

Asha pocketed her phone, took her two girls' hands and headed across busy Geary Street toward the art gallery she intended to visit. Politics bored her in general, but the idea of her father-in-law becoming Prime Minister of India was exciting, and she knew it would be very good for her children. All doors around the world would open for them, should Nirad become prime minister.

"I was interested in the landscape in the window," Asha said.

"It's a Piazzoni. Hello, I'm Robert Thomas, the owner," the well-dressed young man said, walking out of the gallery's Rare Book Room and into a flimsy-feeling light. "Gottardo Piazzoni. Perhaps you've heard of him?"

Asha was wearing black yoga pants and an expensive white blouse she'd bought at Banana Republic the day before. She looked elegant and chic. She was clutching her iPhone, waiting for her husband to return a text about when she could expect him back at the hotel.

"Do you like it?" Thomas asked from across the still-cold salon. The heater had just kicked in. The young man was a slight, handsome in an old-school way. His mother's friends all said he looked like the '60s-era movie star Montgomery Clift, lean and dark-haired and somewhat fragile looking. Asha thought at first he was gay, but something about his smile changed her mind. It was slightly feral, and vibed straight.

Thomas flipped on the light switch next to him, lighting up an entire wall behind him, hung with forty or more landscape paintings, mostly California artists from the 19th and early 20th centuries. It was a dazzling display. Scores of Tonalist and Pasadena School paintings appeared out of the gloom, caught in spotlights designed to show them to their best effect: desert scenes of Palm Springs before it turned into the cheesy resort town; pristine Southern California seashores, before cars and black-top highways invaded, a time when there were still "Pismo clams" at Malibu; Yosemite's famous Half-Dome in winter: fabulous rose gardens of the wealthy in Pasadena of the 1920s: the wondrous almond and orange orchards of San Jose before it became home to the Pentagon's techno-military-industrial complex. The paintings captured all of early 20th century California's once varied, heart-stopping landscapes, long past and forgotten, buried by freeways and McDonalds restaurants.

The art startled her. It was almost as if each painting were only part of a panel in one monumental work, a masterpiece that stretched across 40 feet of gallery wall: California. It opened up something in her.

"I'm looking for a gift, for my husband. For Christmas," Asha said, standing near the entrance as if afraid to come in a step further. Her daughters had pulled away and were exploring a still-dark cavernous second room to Asha's left. "And we've a new place to furnish as well. Terribly exciting, but quite daunting in its scope."

Asha looked down to see a luxe red carpet that gave the place a sumptuous quality, something between a Turkish pasha's harem quarters and the office of a powerful dictator. She felt warm air pour down over her shoulders, from a heating vent in the ceiling directly above her.

The young man looked at her as if she had fallen from the sky instead of walking through the door. She was used to being ogled by men, young and old, and she took it in stride. It had been going on since she was a very young girl. She had the kind of perfect body men couldn't help but stare at or want in the most basic and physical way.

The gallery owner had not noticed her two girls, but now he heard them playing in the adjoining room. The two were sitting in a '60s hoop chair, having a gay time of it.

Robert Thomas stopped smiling and looked at them. He deliberately lit the room the girls were in from the array of light switches behind him. The girls looked at him, caught out.

"But it's the painting in the window that caught my eye," Asha said. "It would be perfect for our new place, I think."

Thomas walked Asha toward the painting in the window. He climbed up into the display and turned the canvas toward her. Something about him was athletic and confident. He is the King of this empire, she thought.

Robert Thomas had designed the window display himself with the utmost care. It was meticulous and enchanting. It was the gallery's special holiday display, and he'd taken great pains to make it look attractive and inviting. He'd arranged a kind of tableau with a mid-century couch and the Piazzoni landscape tilted against it. He'd draped a long string of real antique black pearls off the painting's gilded frame. He'd placed a bottle of French Champagne—one of the large magnums—in an antique silver ice bucket on a silver tray off to its side. He'd laced the scene with tiny Christmas lights. He'd managed to make the old-school painting sexy and modern by combining it with hip furniture. He had a knack with things like that.

The painting impressed Asha again when he turned it toward her. It looked even better in the strange demi-light of morning. The dull winter's light from Geary Street infused it with something special, adding to its delicious moody quality.

He brought the painting closer so she could view it. People walked by the gallery, looking in at them as they passed. He said nothing, letting her enjoy what she was so taken with. He'd seen customers look at paintings like that before. He knew she loved it in a way that was personal and intense, and could lead to a quick sale.

Something about the painting was haunting and profound, Asha had thought the moment she'd first seen it. She'd found herself staring at it from the sidewalk the day before, on the way to lunch. It was of a bay somewhere, with something quietly, intensely intimate about it. The color scheme was classic Tonalist work in different muted gold and green tones, one color fading into the next, dreamlike and sublime. It was as if the painter had assigned this landscape to stand in for some deep emotion he'd felt—a kind of secret between the painter and the landscape that would be impossible to share completely.

You would have to have some key to its meaning, she thought, studying it again. Or have known the artist, been his lover even. Or been with him that day he'd painted it, at least. Before knowing who the painter was, she'd been sure it had been painted by a man and not a woman. Something about it was very male. And then he might only have whispered it to you.

Without intending to she had a quasi-sexual fantasy about the painter, working that day. In her fantasy she sat down next to him and listened to him explain things, things that would otherwise have been unknown to her. It was magical. They were together alone with the landscape, becoming part of it.

He, the painter, turned and looked into her eyes. "Where are you from?" he asked.

"India. I'm from India," she'd said. They'd kissed. The painter touched her breast. His palm was warm. It felt as if he'd touched the very center of her being and flipped the switch, the one that had been there waiting to be turned on without her even knowing it.

The painting sparked something, perhaps just a recognition of nature's power, including her own power. She wondered if she could be pregnant again. Her prior pregnancy had brought on intense emotions: sexual, a strong human compassion too, and at odd times. Since they'd arrived she was constantly buying food for homeless people on Geary Street. If I were pregnant that would explain it. I would blame this weird feeling on a sudden splash of mother-chemicals. But I'm not pregnant. It's something else.

"Where is this bay, so enchanting? It's so — intriguing," Asha asked. The young man had not said a word since he climbed into the display.

"Tomales Bay," Thomas said. "Have you ever been?"

"No. We've just moved here from India. Is it close, Tomales Bay? Perhaps we'll visit."

"About two hours from the City, maybe less. To the North. Marin County." He put the painting back in its place and climbed out of the display window. "Would you like to buy it?"

"Yes, very much," she said, smiling, knowing she could never explain the purchase to her husband. He didn't care much for figurative landscape paintings. When it came to Western paintings, he was attracted to abstract expressionist work. "It's so — relaxing. Is it terribly expensive?"

"No, not at all. Sixty thousand dollars. A steal, really." Robert mugged straight-faced for a moment, then cracked a half-smile. "Should I have it wrapped up and sent along?" He was going to say fifty thousand, which was what he'd been quoting, but something told him to push it higher. She struck him as some guy's heart-stopping trophy wife.

The Chaundhrys had only been in San Francisco for a month. Asha was happy to be out of India—Mumbai, especially, where they'd lived since they were married. She'd found Mumbai claustrophobic. San Francisco was just the opposite. She loved it. They were living in the Clift Hotel while waiting for their new house to be remodeled. She had insisted on living in the City despite the fact that her husband was setting up a new plant near Silicon Valley, to be part of his family's electronics empire.

The Chaundhry family had three massive electronics plants in India—motherboard producers for Dell and others, including secret work for the Indian government. They had decided it was time to expand their motherboard production into the US and had sent their eldest son, Rishi, to make it happen. At least that was what the Indian business press had reported, in countless glowing stories.

Rishi was older than she by almost fifteen years. It was what she'd found attractive about him. He was secure, with that attitude of entitlement the rich have everywhere. His brother was a notorious playboy who dated Bollywood film stars and ran from one bedroom to the next. Rishi was just the opposite. He'd been the perfect Indian son, tending to the business, working with his father and staying out of the newspapers. Asha's parents had found no fault in the man. The fact that he was slightly older than their daughter they viewed as a positive.

When she'd said yes to the marriage—they'd had only really one date, and it had been chaperoned—she knew that her children would have the best of everything. That had made her feel profoundly secure. They had two beautiful daughters, and they hoped to have a third child, a boy.

"I see. Sixty thousand dollars. Well —" Her English was British English, and Robert thought it sounded posh. She was extremely attractive, model quality. He was a ladies' man and considered himself a connoisseur of beauty, as well as number of other things.

He'd skipped college altogether, deciding instead to learn the gallery business from his grandfather, who had been a hard taskmaster but a very good teacher. By the time he was nineteen Robert had become an acknowledged expert, not just in 19th century landscape painting, but in rare books and mid-century furniture, both of which he avidly collected and had a passion for, especially rare books. At the moment he was trying to acquire a manuscript of Kafka's novel The Castle. He thought of himself as a playboy with very good taste. And it was probably true. That he had a serious personality disorder was lost on him.

Robert Thomas had been diagnosed in high school with narcissistic personality disorder by a psychiatrist who thought he was clearest example of the disorder he'd ever seen. Robert's mother had insisted he see someone after a series of outbursts and fights between them about his behavior at school. The doctor had, unfortunately, missed some of Robert's other disturbing personality traits.

"The painter is quite famous in the Bay Area. Swiss. Came to San Francisco when he was only fifteen," Robert said. "Tonalist. Well, some refer to that school as Luminists. But I prefer Tonalist."

He loved to educate people who came into the gallery. He did it nicely and without sounding pompous. It was one of the first things his grandfather had taught him about the art business. "Nobody likes to be lectured," his grandfather had warned him. "Even uneducated people, who should be." He learned that if he smiled and spoke softly, it went down well with the average wealthy person. Poor people didn't wander into the Thomas gallery.

Robert was watching her two little girls like a hawk as he spoke; the girls had come in with her, and were obviously her children. He didn't like it when people brought children into the gallery. But the woman looked well-heeled and he'd decided to be nice to her, in part because she was so attractive. He had a prejudice toward attractive people. He always treated them with respect. He believed they, like himself, were naturally superior.

Robert began to prattle on about the artist again, but Asha stopped listening and looked for her girls in the gloomy room next to them. She spotted them wandering through the salon and relaxed again. She faced the young man, who was standing next to her now, quite close. She thought his smile a strange one. It had a slightly plastered-on quality, as if you could lift it off like wallpaper and see another, older, pattern under it. He was handsome, no doubt, in the way of young white Americans.

"I was also interested in the library chairs you have," she said, interrupting. "I came in yesterday, but your salesperson said I should come back. They're so chic. I know my husband would love them as well." She'd started to feel queer for some reason. He was looking at her in an all too familiar way. It was unmistakable, and beginning to bother her. Is he undressing me?

"The library set? Yes. Pierre Jeanneret. They're from India, in fact — Punjab Central University. Recovered," the young man told her.

"Really?" she said, surprised. "They're so beautiful. That Jeanneret? The architect, of course. I've heard of him. The chairs fold, then?"

"Yes, of course they fold," Robert said. The young man had a perfect face, a symmetry hard to find in nature. His was a classic beauty, the male equivalent of Botticelli's famous Venus. Almost girlish, Asha decided.

Robert was going to go on about the designer Jeanneret and his famous cousin, but stopped himself. He smiled again and began to turn up the charm, which he could do effortlessly. He was only twenty-four and especially effective with older women, who were overwhelmed by his good looks.

On more than one occasion he'd hooked up in the back of the gallery, where he kept a small apartment. The seduced women often wondered how they'd ended up splayed over his antique library table, having sex with a complete stranger. But they'd let themselves be seduced. He had a raw sexual appeal. Part of it was his youth, and part his intellectual swagger, flaunted while showing them hulking and expensive paintings. It worked, most of the time. He had the best luck with married women who came to San Francisco as tourists. Rich women from Southern California were especially susceptible. They wanted a fling with a cute smart guy, and he'd give them a good one. He was the proverbial pool boy, albeit with a necktie and a whopping IQ. The women usually bought something, too.

"I thought the chairs would be perfect for the new place. But I love this painting, I must say. Stunning. Really." Asha meant it.

"Take them all," Robert suggested.

"I wish I could," she said, but immediately regretted it. he felt uncomfortable, and wasn't sure exactly why. He's not gay … You can tell.

He looked at her in a way that frightened her. Something about his look, she thought, something was off, something slightly evil. Perhaps it was his mouth, which had tightened as he spoke. She had a sixth sense and always paid it special heed, especially regarding feelings like this. And especially feelings about weird men. (Since she was a young girl, perverts of every type — young and old — had been attracted to her, trying to "interfere." She'd been smart enough to keep one step ahead of them.)

"We specialize in 19th century California plein air paintings, like the Piazzoni. That's what we're known for. I've added the furniture and modern art since my mother died. Time to freshen up our focus, I think. And I love the mid-century period. I'm a collector myself," he said.

She could tell he was full of himself and this place, as if the artwork were an extension of his own ego.

The young man looked at her daughters who were playing near an Andy Warhol print, the artist's signature Campbell Soup Can, in the next room. He'd started to bring in the Andy Warhol because younger rich people wanted Pop Art. They didn't even look at the oil paintings. Oil paintings, to the young, seemed absurd and old-fashioned, like rotary dial telephones or reruns of old black and white TV shows.

He'd overheard an obviously well-heeled twenty-something couple who'd wandered in, and it had shocked him. There was a profound change in the nature of the rich, he'd decided. They wanted "weird" art and would pay a lot for it. The less craftsmanship it displayed, the better they liked it. Mid-century anything, he could sell, and for top dollar. He referred to them as the hula-hoop crowd.

"Your daughters, they're twins?" Robert said.

"Yes. Identical," Asha said. "I can tell them apart, but sometimes my husband can't."

She made a motion for the girls, who were exploring the place, to come to her. It was unconscious motherly reaction. The girls looked up but didn't come at once, having too much fun picking up curios: a Jouve ceramic vase with a woman's face. One of the twins fumbled the vase. It landed, luckily, on the cushion of the hoop chair and bounced unhurt.

Robert missed it all, his focus again on their mother. The girls, having startled themselves with the fumbled vase, decided it would be a good idea to heed their mother's call. They left the vase where it was, afraid to touch it, and walked quickly to the safety of their mother's side. Asha made an excuse and left the shop, saying she would come back with her husband. Her abrupt leaving annoyed Thomas. After she left, he couldn't stop thinking about her. He didn't handle rejection well; it was one of the first things the psychiatrist had explained to his mother.

A day later Robert saw Asha come out of the Clift Hotel with her husband and jump into a taxi. They were well dressed and obviously going to a party, or perhaps the opera. He was shocked at how much older her husband was. Robert convinced himself that he and the Indian beauty had a connection, that she had been attracted to him. He only needed to impress her, and she would come around. He would "hit it and quit it."

Robert knew one of the girls who worked the Clift's front desk at night. He asked about the Indian family, telling his friend that the mother and her two girls had been in the gallery and he'd discovered something broken, and wanted to speak to the parents about it.

She gave him the family's name and room number. It was all he needed. He rang the next morning, explaining to Asha that the girls had broken a vase. Would she mind coming in and paying for it? He'd made up the lie solely so he could see her again.

When she came back to the shop he tried to seduce her, asking her to come look at his collection of rare books. She thought it corny and obvious. She'd refused, of course, and left a little shocked, after paying $900 for the "Jouve ceramic vase with a woman's face." She said nothing, but did not believe her girls had broken anything.

He handed her the pieces in a box after smashing the vase in his back apartment while she waited at the counter, disconcerted. He'd expected to seduce her, and was sure he was going to succeed. He had not. He'd liked the vase, but enjoyed smashing it to bits.

Asha promised herself she'd never return to the gallery. Three days later they moved into their new fabulous home on Broadway and she forgot all about what happened. Christmas came, with the tree, parties, and the rest of it. They went to Tahoe for New Year's and had a wonderful holiday. The girls learned to snowboard.

She was shocked to find the Piazzoni that she'd so admired at the gallery had been delivered to their house by special courier while they were away. It was a gift, the accompanying card said—from Robert Thomas.

Dear Asha,

I hope you had a great holiday. I was in the Sierras skiing at our place in Tahoe. (You must see it. Perhaps you and your husband would like to use it some time?)

Please accept this painting as a gift. I know you love it. That was so obvious the day we met. Consider it a housewarming gift.

Warm Regards, Robert

Asha had the painting returned immediately, with a curt note.

Dear Mr. Thomas,

My husband and I couldn't possibly accept such an expensive gift. We're sending it back to the gallery.

Mrs. Chaundhry

She was going to add a "thank you" to the note, out of politeness, but decided not to. She was hoping she'd never hear from the strange man again. She wondered how on earth he'd found their home address, or the fact they'd been on holiday in the Sierras.

CHAPTER 8

Marvin asked the coroner's investigator, Paul Millikin, to allow him to go through the victim's pockets before they placed Rishi Chaundhry's body in the black-rubber body bag and removed it from the scene. The coroner's investigator, a seen-it-all older white man with a shock of red hair, was on his cell phone. He agreed with a curt nod.

Millikin, in jeans and a windbreaker, had been taking photos from outside the elevator of the body with a small digital camera. His job was to document the immediate position and physical context the body had been found in through photos and notes, so the coroner's medical examiner could get up-to-speed.

Two burly older black men from the city-contracted mortuary on Fillmore Street came up the stairs, ready to remove the bodies to the morgue—body handlers, they were called in the homicide business.

"In the elevator," Millikin said. "How you been, Paul?"

One of the black men reached over and shook Millikin's hand.

"Nice place," the older of the two men said.

"Yeah. You should see the view," Millikin said. "There's a body up on the third floor as well. It's a double."

Marvin stepped over the body tarp the two morgue attendants spread out in the hallway. Marvin watched as they lifted

Rishi Chaundhry's body unceremoniously from the floor of the blood-slick elevator and out onto the heavy plastic in the hallway. Livor mortis had set in. Blood had pooled on the lowest points, discoloring the victim's neck and palms. Blood from his wounds, under him, had yellowish-red, with a jelly-like consistency.

"Okay, you want to look for a phone, knock yourself out, Marvin," Millikin said.

Marvin nodded and asked the body handlers to help him turn Chaundhry onto his stomach. The body made ugly sounds, gas having built up. Manhandling the body was distasteful, but the men pretended it was routine.

Marvin dug through Chaundhry's pockets, finding a wallet with a California driver's license and three credit cards. That was all: no cell phone.

"Okay." Marvin backed away. "Let's see if he was stabbed anywhere else."

Millikin moved in and stood over the body. He cut the shirt open, slitting the man's once-white shirt down the back. He peeled back the shirt to expose Chaundhry's naked and discolored back. There were no other obvious wounds.

Marvin backed up and watched Millikin cut the man's blood-soaked trousers, exposing the back of his legs and buttocks. When they were satisfied there was nothing more to examine, Marvin nodded to Millikin and he had the body put in the body bag. Millikin zipped it up and signaled to the two black men to take it away on a special narrow rolling gurney brought for the purpose.

As soon as the first body was gone the two female criminalists, unable to dust the elevator for prints before, climbed in and started to work. They held a high intensity light at an angle to spot possible prints left on the elevator's walls, for dusting. Marvin watched as the two went to work.

Millikin and the body handlers went up after Kumar's body. Marvin didn't want to see the young woman's naked body, so horribly crumpled, put into the body bag. He didn't want to see the men handling the girl later in his dreams, which were vivid and frightening, despite all the murder scenes he'd worked. He often had dreams about victims. Sometimes they would speak to him in a queer way, off-handedly. One woman, in a dream, asked him if he "felt bad" about her being raped.

He signaled them to go on without him. Then he did what he'd promised his wife he wouldn't do: he went outside and had a cigarette in the Chaundhrys' backyard, looking out on the Bay. He noticed red stains on the cigarette along the filter, despite having washed his hands after handling the body. He dropped it immediately and snuffed it out with the heel of his polished shoe.

"My name is Nirad Chaundhry. I'm Rishi Chaundhry's father," the man said over the phone. "The girls are safe. They're staying at the Indian Consulate. I've received all your messages."

"We need to speak," O'Higgins said. "Where are you?"

O'Higgins was driving to the scene on Broadway. The scene was still locked down. The press in India had gotten hold of the story, publishing the names of the victims. The murders were already headline news in the Times of India. He'd seen the headline on Yahoo News that morning on his phone. He was startled to read that Nirad Chaundhry was, from the looks of it, likely to be India's next Prime Minister.

"Yes. All right. I'll need access to Rishi's house very soon," Nirad Chaundhry said. "When can we have it back—the house?"

"I don't know," O'Higgins said, surprised at the man's cold, all-business tone of voice.

"We are a very busy family. My son's office, it's crucial that we have access. I must be able to access his office and conduct business. You can understand, Detective, I'm sure," Chaundhry said.

"Have you seen your son's cell phone? Do you know where we might find it? It's very important we get hold of it," O'Higgins said, ignoring Chaundhry's attempt to bully him.

"Yes," Chaundhry said. "I have it."

"You have it? It's important that we have a chance to examine your son's phone."

"I'll explain when we meet. Why don't you come to my lawyer's office on Sansome Street? Pandit Singh LLC. Fourth floor, eleven a.m. Goodbye, detective." Chaundhry hung up without waiting for a response.

O'Higgins pressed the button on his steering wheel to end the call. He drove down Webster Street toward Broadway. He replayed the conversation back in his head. Nirad Chaundhry was not showing the normal signs of grief from a close family member of a murder victim.

O'Higgins called Chaundhry's number, but it went direct to voice mail. He swore out loud and rolled through a stop sign. He slammed the steering wheel with his palm and punched the gas. His battered Ford raced by a white Bentley whose driver was texting. He pulled alongside and gave the young driver a dirty look. His phone rang again, and he took the call. It was Marvin.

"We may have found the murder weapon," Marvin said. "It was part of a collection of antique knives. Luna is testing it. Where are you, man? I'm at the scene. The coroner took the bodies. There was no phone on Rishi Chaundhry. No other wounds, either. And still no phone for the nanny, Kumar."

"I'm five minutes away," O'Higgins said.

"All right, then."

"I just heard from the father. He has the kids, he said they're staying at the Indian Consulate. Can you call the Consulate and confirm that the Chaundhry girls are there? We should send Social Services to check on them."

"Yeah. Okay. Good news. We don't have a kidnapping, on top of this mess." Marvin rang off.

He and Marvin went into Rishi Chaundhry's home office to review the case. The man had a collection of antique daggers that decorators were installing in a fancy glass display case. The display case had been resting on the floor of a utility room on the first floor. Woo had found the knives while searching for a bathroom.

Marvin had gone home, but just for breakfast and to see his kids off to school. His wife, a stewardess for Southwest, was on a flight to Puerto Rico. Marvin didn't like his girls to wake up in an empty house.

"Okay, I called. The two Chaundhry girls are at the Indian Consulate 'under special protection,' an official told me. Whatever that means. The girls are Indian citizens, as are their parents. We can go see them for an interview. But they're in India now as far as that goes, so the official says we can't remove them from the Consulate. I got a call from the assistant DA. I guess this guy Nirad Chaundhry is a real heavyweight.

"The DA's office got a call last night from the State Department. State wants the FBI to take over the case because of its importance to national security. If it had turned into a kidnapping, the feds would have already taken over by now. They were waiting to hear. I'm guessing that the FBI don't want any part of it."

"Not a kidnapping now. I'll call Social Services and have them send someone to check on the kids this morning," O'Higgins said.

"We should try to interview the girls," Marvin said.

"Right. I know. Okay, suspects as of this morning?" Michael asked.

"The victim's wife and the father are at the top of the list. No forced entry. Not a robbery. The safe is here, and untouched. The father and the wife both had the opportunity to kill Chaundhry and Kumar, and then call it in. I checked the call to SFPD. It came from here, the landline number. The caller didn't leave his name, but it was a man. So."

"Who else?" Michael said.

"You tell me, doctor," Marvin said. Marvin had changed into a dark grey suit and looked put together, but his eyes were red and puffy from lack of sleep.

"There was a guy who has been texting the wife. She never answered him. He wanted to meet her for coffee," Michael said.

"Who is it?"

"Name is Robert Thomas. I had the phone number looked up. He's a local society brat, owns a gallery on Geary Street. I Googled him. The Thomas Gallery."

"Sounds like he's gay? Gallery business."

"Can you sing and dance?" Michael said.

"Sing? No. I'm a hell of a dancer, though, 'cause I black."

"Okay, I'll swing by, see what he's about. We both should interview Chaundhry senior. I want you there with me this morning."

"Did you ask him to come down to Bryant Street?"

"Didn't get a chance to. He said he'd meet us at his lawyer's office downtown."

"He lawyered up quick," Marvin said. "And where was he yesterday, I wonder? He took the kids and left the scene?"

"It looks that way. The wife said her father-in-law was expected home for dinner, but she didn't see him when she got back from the store. What about keeping the scene shut down?"

"Another day at least," Marvin said.

"Nirad Chaundhry wants it back," O'Higgins said.

"This is a high profile case. We have two suspects who we've not locked into a story yet. I want to interview them before this all gets disturbed and someone comes in here and starts contaminating our scene."

Fields stuck her head into the room. "Okay, I've got the orientation maps. You want to see them?" She was a tall woman in her early thirties and a mountain-bike racer in her off time. It showed; all the single cops got nervous around her because she was pretty, athletic and unavailable.

"Yeah. Okay," Marvin said.

Marvin went into the hallway with Fields to review the sketches she'd done of the bodies, giving their orientation North, East, West, and South with notes: position of wounds, blood cast off from the murder weapon, and other details.

The criminalists' photographs of the scene would be burnt to disk and those disks assigned a number that would appear in the "murder book." These notes, sketches, and photos were critical to get right, as the District Attorney's office would need them. They were the spine of the murder book, and would be shared with the defense, with the rest of the murder book's contents if and when the case went to trial.

O'Higgins walked to the window and looked out on the bay.

His mind was full of random details, trying to organize them for the preliminary report they would soon have to write. He didn't react to the sight of the bay, grey-blue that morning.

He turned away from the window and dialed Robert Thomas' cell number. It went to voice mail. He left a message asking him to call Detective Michael O'Higgins from the SFPD at his earliest convenience.

Almost immediately, his phone rang. It was the District Attorney's office, saying that the Indian Consulate was not going to allow Asha Chaundhry's daughters to be interviewed by anyone, including Social Services. Members of the family would be taking the two girls back to India in the next 24 hours. It was all very imperious and final, as if the SFPD's murder investigation was of no importance.

O'Higgins ended the call realizing this was not going to be a normal murder investigation.

CHAPTER 9

Pandit Singh LLC was not a lawyer, but the name of a huge international law firm representing various transnational Indian corporations and elite Indian families. It had ties to Indian intelligence, but these were unknown to the general public.

The CIA and other foreign intelligence agencies had found that law firms—like the Dulles brothers' firm, Sullivan & Cromwell—were the perfect cover, and useful tools. Vladimir Putin had been trained as a lawyer as well as a KGB officer. Law, espionage, and investment banking were fingers of the hand that held the reins of the modern nation state. India was no different from America or England in that regard.

The public did know that Pandit Singh LLC was started in the 1920's by young Indian lawyers in order to better represent radical elements who opposed the British Raj. Ironically, it had started in London. Singh was now one of India's premier corporate law firms. It occupied two floors in the same building as the Mandarin Hotel in San Francisco's financial district.

Det. Marvin Lee and Det. O'Higgins were ushered into a stunning conference room on the thirty-second floor, with a fabulous view of Coit Tower and beyond it the East Bay. O'Higgins noticed that all the employees, including the young woman who'd shown them to the conference room, were Indians.

Nirad Chaundhry was sixty years old, according to O'Higgins' Google search. His hair was coal black, and Michael thought he was dyeing it. He was bigger physically than he'd sounded on the phone. He used a cane, O'Higgins had read, as the result of a terrible automobile accident in his youth. His eyes were wide set and the lids heavy with dark circles under them that looked almost blue. His pock-marked skin was leathery. That morning he looked like a man who'd not slept in days, or had been drinking a great deal, or both. He also looked like a man who was used to being obeyed.

Next to Chaundhry was a young, eager-looking Indian lawyer in a thousand-dollar suit. The lawyer's hair was slicked down and combed straight back. A cup of chai in a porcelain cup rested on the table in front of him. In contrast, Chaundhry wore a black turtleneck sweater and slacks and looked rumbled, certainly for a captain of industry and reputedly the richest man in South Asia.

"This is Mr. Nath," Chaundhry said. "He works for the family." He smiled curtly, as if the detectives were there for a business meeting and not an interview about a double homicide in his family.

"Pleased to meet you," Nath said without moving his face muscles. Then the young lawyer smiled. It wasn't genuine; it was a lips-only smile, and phony. The lawyer was twenty-five, if that. He looked out of his depth but quick-witted and eager to please his boss. His teeth, O'Higgins noticed, had been over-bleached to an eggshell white, and seemed too big for his mouth.

"Thank you for meeting with us," O'Higgins said. "We'd like to ask you some questions, Mr. Chaundhry."

"Please, sit down," Chaundhry said. "Speak freely. I'm here to help. Anything I can do to help — under the circumstances."

Michael sat down on the other side of the wide conference table. Marvin slipped into the seat next to him. Chaundhry didn't seem particularly upset by the circumstances he was referring to. He took a sip from his cup like an animal holding its prey, looking at O'Higgins as he did.

The huge boardroom style conference table had a glassy finish and appeared as if it was never used, not a scratch on its polished surface. The lawyer picked up his pen, looked down at a fresh yellow legal pad and noted the time. Michael watched him glance at his big expensive watch. He remembered how his wife used to make fun of big-dick watches.

"I'm sorry about your son," Michael said.

"It's a terrible tragedy. Yes. Thank you," Chaundhry said. He put his cup back on the saucer carefully, as if it might break.

"Were you in the house yesterday when your son was attacked?" O'Higgins asked.

"No. I'd gone out. I got to Broadway around five and found my son in the elevator. He was dead."

"Where were you yesterday?" O'Higgins asked.

"I was organizing our new corporate offices here in this building — meeting with Mr. Nath, in fact, and others. I was here all day," Chaundhry said.

"You called the police when you got to the house?"

"Yes. I came home about five or so, and found my son already dead. I called the police immediately. I found the children across the street at a neighbor's and took them away before they could find out what had happened to their father. Their safety was, of course, my chief concern. That's why I left and went straight to the Indian Consulate. I know the Consul General. He's a personal friend."

"So the children weren't in the house when you arrived?" Marvin asked.

"No. They were across the street at the neighbors', the Gilberts. They had a play date, I think you call it here. The Gilberts have a daughter their age. My daughter-in-law keeps a white board in the kitchen with the girls' schedule. She keeps them very busy. I checked the board as soon as I found Rishi's body. I was afraid the children were in the house. Terrified, in fact — that Asha had done something to them, too. I saw they were scheduled to be across the street and got them."

O'Higgins turned and looked at Marvin. Chaundhry was accusing his daughter-in-law of the murders.

"After you called 911, you went and got the girls from the Gilberts' place?"

"Yes," Chaundhry said. O'Higgins saw the lawyer was writing each of his questions down on his notepad.

"Did you know that the girls' nanny had been attacked as well?"

"Yes. I found her body while I was looking for my grandchildren."

"And after you called 911?"

"I don't remember. I was upset, of course. I may have found Miss Kumar after I called."

"Do you know who might have wanted to harm your son? Or the nanny?"

"I'm afraid — Asha. Rishi's wife. I believe she killed my son. And Miss Kumar."

"Why do you say that?" Michael asked.

"Because I think Rishi was having an affair with Miss Kumar. I suspected it, anyway."

"Why did you believe your son and Ms. Kumar were having an affair?"

"I caught Rishi coming from the girl's room one afternoon when Asha and the children were out. It was clear to me then. They were both bare-footed, and the girl was dressed inappropriately. I was obviously not expected."

"Did you confront your son about what you suspected?" Marvin said.

"No."

"But you believe it was going on, this affair?" Michael said.

"Yes. The girl was very pretty. You couldn't blame him, not really. Asha must have caught them, or somehow found out about it. If they were so foolish that I caught them, Asha certainly must have realized what was going on in her own home."

"So you think your daughter-in-law killed your son? That's what you're saying?"

"Yes. Asha has a violent temper. I've seen it many times myself."

That registered as a lie to O'Higgins, and he noted it. The woman he'd met that day on the ferry did not seem to be that type at all. She seemed gentle and kind. He'd seen her with her two girls and with her husband. He didn't believe it. Chaundhry's expression — his tightly pressed lips — said "lie," too.

"So you went and got your grandchildren and left — in an Uber cab?"

"Yes, directly to the Indian Consulate. I wanted the girls to be protected from the press, and, of course, from their mother. Especially the Indian press. I knew my son's death was going to be — well, a mess. It's all over the Indian media today, in fact. They'll be sending reporters. I don't want the girls' pictures taken for obvious reasons," Nirad said. "Right now the girls think their father is in India."

"What time did you arrive at your son's house yesterday, exactly?" O'Higgins said.

"Five, maybe a little before. As I said."

"You're sure of the time?" Marvin said.

"No, not exactly, sure. I didn't look at my phone until I was in a cab with the girls on the way to the Consulate. When I called the Consul General, I noticed the time."

"And when you arrived at the house and found your son's body, Mrs. Chaundhry wasn't at home yet?" Marvin said.

"No, she was not there. The house was empty when I got there."

"So you never saw her at the house, after you arrived?" O'Higgins said.

"No."

"When was the last time you saw her — Asha Chaundhry?" O'Higgins said.

"I saw her yesterday morning, around eight in the morning. We all had breakfast together. The three of us. The girls had been driven to school. There is a car service that picks them up and brings them home."

"How about your son?" O'Higgins said.

"I saw him at breakfast as well."

"He didn't go to the office with you?" Marvin said.

"No. He was going to the new plant. He was to take a helicopter at ten a.m., I believe."

"A helicopter?" O'Higgins said.

"Yes. It saves time. We take it from San Francisco International to the plant, near Gilroy. He went to the plant and came home in the afternoon. We spoke on the phone, twice."

"I see. So you came home around five p.m. and found your son's body in the elevator?"

"Yes. I was going to use the elevator to go up to the guest room. My room is on the third floor."

"The same floor as the nanny's room?" O'Higgins said.

"Yes."

"And you called the police — when, exactly?"

"I called almost immediately, of course."

"911 got the call at 5:31 PM," O'Higgins said.

"Well — I was in shock. I may have called from the Uber car. I was naturally upset."

"And after you picked up the girls?" O'Higgins said.

"Yes. I think so. I'm not sure. I was upset, of course. I can't say now exactly when I called. I believe I called from the house."

"You don't remember when you called the police?" Marvin said.

"No, not exactly. But you say it was 5:31?"

"Yes."

O'Higgins was in possession of all the important time stamps in the case to date. He watched Chaundhry's face for a micro expression and saw one. Since the accident he'd read a great deal more about the human face, and he'd taken classes on micro expressions in order to make detective. They could betray real truths.

The question, Michael thought, had produced a look of concern. Before that, the man's face had worn a placid expression — what behavioral scientist called a "neutral" expression —and what Michael had learned was a forced, inappropriate smile when he and Marvin walked in.

Chaundhry hadn't seemed upset that his son had been murdered. Nirad Chaundhry seemed, instead, to be prepared for a business meeting with underlings, and not an interview with the police about a murder of a family member.

Nirad looked at his lawyer, who was busy writing down the detective's questions, not bothering to look up.

"You had your cell phone with you?" O'Higgins said.

"Yes."

"You didn't use your phone in the cab on the way to your son's house?" O'Higgins said.

"No. I was tired. I simply wanted to take in the drive and relax."

"Did you receive any text messages or emails while you were in the house?" O'Higgins said.

"No. I don't know. A text may have come in as I was paying the Uber driver," Nirad said. "But I didn't respond. As I said, I was tired. I didn't look at my phone."

"Did you call anyone after you had the children with you?" Marvin said.

"Yes. I called my wife in India from the consulate and told her what happened to our son. I wanted to be the one to tell her what Asha had done."

"Did you call your son's wife to let her know her children were safe?"

"I don't know. I might have. I don't remember. I think not. I was angry. I believed she killed Rishi. No, I don't think I did," Nirad said.

"You might have? You don't know? Or you didn't? Which is it?" O'Higgins said.

"My concern was for the safety of the children. That was my

focus. No, I don't think I did."

"Are you implying that Mrs. Chaundhry might have been a threat to her own children?" O'Higgins said.

"One never knows in these cases. Jealousy is a frightening emotion. I had to be sure the children were safe," Chaundhry said. His expression was placid again.

"So you believe Mrs. Asha Chaundhry murdered your son and Ms. Kumar?" O'Higgins said.

"Yes. I think so. That's the second time you've asked me the question, Detective. The front door was locked when I came in. I had to punch in the code. There didn't seem to be any sign of a robbery as I looked for my grandchildren. My son was having an affair with the children's nanny. It seemed obvious what happened from the moment I opened the elevator door."

"Obvious. I see. But you went around the house checking for a break-in?" O'Higgins said.

"I was looking for the children. I couldn't help but notice — I was looking for both, I suppose."

"Your daughter-in-law, Asha Chaundhry, murdered your son because she found out about Rishi and her nanny, Bharti Kumar, having an affair? Is that what you're telling us?"

"Yes. That's what I believe. If Ben Affleck did it, why not my son? He was only human. I told him that Miss Kumar might not be the right choice for a nanny. I always thought she was too pretty."

"You said you had your son's cell phone?" Michael said.

"Yes."

"Why did you take it from the scene?"

"I'm not sure," Nirad said. "I just did."

"Where was it? His phone?"

"I saw it in the office, on his desk. I knew I would have to take on his responsibilities, so I took it. After all, he was dead."

"So you went into your son's office?"

"Yes. I was looking for the girls. I told you. I didn't know what had happened. I saw the door was open to the office and I went in and saw Rishi's phone."

"You didn't come back into the house once you found the girls at the neighbors?"

"No. I sent a message to Uber from the Gilberts."

"Did you tell the neighbors—the Gilberts—what had happened?"

"No. Of course not. The children were there. I said nothing."

"Why are your grandchildren being taken to India?"

"We thought it best under the circumstances. My wife is coming to pick them up. She's taking them back to India on our company plane."

"Does Asha Chaundhry know you plan to take her daughters to India?" O'Higgins said.

"I'm not sure. I believe my wife got Asha's permission on the phone." That seemed impossible, given Asha Chaundhry's insistence that her daughters be brought to the hospital.

Michael glanced at Marvin. "Can I have your son's cell phone? We will need it for our investigation."

"I'm afraid the Indian government took possession of it."

"The Indian government?"

"Yes."

"I don't understand," Michael said. He looked again at Marvin, who was studying Chaundhry.

"I'm afraid I can't comment on this," Chaundhry said. "You will have to take it up with the Indian Embassy in Washington."

"Was the phone you took your son's primary cell phone?" Marvin said.

"I believe so. It's what was on his desk. And it's what I've seen him use."

"How long were you in the house after you discovered your son's body?" Marvin asked.

"I couldn't have been more than ten minutes. I'm not sure exactly. I was upset. It seemed an eternity."

"You searched the entire house in ten minutes?"

"Yes, looking for the girls, as I said."

"You didn't go into the elevator, step inside and try to help your son?"

"It was obvious to me he was dead. I thought it prudent not to disturb things."

"You weren't afraid someone was in the house? The person who had attacked your son?"

"No."

"Why not?" O'Higgins said.

"I'm not sure, really. Perhaps because I knew who had done it," Chaundhry said, and smiled.

It was a horrible smile, O'Higgins thought, deprecating and inappropriate. He may be crazy. He'd seen a similar smile on the face of the serial killer he'd roughed up. It was a smile designed to egg him on. It was arrogance personified.

"How about the nanny," O'Higgins said. "Did you know her? Bharti Kumar?"

"She was the nanny. Of course I knew her," Chaundhry said. The man looked at his lawyer. The lawyer was busy writing down the question, but he looked up.

O'Higgins thought he caught a micro expression of shame on

Nirad's face, but because Chaundhry had turned his head to the side, to look at his lawyer, he wasn't sure. Shame's micro expression was difficult to catch, one of the harder ones.

"We would like the police to release the house," Nath said. "Failure to do so might create an international incident between our two countries."

"Well, gentlemen, I've got an important lunch date," Chaundhry said. "Thank you for coming."

"We would like you to stay in San Francisco for the time being. Thank you for your time," O'Higgins said.

The two looked at each other. It was clear that Nirad Chaundhry not only didn't like him for questioning him about something so trivial as the murder of his son, but Chaundhry probably thought him stupid to boot.

"I'm scheduled to return to India at the end of next week," Chaundhry said. "I don't see any reason to change my plans."

CHAPTER 10

Homicide Division was set to move in a week, out of its storied headquarters at 850 Bryant Street to the SFPD's new "Public Safety Building" in Mission Bay. The new headquarters, a soulless glass-and-steel edifice in an East Coast style, represented the City's transition from a rough-and-tumble legendary west coast port city, to the rudely homogenized and bland one-size-fits-all New America. Marvin Lee didn't like the building, and told his wife it made him feel uncomfortable every time he drove by it. His younger partner had loved it calling it "cool" when they'd driven by.

"Close the door please, Marvin," Captain Towler said. Marvin closed the inner office door behind him. The Hall Of Justice building had an old San Francisco feel to it that Marvin liked, complete with opaque glass doors with hand-painted black numbers and lettering: Homicide Division, Vice, Traffic, and the rest of the force's divisions marked in a typeface reminiscent of when the San Francisco police were almost entirely male, Irish and white. And it smelled oddly like his father's pool hall in West Oakland. Marvin had come up the department's ranks from patrol to detective, so the building meant something to him, personally. It had not been easy for a black man to climb the SFPD's ranks.

"How are you, Marvin?" Towler said. Towler was an old-school cop who had started working as a beat cop when the department truly was the Wild West. Eastwood had chosen the SFPD as the Dirty Harry's department for a reason.

"Good, boss. Caught a high-profile double."

"Yeah, I know. The wealthy Indian family. Thanks for coming in."

"What is it you wanted to see me about?" Marvin asked.

"Couple things. First, how's your gorgeous wife?" Towler smiled. He had the Irish gift for leveling tension.

"She's good," Marvin said, smiling back. "She's working too much, but — that's how we can pay for all the junk we buy at Costco. And private school. Jesus."

"You're a lucky dog. Do you know that? She's too good-looking for the likes of you," Towler said.

"I know. I know," Marvin said and meant it. His wife had been a swimsuit model who'd traveled in the fast lane in LA, working up to walk-on roles on network TV. But she'd slid into a serious coke addiction, flirting with the LA underworld. She'd found both God and a husband after walking into a random Baptist church in San Francisco's Western Addition, desperately stoned and terrified of what she'd done to herself. She'd slid, disheveled in a short black dress and clutching a $14,000 Louis Vuitton bag, into a pew next to Marvin. She'd run out of a hotel room up at the Fairmont. She'd been the only white person in the place, looking like a "Las Vegas" hooker, Marvin had told her years later. She never confessed to her husband, who she adored, just how close she'd come to that being true.

"What did you do that was so good you got her to marry

you?"

"I go to church. I just had to be there. That's where the girls are. I keep telling everyone that."

"How's Michael doing?" Marvin knew that what was left of the old-boys Irish network was looking after O'Higgins on principle, and not just because of the horrible tragedy. He was one of them.

"Mike's okay," Marvin said.

"You're sure? I know you've been partners for a long time. But you have to tell me if — if you think he's not up to the job. For everyone's sake. This is a high-profile case. Maybe it's too much to come back to, so soon after what happened."

"He's fine," Marvin said, not sure he meant it.

"He's coming in for a scheduled review next week. A talk, really. I didn't expect you guys to catch a big high-profile case right off the bat, obviously," Towler said.

"Luck of the draw," Marvin said.

The two men looked at each other. Towler was tall and thin and drank down the street at a famous cops' bar, the 441. It showed on his face: a little bloated, his skin paper thin. Towler's blue eyes seemed very alive, despite that.

"I got a call from Detective Michael Rodriguez from Los Angeles County Sheriff's Department. He and his partner are putting together a task force for high profile murders for the state's Department of Justice. He wanted to know who our best guys were, and who might be right for the task force. I gave him your name, and O'Higgins' name too."

"I know his partner, Rich Tomlin," Marvin said. "He caught the Phil Spector case. He and Rodriguez run the Murder School for LA County."

"Rodriguez said they would work high-profile cases like this Chaundhry case. Run out of the state's Attorney General's office," Towler said. "Are you interested? It's a big deal, career-wise."

"Maybe," Marvin said. "Have to talk to the wife." He suddenly wanted to get up and leave Towler's office. He was harboring a serious fear that his partner wasn't well at all. Several times in the last few days, he'd seen O'Higgins drift away in a kind of trance. Marvin could just tell he wasn't present even when Michael was in the car sitting next to him. It was probably safe to tell Towler that O'Higgins might not be ready for such a high-profile case, but he decided not to roll on his friend.

"How's it progressing?" Towler asked. "The Chaundhry case."

"We need to get our hands on both victims' cell phones. The father in-law took Rishi Chaundhry's cell phone to the Indian Consulate. The Consulate people are holding it, saying it's to do with official state secrets. And we just don't know what happened to the nanny's cell phone. We can't find it. We know she had one, the neighbor said the girl always carried one. They'd seen her on it. But no carrier has her listed. There are thousands of Kumars in the Bay Area."

"Marvin, the feds are watching this case, closely. I had someone from the State Department call to tell me how sensitive this case is. And they support the Indian government holding Rishi's phone," Towler said. "It's one of the reasons I wanted to see you today."

"Two people dead," Marvin said. "We need both victims' phones. You know that. Phones are key."

"And the Indian Consul General here in town wants to know why we haven't released the scene. The father has some big-shit law firm calling the DA every day, asking the same question,"

Towler said.

"Rene and everyone just finished up. And we have not locked the principal suspects into stories yet," Marvin said. "The wife has been in the hospital. We're waiting to do a formal interview. Maybe we'll try again tonight. The wife was still out of it when we spoke to her at the hospital yesterday."

"You know the victim's father is one of the richest men in India? And he's close to their government, and ours." Towler leaned forward to make his point.

Marvin got the feeling that this was why he'd been called into Bryant Street—to be sent a message, obliquely, from the DA's office.

"Yeah, I know about the father. But I don't understand what the rush is about the scene," Marvin said. He did understand, but he wanted Towler's take on the situation—exactly—so he could see how far he could challenge the pressure coming from outside to release the scene.

"My feeling is that the victim worked for our government in some way. The father, too. I don't get calls from Washington about nobodies. And that's what this is really about."

"Works for us?"

"Just a guess, but everything the woman said on the phone hinted at that, without coming right out and saying it." Towler made air quotation marks. "Good friend of America. Important political ally in the War on Terror. Nirad Chaundhry may be the next Prime Minister of India. We shouldn't strain the relationship over this tragedy."

"Yeah? No shit," Marvin said.

"The State Department wants us to release the scene as soon as possible. They called the prosecutor's office, too. Just in case I didn't understand English," Towler said.

"Okay, I got it," Marvin said. "They want the house back."

"Who are your suspects?" Towler asked.

"Right now we have the wife and our friend the next prime minister of India, I guess."

"I'll make a call about the phone," Towler said. "See what I can do. Maybe they'll at least let you take a look at it."

"Great. That would help."

"Let me know if Michael is holding up his end. And Marvin, sometimes — sometimes when it gets like this, investigations can go sideways. You know what I mean. It won't be your fault."

Marvin got up and left, not saying anything. He knew what Towler had said was bullshit. They would be blamed, and quickly.

***

O'Higgins called Officer Madrone's cell number and waited for her to pick up. He'd read her short report while sitting alone in Rishi Chaundhry's office, after speaking to the Gilberts, the Chaudhrys' neighbors, on the phone. He'd caught a contradiction between the Gilberts' interviews, given to Madrone the night before, and what Mrs. Gilbert had just told him.

They'd gotten a call from Social Services saying that the Indian Consulate had turned them away, not allowing them to interview the Chaundhry girls. The social workers had seen photos of the girls playing inside the Consulate, and the girls seemed fine physically. A consular official had told the social workers that the children were going to be sent back to India soon.

It seemed strange to both him and Marvin that the girls were being sent out of the country so soon, and before they'd seen their mother. It wasn't clear at all, either, that Asha Chaundhry was aware that her daughters were going to be taken to India.

The fact that the police might want to interview the girls seemed to be of no interest to the Indian government.

Something in Madrone's voice was different from when she was on duty, a softer feminine quality. O'Higgins thought he heard music, Dolly Parton playing in the background.

"It's Detective O'Higgins."

"Yes sir," Madrone said.

"Listen, you've got here, in your report, that the Gilbert family, when you interviewed them last night, said that the father —"

"Hold on a moment, sir." Madrone left the line, and the music playing in the background stopped. "Sorry, sir. I wanted to hear. I'm at home this morning. It's my day off."

"Sorry."

"No, that's fine," Madrone said.

"It says here, in your report, that — Paul Gilbert told you Mr. Chaundhry, the victim's father, came for the two girls at 5:45. Is that right?"

"Yes, if that's what I wrote. Yes, that's what Gilbert said. I remember now. His wife was cooking something and had just noted the time when the girls' grandfather rang their bell. The husband answered. He didn't know exactly what time it was, but the wife said she did. I spoke to them both."

"I was on the phone with Mrs. Gilbert, just now. She says that the grandfather was there at 5:15. That's a big difference. Are you sure you caught the time right last night?" O'Higgins said.

"Yes, sir."

"Could I see you sometime?" O'Higgins said. "Drink or something?" It came out of his mouth before he realized he'd said it. It was as if someone else had broken into the conversation and interrupted him.

"Sure. Yeah."

"It's Michael. Call me Michael."

"Sure — Michael."

"Today at five, the bar at Kokkari? You know where it is? The Greek place downtown."

"Yeah. I know. On Jackson." She was surprised, he could tell.

"Okay. Listen, I'm going to go over there and interview the wife. Five forty-five is what she told you? You're sure?"

"She was cooking — pasta, she said. They were going to eat at six because they had to go to a parent-teacher night at their daughter's school. It's the same school the Chaundhry kids go to. I remember what she said. Five forty-five," Madrone said. "I'm positive."

"Okay. Thanks. I'll see you there — at Kokkari, then."

He ended the call before she could answer. He looked around him as if he'd dropped something. He realized he'd wanted to have sex with Madrone from the moment he'd seen her. He wasn't sure why, exactly. She was attractive, petite, a blonde. And then it hit him: she looked like his wife.

He stood up and moved away from the desk, out of the office, down the stairs. He had a crazy idea that he would call his psychiatrist and tell her what he'd just done. How strange it seemed. But he didn't.

He crossed the street and went to the Gilbert house. Their house was directly across from the Chaundhry's. It was foggy out, the street painted in grey tones. It was three in the afternoon and he wasn't sure anyone would be home.

"Hello, my name is Detective O'Higgins. We spoke earlier on the phone."

"Hello, Detective."

The woman who answered the door was about 35. Pretty, tall, athletic looking. He'd noticed the wives in the neighborhood were younger than their husbands, for the most part. He'd checked several of the names in Madrone's report, looking for anyone with a record. It had been a random search, but he wanted to start ruling out the possibility that despite the neighborhood, they had someone who was known to the police, a Peeping Tom or the like. Patrol had interviewed several of the neighbors on the block. Some of the houses that had not been contacted were owned by foreign corporations and had been a dead end when he looked into them. Two, side by side, were owned by Aramco in Saudi Arabia. No one living on the block had any kind of police record.

"I'm Detective O'Higgins," he said again. He showed her his ID. "Are you Mrs. Gilbert?"

"Yes."

"Can I ask you a few questions?"

"Yes, of course, Detective. Come in."

Like the Chaundhry mansion, the Gilberts' place was plush and huge. Modern art hung on the walls, cold and slightly corporate in feel with a lot of abstract works in black and white. Mrs. Gilbert was wearing teal yoga pants, and her butt was pressed up against them. He tried not to look at her ass.

She walked him to the back of the house, into an oversized kitchen that was cavernous. He could see a pool in the backyard, which didn't surprise him. It was a lap pool, and its warm surface was throwing off steam, the steam mixing with the fog.

"Can I offer you a cup of coffee, Detective?" The kitchen was all white with black marble countertops. Mrs. Gilbert went to a sleek coffee maker and popped in a cartridge. "It's so — God, I can't even find the words to describe it. What happened to Rishi and Bharti. Surreal," Mrs. Gilbert said.

"Yes," he said automatically. He was looking around. He couldn't see the street from back here, and the hallway leading to the kitchen was forty feet long, at least.

She turned and faced him. "Now, Detective, how can I help you? Ask me anything."

"Do you know the Chaundhrys well?"

"No, not well. They've only been in the house a few months, since the holidays. But we had them over for dinner, after they moved in. We wanted to introduce ourselves. And our daughter, Clair, and their twins hit it off right away. They go to the same school."

"Did they seem to get along, the parents?"

The coffee machine signaled the coffee was done with a beep. Mrs. Gilbert looked at him. She turned and poured his coffee and put the cup down on the marble counter near him.

"Cream and sugar, Detective?"

"No, thank you. Black is fine."

"Yes. Asha is so sweet. You can't imagine. She's darling. She and I hit it off. We take a yoga class together in the Marina."

"Have you lived here long?" O'Higgins asked.

"Three years, next month."

"What does your husband do?" O'Higgins asked.

"He was a banker. JP Morgan in New York, for years. He's a property developer now. We came out west after he left the bank. It's been a dream of ours to live in San Francisco."

"I see. Have you seen anyone in the neighborhood you'd consider strange, or anyone acting strangely in the last few days?"

"No, not really. They had a lot of people coming and going

across the street. Contractors. Rishi worked a lot from home, Asha said. They seemed to have a lot of visitors. Indian people, mostly," she said. "People with funny head gear, that kind of thing."

"What time did the girls come over yesterday?"

"About three, I think. Bharti brought them. I can't — she was a lovely girl. She didn't speak much English. But I liked her. I saw her a lot."

"Did you speak to Ms. Kumar — Bharti? Did she ever confide in you about the family?"

"As I said, she didn't speak much English. Or not very well. I'd said hello. Lots of hand signs. She dropped the girls off and left. So, no, we didn't develop that kind of relationship."

"The Chaundhrys' girls arrived at what time?" he asked.

"Three. The play date was for three to five. Asha texted and said she would send Bharti to pick the girls up. She had to run to the store or something."

"You told one of the patrol officers last night that the girls' grandfather came to get them at 5:45."

"Did I?" Mrs. Gilbert said. "No, I think I said 5:15."

He looked down at his notebook. "Yes. You told the patrol officer 5:45."

"No. I don't think so. It was earlier than that. It was around 5:15," she said.

He decided to let it go. "Did he seem upset? Mr. Chaundhry. When he was here."

"I didn't really see him. My husband had just come home from work and got the girls down for him. They were upstairs in the playroom. I was in here, cooking dinner."

"But you're sure of the time. 5:15?" He gave her one more

chance to change her story.

"Yes. I heard the front bell ring while I was in the kitchen. I expected the girls to be gone by five or so. We had to leave the house for a meeting at my daughter's school."

"You heard the doorbell, in here?"

"Yes. I may have poked my head out into the hallway," she said. She moved back to the coffee machine, took out the cartridge she'd used to make his coffee and threw it into the garbage under the sink. The kitchen was immaculate and seemed hardly used.

A short Latin woman walked into the kitchen. She was carrying a white plastic laundry basket loaded with dirty clothes. The Latina, dressed in an old-school maid's uniform, glanced at him quickly and disappeared into a room at the back of the kitchen.

"I noticed you have a front-door knocker, too. Did you hear that? Or did Chaundhry use the bell?"

"I — I don't remember, Detective. Is that important?"

"The nanny, did she seem — did she seem upset when she dropped the girls off?"

Mrs. Gilbert leaned on the counter a few feet from him. The woman looked very thin. He could see the blue of veins in her exposed shoulders. Her stomach was ironing-board flat. She was in good shape and looked the epitome of what she was, an exceedingly privileged woman with a sense of entitlement. Very different from the poor people of the Mission or Hunter's Point, who were afraid of the police and never made eye contact if they could avoid it.

She looked at him for a moment. "No. Bharti seemed fine."

He watched her lips. A lie printed across her face. Her micro expression made it clear: her lips pursed subtly but classically, betraying her lie.

"Would you mind if I checked the doorbell," he said, "rang it?"

"I don't understand, Detective," she said. "You're confusing me. Are we — suspects? Do you think we had something to do with this awful —?"

A second micro expression moved quickly across her face: regret. It was the same expression he'd had in the class he'd taken at Mills College, as part of the continuing education SFPD required of all its detectives. Many of the professor's examples of micro expressions were of Amanda Knox or Bill Clinton speaking in public, especially when the subject of his professor's slides had to do with lies and their facial "tells."

The one for regret had been subtle and hard for him to learn. He'd had to work on recognizing it, with repeated views of the slide over and over, mixing the regret "tell" in with countless neutral expressions from countless faces of various ethnicities. But he'd finally learned it. The cover of the eyes always turned down.

They looked at each other. Mrs. Gilbert's pretty face showed that she was annoyed, and tired of being questioned. Her expression turned from affable to steely.

He looked around for a clock in the kitchen and didn't see one. As in most households, old-school clocks had disappeared along with landlines. Rich or poor, most people relied on their cell phones to tell them the time. He glanced at the fancy six-burner, restaurant-style stove but didn't see a clock there either. So she would have had to stop what she was doing and look at her phone when the doorbell rang? Why would she, if she was cooking and was expecting the girls to be picked up?

"Did I help?" Mrs. Gilbert asked.

"Yes, thank you. One more thing: did you hear the doorbell in here? When Mr. Chaundhry came to the door?"

"No, I don't think so. It's hard to hear from back here, usually. My husband answered the door. I don't think I heard it ring."

"But you're sure it was 5:15 when he came to pick up the girls?"

"Yes. I'm sure. I was on my phone and had to end the call because my husband wanted me to come meet Mr. Chaundhry. I noticed the time then — we'd heard so much about him when my husband was still at the bank. It's not every day you meet a billionaire, is it, Detective? My husband said he's probably going to be president, or whatever it is they have there."

"I see."

He thanked her for the coffee. She smiled stiffly and walked him to the door. It was a forced smile, the woman's eye muscles not involved in the least—the ultimate tell of a phony smile. He asked if he could have her husband's cell number in case he had any more questions, and she gave it to him. He put her husband's number into his cell phone as he crossed the foggy street.

CHAPTER 11

One week before the murders

"You should sit with us," the well-dressed Indian said.

They had been together at the head of the line, so naturally found themselves going up the ferry's steep steps, leading up from its interior below-deck space, where the gang of young lesbians were parking their bikes, and where some of the older people, less adventurous retired types, were heading. Above deck was where the younger people rode, not put off by the cold March air.

The Indian family headed immediately to the top deck and he'd followed as if he were a member, their American cousin. He had no explanation for it, but he wanted to follow them. He felt that somehow they would help him manage the crossing. They all settled on the long metal bench just under the pilot house, facing away from the water.

Thank God, O'Higgins thought.

They made room for him, the father on the edge of his seat. The Indian man's attractive wife smiled at him, welcoming him and seeming to be genuinely pleased that he'd followed them. They had had an instant rapport.

"What's your name?" the father asked, after they'd sat down.

The question surprised him. "Michael," he said.

The father nodded as if it was the first time he'd heard the name. "Michael. Excellent. I'm Rishi, this is my wife, Asha. Pleased to meet you," the man said.

"Nice to meet you," Michael said. He turned and looked at the wife. She was even younger than he'd first thought. She might have only been 25, if that. She had the big Indian eyes he remembered seeing at the murals at Angkor Wat, on a trip he and his wife had taken before they were married. They had been surprisingly erotic murals. The man's young wife had the same captivating eyes.

"Are you a tourist, too, Michael?" the wife asked. It was the first time he'd heard her speak English.

"No. No. I was bo— born here."

He'd caught a glimpse of the open water behind the husband's shoulder. The ferry had pulled away from the dock, turning slowly, and was heading into the bay. His view was changing, the water coming up as they pulled away from the dock. He'd was careful to keep his eyes pegged to the deck, or on the railing, or on the husband's face. The sight of the open water when he'd lifted his head to answer the woman hit him all at once. What had he done? Foolishly come top deck when he shouldn't have.

His doctor had told him to go slow. Was the ride out onto San Francisco Bay slow?

"Just sit by the water, Michael," Dr. Schneider had said. "Try that."

He'd decided to take the ferry to Angel Island early that morning while staring at the ceiling in his bedroom. Normally he would have taken another Valium, rolled over and slept on until 2:00 p.m., and then taken a second Valium and woken before dinner. He'd been doing that for months. But this morning, for whatever reason, he was tired of it. He'd stared at the vial, reached for it. He wanted to dream — didn't he?

Instead he'd thrown the vial of Valium across the dark bedroom, made tomb-dark by the hotel-style blackout curtains he'd had installed. He heard the vial of pills roll across the hardwood floor.

He'd woken up angry. It was something that had started after the accident. He would sit bolt upright, ready to attack, punch someone — seething. Angry at what the world had served up to him and his daughter.

The anger was getting worse. Even the Valium no longer stifled it. It was a horrible anger that ran through him like fire. It hurt, physically. When it came on him, it was overwhelming. Debilitating.

He'd bought a new pistol. The new pistol, kept fully loaded, was on the kitchen table, buried under stacks of unopened mail, newspapers, delinquent bill notices of all kinds, their threats meaningless. Twice his power had been cut off. He'd had to go down to PG&E's local offices and pay off the due-months in person, all his finances a shambles.

One afternoon he'd gotten up out of bed and decided to drive. He'd kept driving all day toward Arizona without questioning it. He'd stopped and bought the new pistol as soon as he crossed the border into Arizona, near Yuma. He had every intention of getting back on the freeway, finding a rest stop and just doing it. Ending it, finally. The way it should have ended the day of the accident.

His life hung in the balance for hours and could have been over countless times, at any moment, but he'd driven toward the setting sun unable to pull over and do it. Why? He had good reasons not to. His daughter needed him after all. And there were prevarications: the sight of a jalopy with happy Mexican kids in the back seat, the sight of a young woman driving alone that looked a little like his wife. An empty random building on the edge of the desert had given him an excuse to wonder why it had been built, and by whom.

And it was the desert sunset's fault, too. It had been a particularly violent and beautiful one you get sometimes in August in Arizona, during the monsoon season. He'd driven back toward it, its mash-up colors: red with glass-green streaks across the sky, unusual and captivating. What produced the green color? It reminded him of a vintage car color from his parents' day, emerald green. He'd always liked that color. Was it a message? Why was he looking for messages this late in what should have been his last day? He drove through a quick downpour, indifferent to the rain pounding the oil-stained freeway. He tried to convince himself his daughter would be better off without him but it wasn't working. It was a lie and he knew it.

And so he'd driven on, grabbed by ideas keeping him alive: his father, a well-known San Francisco attorney, had an office painted green. He'd had a pencil box in fourth grade that was green. It had two dials that, when synchronized, gave the capitals of all the states; it had once been his prized possession. He realized what a good child he'd been, studious and quiet, eager to learn about the world. He'd overheard his parents talking about his being overly sensitive. His mother had been shocked when he joined the Marine Corps.

His eldest sister wore greenish toe-shoes when she went off to dance class. Bits of dried blood, where she'd worked her toes raw, had left rose-red stains. She had become a ballerina and had moved to New York City to dance in the New York City's ballet company's corps de ballet. It was she who had gotten his daughter interested in dance. His sister had come to visit him after the accident, but it had been useless. She'd said "I'm sorry," and he'd gotten upset with her. He'd sent her away, and afterwards felt guilty for acting out, but he'd hated those words. It had been irrational, but platitudes sent him into fury.

His grandmother, who lived on Capp Street had green Depression-era glass plates she brought out for Thanksgiving dinners. She'd left them to his wife when she died. He didn't know where they were now. Somewhere.

Twice he'd pulled over and stared at the short-barreled .38 revolver he'd bought in Yuma. They were common as dirt and cheap compared to the fancy automatics so in vogue now. He'd picked the weapon for its short, mouth-friendly barrel. He'd thought it would be easily inserted. With the right "cop-killer" ammo, the smaller weapon would do the job just fine. It would take off the back of his head, passing by the amygdala to the posterior of the brain, the oldest part of the brain stem. His brother had explained it once while they'd been fishing. It would look like the strange trailer he'd seen for "Sons of Anarchy" TV show—a bullet shown busting out the back of a skull. And then it would finally be done—show over.

He'd bought the weapon from a Korean in one of the biggest gun stores he'd ever been in. The short, all-about-the-money salesman would have sold Charlie Manson a handgun and a map to the stars' homes. The Korean wore a sidearm. Who needs to wear a sidearm in a gun shop, O'Higgins wondered. Robbery was unlikely.

Twice he'd picked up the .38 and stuck the awful-tasting

barrel in his mouth, ignoring the other people milling about the dusk-orange rest stop. Twice he'd unlocked his car doors, so the first responders could pull his dead body out without a lot of hassle. Why make it hard on them? Lock, unlock. He'd been at the scene of countless suicides. They always had a respectful air, perhaps more than any other crime scene. The murderer and victim one and the same. Suicide frightened cops because so many fell victim to it themselves.

He'd heard the definitive click of the locks. Next, the idea of infinity and the look of his wife as the wave hit the boat, washing her violently into the water.

He pulled the barrel out of his mouth, thinking it was wrong to scare people. He knew, too, his wife wouldn't approve at all. She was a Catholic. She'd believed in all that nonsense. Did he believe? No. What if some kid found him? He locked the doors. Heard the pop of the locks locking electrically. It was a relief. It was the wrong place.

He decided to pull over as soon as night fell and do it in the desert, on some isolated dark dirt road where no one would see or find him for days. He was going to go out looking up at the stars. That would be right, he thought. If you concentrated on the Milky Way, the way he had as a child when he'd gotten a telescope for his thirteenth birthday, it would be a good way to go. Say hello to infinity. Say hello to the galaxy. Say hello to oblivion. Bang! Game over. New player. Your score is 37 years.

"Is it pretty, the island?" Asha said, smiling at him.

The wife had a sweet-sounding voice. Her skin was brown, light-chocolate brown. He looked into her eyes. He couldn't help himself. It was like listening to some kind of wild, satisfying, music. He couldn't stop listening/looking at her. Like her husband's, her eyes were kind. He was attracted to her. He had not thought of any women—at all, or in any way—since the accident, certainly not sexually. It was the first time since the accident that he'd had that kind of thought. It shocked him. Repulsed him.

He turned away from her. How could he? It was music he didn't want to hear.

"Yes. Yes, very pretty," Michael said. He got out simple words without muffing them, and he was proud of it.

One of the couple's daughters came running up and said something in Hindi and then English. She turned, looked at him and smiled. He smiled back. Second smile, he realized in the space of a few moments. Life was smacking him in the face, and on a boat on the water, of all places.

"Do you have children, Michael?" the husband asked.

"I — I — I — " he tried to answer. He was going to say yes, he had a daughter. Although it seemed like a thousand years since she'd been with him. Was he dreaming this? This whole thing, now on the ferry, was it a dream? He would wake up. The digital clock by his nightstand would read 6:00 a.m. He would roll over and look across at the Valium vial and at the water glass he kept on his wife's side of the bed where he slept. Yes, I'll wake up. Not a bad dream.

He looked directly out at the bay, at the open water. He could feel the rumble of the ferry's twin diesel engines come up through the thick steel bench, the cold sun on his face as they headed east toward the green island.

"I — I — ye — yes."

The wife turned and looked at her husband. Their daughter was afraid of him now. She rolled further into her mother's arms, seeking protection.

"Yes, well. It won't be long and we'll be there," the husband said. He was looking at Michael more carefully.

Michael had stopped trying to make words. It was useless. The connection between his mouth and his brain seemed to be severed. He just nodded and smiled, making sure he didn't glance toward the open water again. He glanced again at the mother and daughter, who were looking at him with a kind of pity. It was a pity people displayed for the mentally slow, or the homeless.

They think I'm slow.

"We love San Francisco," the man's wife said, talking really more to herself, trying to keep the awkward conversation going — for his sake? Or hers? "The girls love it too. We love Italian food. We can't get good Italian food at home. I had it while in England in school."

The three of them were looking at him, the wife's look clinical. She was trying to categorize his problem: mentally deficient, drunk, head injury?

"What do you do?" The husband seemed to want to soldier on with conversation, thinking it would help pave over the awkwardness of his stuttering.

Most people would have just dropped him by now. He'd been through this before with strangers. It wasn't the first time people thought him slow — "touched" was the word someone had used, thinking he couldn't understand English.

The wife turned toward her husband and shook her head slightly. She'd decided it was time to leave the poor man alone.

"Po — po —"

"Policeman!" her husband exclaimed, filling the rest of the word in for him. "Cops and robbers!"

"Yes," he answered, smiling again for the third time in almost a year, and not realizing it this time.

The little girl wiggled out of her mother's arms, bored with the big white man's stuttering.

"Go with her, Rishi. I'm afraid she'll fall in," the mother said.

Michael stood bolt upright, as if he'd been shot. He towered over them. They noticed how tall he was. He seemed a giant to them.

"Yes, go with her," O'Higgins said. The words came out perfectly, as if nothing was wrong with him at all. The tone was the old tone he'd used on the streets when talking to civilians, full of cop authority.

The father looked at him, shocked by both his tone and his having stood up so quickly, as if there was some great emergency.

"Accidents happen," Michael said. He sat down again, realizing that he was scaring the couple.

"Yes. Of course," the husband said. He and his wife exchanged a look, and the father took his daughter's hand. The wife stood up, looking for her other daughter, and saw her by the railing. She was taking pictures with their father's iPad of random sailboats leaving from the Tiburon Yacht Club.

Michael watched the wind catch the mother's jacket as she stood, and whip it. She grabbed at it. He could see the outline of her slender body, the outline of her breasts. Something about her was startlingly beautiful, something perfect that he would always remember: the wind, the dance of her long thick black hair being blown about, the sight of her slender brown arm against the bright orange of her blouse. He stared at her, afraid he would see the open water again but risking it. He leaned into the seat and felt more of the reassuring vibrations from the boat's engine move along the steel at his back. When he stood up, he'd gotten the whole picture of Raccoon Strait.

The only noise was the heavy sound of ferry's big diesel engines. The young mother sat down. Perhaps she was afraid of him? Certainly caution had moved in. He closed his eyes and heard the sound of gulls and the sound of people's voices over the engines. He let himself sink into the sounds.

He opened his eyes with the intention of rescuing the conversation. I need to talk to people, he realized. I'll call Marvin when I get home. I will call Marvin when I get home. I love Marvin. He knows me. I love my daughter. She knows me. He turned toward the wife.

At that instant a man came around the corner and sat on the other side of her. Something about him was off, some vibe. His cop senses went off. The man was white and about forty, but could have been younger. It was hard to tell as he pulled a black hoodie over his head. He'd given them a quick but deliberate look.

The man turned and glanced again at the mother, who was looking at Michael and smiling. The man didn't smile or show any emotion. It was a glance of appraisal. Then, without warning, the man glanced his way. It was a flat look he'd seen before in the streets. The man's eyes narrowed, atavistic and threatening. He had the eyes of a shark, cold and if not exactly dead, without life's brightness either.

The man turned away. He got up quickly and slipped into the crowd standing at the railings, moving off through it and finally disappearing. Michael thought he noticed the outline of a side arm's profile on the man's right hip.

"Are you okay, Michael?" the wife asked him. He nodded yes.

***

"I want to come back to work," Michael said.

"Are you sure you're ready, Mike?" Marvin said. He tucked into his bowl of chili. He'd smashed saltines onto the top of the chili, which Michael had seen him do a hundred times before. He liked seeing it again. Seeing Marvin's big hands crush the white crackers was reassuring, familiar. Marvin Lee was one part of his old life that he wanted back. Normalcy. It was two days before he was scheduled to go back to work at SFPD.

"You haven't asked me anything about what happened," Michael said.

"No, I haven't," Marvin said.

"Why not?"

"I don't want to know," Marvin said. "Selfish on my part, really. But I don't."

"Why?"

"I don't know exactly. Too painful. Too much. I'm too old. I don't know," Marvin said. "I had a rough time thinking about you and Rebecca without Jennifer."

"Rough is right," Michael said, trying to sum it all up, the last nine months.

"Yeah. I still sometimes think — I don't know, that it didn't happen. It's crazy," Marvin said.

"You can ask me," Michael said. "Maybe I want you to ask me about it."

"No, you don't. I can tell."

"I've got another weapon. It's at the house. I've tried to use it on myself, but can't," Michael said.

Marvin stopped eating. "Okay. What happened out there?" Marvin was looking directly at him.

"I'm not sure. A wave. Rogue wave. The tiller busted, so we

went sideways into a trough. Jennifer was in the galley. It was calm. July is safe. Calm seas. Nothing. It was always calm in July. I remember there was a red sky the night before, as I was driving to the store. Red sky at night, sailors' delight — I don't know if I can make it," Michael said. "I'm seeing a doctor, but I don't know if I can make it."

"But you want to come back," Marvin said.

"Yes. I think so."

"You don't have to, not yet. You can extend it, the leave," Marvin said.

"I want to come back, or I'm never going to come back. I want you to be my partner again. I can't deal with anyone else. No rookies. No kids with something to prove. No burnt-out drunks I have to watch out for."

"Okay. Okay," Marvin said.

"I don't want to die and I do want to die. Does that surprise you?"

"Stop that bullshit. You got a daughter to live for. I don't want to hear any more of that silly shit." Marvin tucked back into his bowl of chili. "Stop feeling sorry for yourself, Mike. Cut it out."

"Will you really have me as a full-on partner, or are you going to be afraid I'm a nut job? I need to know. I don't want to be treated like there's something wrong with me. I want to be treated like before this all happened. I don't want you walking on eggshells. I don't want you to look at me like I'm crazy. And there's something else — I'm afraid of open water. It's some kind of reaction. It's like vertigo. I get sick when I see open water. Can't even talk right." He'd not spoken so much in months to anyone but the doctor.

"I don't care. We're not in the navy." Marvin smiled at him.

"What if we have to go near the water, Marvin?"

"I said, I — don't — give — a — fuck. Do you still understand English?"

"Yes, I understand English," he said.

"Good. That's a start, then. Come back. I've been working with a twenty-five year old kid who just stares at his phone all the fucking time. He makes me feel old, besides. You Irish dick."

CHAPTER 12

It had begun to rain, one of those surprisingly violent rains that come to the Bay Area in the beginning of March and leave the sky swept clean and blue afterwards, laying the groundwork for spring.

He had been staring at the huge landscape painting in the Chaundhrys' foyer. It was a place he recognized, Duxbury Reef. He could hear the rain hitting the mansion and realized that it was striking the windows along the living room. A lone black-and-white patrol car sat in the Chaundhrys' driveway, protecting the scene of the crimes. The number on the patrol car's roof was just visible from where he was standing in the foyer.

The painting fascinated him. It covered the whole wall. It had a silent feel and was intensely dramatic. It felt as if you were standing with the artist, watching the waves crash along the reef. It was captivating.

Because it was of the ocean, he'd been almost afraid to appreciate it. The first time he'd seen it he'd turned away but now, alone in the house for the first time, he took it in. Something about it told of the ocean's brutality, what he knew so well about it. Something in the painting said that brutality was basic to nature and fundamental to life. He had a funny impulse to steal the painting and bring it home so he could better understand what the artist was trying to say. Perhaps studying it, he could find out what was wrong with him. Had he become brutish because of the tragedy? Yes, he thought, and it frightened him. His anger he recognized as brutish and terrifying.

He knew the place: Bolinas' Duxbury reef. It was a spot he knew well as his brother, the surgeon, had a place overlooking it. When he'd first bought his sailboat, he'd sailed by the reef many times on the way to Tomales Bay. He'd seen the famous reef from both the ocean and the land, in summer and in winter.

He heard the front door open and saw Marvin walk in. He was wearing a grey raincoat, the shoulders stained dark, proof that it was still raining hard.

"What's up, buttercup?" Marvin asked.

"Waiting for you."

"They're cute girls," Marvin said. "Twins. You can't tell them apart." He'd gone to interview the two Chaundhry girls at the Indian Consulate after seeing Towler. He forced his way in, causing a scene. The Consulate staff had relented and allowed him to talk to the girls in person, afraid perhaps that the press would get wind of them keeping the girls locked up and away from the police.

Michael walked into the family's grand living room. Its stained mahogany wide-plank hardwood floors were brand new. It was the kind of house his wife would have loved, he thought. It had been his wife's dream to buy a vacation home somewhere and decorate it. He looked around, taking it all in.

The windows facing the view to the west were wet and streaked, glistening in places, the rain driven sideways by the wind. Everything was perfect: the art, the caramel-colored furniture worth tens of thousands of dollars. Even an average person would feel like a somebody sitting here. World class. He crossed the room and went to the fireplace. With a control he found on the mantle, he turned on the gas-insert. A fire sprung to life, seeding the iron "faux" logs and making them start to glow like real wood.

"This is cool." He thought he heard his wife's voice. It startled him. He put the fireplace control down. He knew he'd jumped, and hoped Marvin hadn't noticed it.

"Are you okay?" Marvin said. "Getting comfortable? I wouldn't." He came into the room behind his partner. Marvin's phone rang and he took the call, walking back out to the hallway while taking off his raincoat. Michael could tell Marvin was talking to his wife.

O'Higgins sat down and opened his iPad. He began to flip through the photos of the scene Rene Fields had emailed him. There were dozens. How was it they'd not found the nanny's phone, he wondered. He studied shots of the elevator's mechanicals, which were covered in Rishi Chaundhry's blood. The blood had run into the gap and down the elevator's shaft, pooling around its brand new motor. The photographs told him nothing, he thought, about who had killed his victims. He was getting frustrated.

"They're okay, the Chaundhry kids?" Michael said, looking up from the iPad when Marvin came back into the room.

"Yeah. They want to come home. And they want to see their mother, of course. She's talked to them on the phone. But — it's strange. The Consulate twits said they were going to India in a few hours."

"What time did their grandfather pick them up?" Michael asked. "Did they say?"

"They didn't have a clue. They're just little girls. They're upset. They haven't been allowed to visit their mom. They're living with strangers, and they're set to be taken to India. I felt sorry for them."

"I don't get that," Michael said. "How can Nirad Chaundhry just take them out of the country like that?"

"The grandfather is calling the shots. He's flying them home on a private jet. That's what the guy in the turban said. He's the same guy who was out here last night. He stayed with me the whole time I was in there talking to the girls."

"He can't leave — Chaundhry."

"I know. We've told him," Marvin said.

"He's a flight risk," Michael said.

"You think he did it?" Marvin said.

"I don't know."

"What about the neighbor? How did that go?"

"She's lying about the time. Why she's lying, I don't know. She told patrol, when they interviewed her and her husband, that Nirad Chaundhry had come at 5:45."

"How do you know that they just didn't make a mistake, when they were first interviewed? Why would they lie to us?"

"Trust me. She's lying. Her expressions gave her away. And she told patrol that she heard a bell and went to answer the door. Now she says her husband answered the door. Madrone—the officer who interviewed them—had 5:45 in her report. The wife told Madrone the grandfather came for the girls at 5:45, not 5:15, which is what she's saying now."

"Towler is worried about you," Marvin said. "I was called downtown." He'd decided in the car on the way over that he wasn't going to keep it from O'Higgins. He would tell his partner the truth: their boss was getting worried that the case was too important, too high-profile for Michael to handle.

"Worried? Why?"

"That you're 5150, I guess. Really. I'm not joking, Mike."

"Great."

"I told Towler you're okay. Are you okay, Mike?" Marvin said. He felt guilty asking, but he wanted to know. He sensed something was terribly wrong with his friend. He noticed a stand-off quality that had not been there before the accident, as if O'Higgins was keeping some terrible secret.

"Fine."

"Why don't you look at the wife, Asha Chaundhry? You saw the nanny? That was temptation there, man. She was a very beautiful girl. That's a fact. Rishi was human. Every day he was looking at this young girl, and one day maybe he crossed the line."

"We will look at her. I was waiting for her to be able to talk to us. And have a clear head. She was heavily sedated when we spoke with her."

"You said 'she couldn't have done it.' That's not like you, man. You met the lady once. Come on. She's at the top of the damn list as far as I'm concerned."

"According to patrol there are no security camera recordings. All the neighbors have security camera systems, the five neighbors who were interviewed last night. But their systems just feed live video. No one saw anything. No strange cars, or strange people, nothing out of the ordinary," Michael said.

"They want us to release this place," Marvin said. "The DA is pushing for that. They're getting pressure from the Consulate."

"The nanny's phone is still missing. It could be here, in the house. We shouldn't release the house until we find it," Michael said. He looked down at the iPad. It was automatically scrolling through the crime-scene photos. He saw a series begin of the nanny's room.

"Yeah. Tell me something I don't know. The pressure to release the scene, she is building, amigo," Marvin said.

"It could be here — the nanny's phone. It might tell us something. Who she was texting, who she was talking to, photos. Was there a boyfriend? We need that phone," O'Higgins said. "If we can't get our hands on Rishi's we need Kumar's for Christ's sake."

"We've looked," Marvin said.

"We have to look again," Michael said. "Screw releasing the scene until we find the girl's phone."

"What if the killer took it? It's possible."

"He didn't take it," O'Higgins said.

"Oh, you know that? How do you know the grandfather didn't take it? He took Rishi's."

"I just want to make sure it's not here. There's something weird going on, Marvin. The father of the victim takes the victim's phone and now we can't see it. Why? Why wouldn't he, of all people, want us to see what's on his son's phone? And why is Rishi Chaundhry's cell phone such a big deal to the Indian government? He's a businessman, not a diplomat. Why is the Indian government getting in our way? Why are the two little girls being taken to India, away from their mother?"

"Towler said Chaundhry could be the next Prime Minister of India. That's what Towler said. Chaundhry senior is very tight with our State Department, apparently. I guess our victim was too. Who knows what's going on," Marvin said.

"Well, I don't think the nanny was working for the government."

"Very funny. No, I don't think so."

"Nobody at the Consulate gives a shit about the Kumar girl, is my guess," Michael said.

"We give a shit," Marvin said, and he meant it.

"Why would a random neighbor change her story? There's got to be a reason."

Marvin got a text. Michael heard it hit Marvin's iPhone.

"It's from Towler," Marvin said. "We have to release the scene. We have twenty-four hours."

Michael had glanced down at his iPad. He looked at his partner and stood up. The iPad's slide show was still showing views of the nanny's bedroom. He saw a close photo of the girl's neatly stacked clothes on the end of her bed.

"It might be in the jeans she left on the bed," Michael said suddenly.

"Didn't you look?" Marvin said. "Last night?"

"No. It was the one place I didn't look," Michael said. "I picked up the stack of clothes and looked under them, but I thought the jeans and blouse were clean and unworn. What if they weren't clean? They might have just been folded neatly."

Michael rushed up the house's three flights of stairs. Before the accident, when he was exercising a lot, the run would have been nothing. Now, as he hit the third floor and broke down the hallway toward the nanny's room, he was breathing hard.

The iPhone was in Bharti Kumar's still-folded jeans' back pocket— exactly where she'd left it. The phone's battery icon was red, warning the phone needed to be charged. O'Higgins searched the room and then the closet, looking for the charger. He finally found it in a drawer in the bathroom.

"Put the fucking thing on airplane mode, it will charge quicker," Marvin said.

***

He wasn't even sure why he'd picked the fashionable restaurant to meet Madrone. He'd driven by it several times lately and seen people standing in the bar. It had looked inviting. The bar catered to well-heeled Financial District types and younger people who wanted to be seen, even if they were only working as temps. The bar was always packed by 5:30. He supposed, parking his un-marked Ford in a red zone nearby, that he'd picked this place because he wanted to be buoyed by the young crowd. In a crowd, he'd thought, he could figure out what he'd done and what he was doing asking out a girl—a stranger, really—he'd just met.

"She was sure. She told me 5:45," Madrone said. She looked entirely different for the date. She was wearing a dress, for one thing, and had her hair down. She was pretty and very feminine; she didn't look anything like the way she looked in uniform. Her petite body looked good in a dress.

"She's lying, I think," Madrone said.

"But why?" he said.

She was looking at him. It was a look of appraisal. Was she too wondering why the hell he'd asked her out?

Talking about work was easy. He'd told her about going to the Gilberts' and interviewing the wife. They couldn't get a seat at the bar, it was too crowded, but he managed to get them two glasses of wine. She found them a perch by the windows facing Jackson Street. It was still raining. At times the rain seemed more like a mist that painted the street and the small park beyond.

"Why did you become a cop?" Madrone asked.

"I needed a job." He smiled. It was the same reason he'd given his brother, who never understood why he'd wanted to be a policeman. His brother was an intellectual who, he admitted once, found the police frightening.

"Me too," she said and smiled back.

She had flecks of mica-green in her eyes. He'd never seen that before. He knew why he'd called her. He'd felt a strong physical attraction from the moment she'd handed him the sign-in sheet at the scene. It was the second time he'd felt the physical pull of a woman since the accident. The first time had been with Asha Chaundhry, on the ferry. This one was less complicated because it was hundred-percent carnal.

"I've never seen someone so — hysterical. It was terrible. The wife," Madrone said.

"Yeah." He didn't want to talk about the case, he realized. He wanted to get away from it. Every time he thought about it, he saw Nirad Chaundhry's supercilious look when they'd been at his attorney's office. I'm going to shut down that smile. "Do you like it — patrol?" he asked, taking a sip of the wine. He was relaxed with her, maybe because she wasn't a civilian.

"Yeah, I do. I was in the military, and it's close to what I did in Iraq. MP."

"Yeah, I was there — Iraq."

She looked at him quickly.

"Marine Corps," he said.

"Where are you from?" she asked.

He wanted to touch her arm. He looked at the muscle of her arm. She looked strong. "Here," he said. "I grew up here in town. You?"

"Colorado. Farmington."

A young black couple, the young man in a grey suit, walked by them trying to squeeze into the three-deep bar and buy drinks. The girl gave up and the young man tried his best to get the bartender's attention. He was short, so it was going to be a long night for him.

"I've never been here," Madrone said. "Fun place. Starchy, but fun."

"Greek food. It's good," he said. "I don't know your first name. It's embarrassing."

"Katie," she said. She touched his left hand unexpectedly. "I thought you'd never ask."

"Michael," he said. "My first name. Friends call me Mike."

"Good. I didn't want to call you Detective all night," she said. She let go of his hand. It was a signal, of course, and he understood it. It was what he wanted to know, whether the gate was open to that place. It was.

"I have a boyfriend," she said. "On-and-off type thing. Mortgage broker, wants to be rich. He'd like this place. He wears ties and shoes without socks. Loves the Giants."

"Really," he said, not giving a damn about her boyfriend and knowing the frat-boy type.

"Yes," she said. "So you know. Don't want to — keep it to myself."

"I see. Is he on right now, or off?"

"Not sure about him. Off tonight. I was hoping you'd call. I thought about calling you," she said. "I've trouble with civilians. The boyfriend doesn't know shit about shit — you know what I mean? Can't understand why I joined the Army." She took a drink. Half the glass of wine disappeared in one swallow. She looked at him and then toward the bar.

He took a sip of his drink. The noise in the restaurant was getting to that point where it surrounded you, made you feel good about being alive. He looked out the window. A middle-aged homeless guy with a beard, wearing a clear-plastic poncho, was rolling a shopping cart full of his dilapidated life-stuff into the park across the street to put up for the night.

"I don't care about your boyfriend if you don't," he said.

The boyfriend knocked on her door while they were making love two hours later. Madrone had a place up on Chenery Street in the Mission. It was a small basement apartment. It was like a warren, the ceilings very low. She said she was lucky to have found the place. San Francisco was becoming impossible, rents constantly pushed up by twenty-year-olds working at Twitter or Facebook, or rich kids from all over the country who could afford anything they wanted.

He got high with her. She liked to smoke weed, she told him, looking directly at him when she said it. He couldn't have cared less. He was in the mood to be out of himself, completely. He wanted—needed—to change himself, or just lose himself.

After they made love the first time that night, she told him — half-dressed, lying on her couch — that she wasn't stoned on duty. He thought she was probably lying about that. He could tell from her quick facial expression, her white skin red from the frantic lovemaking after they walked in the door. She handed him the bong, its glass dirty from a lot of use.

Many of the vets he knew were using drugs to get by, narcotizing their PTS symptoms. It turned out she'd gone to Iraq at eighteen, the 82 Airborne Division as an MP during Operation Iraqi Freedom in 2009.

He'd been having a dream before it happened. In his dream he was talking to his wife, trying to explain why he was sleeping with a girl he'd just met. His wife was in jail—SF County jail—and he was talking to her over a phone. A thick Plexiglas divider separated them. All his wife did was nod. The Plexiglas was horribly scratched, almost white. It obscured her face, but he could tell Jennifer was crying. The Plexiglas had one clear spot, unscratched. He could see his wife's eyes were red from crying through the one clear spot in the glass.

"What happened?" Jennifer said finally. "What happened, Michael? Why?"

He'd woken with a start. Madrone had a black-metal bed. It had made a noise while they'd made love, the frame giving and moving along with them. It built toward something with their bodies, its energy, swaying madness, a disjointed kind of swaying movement punctuated by Katie's quiet, breathless "Fuck me!" over and over as a mantra — exciting, but frightening too.

It was early morning, and the light was tinged grey and dirty looking. He was disoriented. Madrone was slamming a baton down on a man's wrist, breaking it instantly and forcing the automatic the intruder was pointing at O'Higgins to fall from his hand.

In shock and pain, the dark-skinned man turned toward the direction of his attacker. Like a mad person, Madrone whipped the black steel baton across the man's temple, opening a dime-wide cut and blinding his right eye. The baton's tip gouged the pupil, splitting it open. The intruder screamed.

By then O'Higgins was standing, also naked, his brain processing the scene all at once in a surreal burst of language-less information coming out of the demi-light: the naked girl-woman striking the intruder with her elbow, directly in the nose, so violently that his head snapped back and to the right. Katie's hair wild, moving counter to her violent motions with the baton.

The intruder was holding Kumar's phone in his other hand. He sagged. O'Higgins dove toward the pistol, which had landed on the foot of the bed. Picking it up, he yelled for the man to get on his knees. He tried to see what kind of weapon it was so he could determine if it was ready to fire. He moved the barrel and pulled the trigger. A round went off and he heard it smash something.

The man, recovering from the elbow to his nose, looked directly at him. Their eyes met.

O'Higgins moved the gun barrel back and centered it on the man's chest. It was over. The man understood that if he attacked, he would shoot him. It was then, as the intruder tried to look for an escape, that Madrone split his skull, whipping the baton straight down on the top of his head as she'd been taught. Then she hit him again, striking him on the side of his knee. He collapsed on his ass, his right knee smashed and unable to hold him up.

O'Higgins picked up Kumar's phone while Madrone, her naked and freckled shoulders hunched, stood directly above the intruder and kept hitting him across the face. The sprung baton hit his face with an awful sound. He finally pulled her off, her own face splattered with the intruder's blood and bits of teeth, all while screaming at the man that she was going to kill him. She was not only out of control, but completely ruthless.

CHAPTER 13

He had come to Dr. Schneider's office without an appointment. It was wrong, but after what had happened at Madrone's the night before, he'd been in a panic. His life seemed to be spinning out of control, or gone into a destructive hyper-speed, crashing through walls.

No, he thought, riding the elevator up to her office, they're crumbling away. I'm not right. Nothing is right.

Katie Madrone had beaten someone to death last night. An intruder, an Indian, had broken in. Had Madrone not stopped the man, O'Higgins would probably have been killed. Madrone had stopped him cold, beating him to death in the most savage way.

O'Higgins believed it was karma, a result of sleeping with the girl. As he looked at the dead man's face, almost completely obliterated, front teeth shattered, O'Higgins was sure he was seeing Death's messenger. Foiled again, countless times, on the ocean and in war. Why was it he who was always saved? Why?

"You know that you can't just come here and expect to see me," Dr. Schneider said.

"Yes, I understand. I'm sorry," he said. "I — something happened, and I felt like I was losing it."

He'd come from the hospital, where Madrone had been admitted after the fight. There would be no charges, but Captain Towler himself had come out to the scene to investigate. He seemed angry at the both of them, despite the obvious case of self-defense.

The intruder had not yet been identified. He'd been armed and was in his thirties or perhaps older, carrying no ID. Prints had matched nothing in any police or agency database, including the FBI's, which included visa applicants from around the world.

He'd knocked on the inner sanctum and Schneider had come to the door, obviously miffed that someone had come to her office without an appointment. He was interrupting a session. She'd opened the door and told him to sit in the waiting room. She would see him when her session was over.

He sat in the small waiting room filled with National Geographic and Conde Nast Traveler magazines with ads for luxury spas. He thumbed through pages filled with what seemed to be sheer out-of-touch gobbledygook. He forced himself to stop on one photo. It showed a perfect white-sugar sand beach, a young svelte couple canoodling alone with the ocean in front of them—tame. He wanted to believe in the photo's promise of happiness and contentment and safe places … Out-of-touch bullshit.

He put the magazine aside and looked down at his shoes. His left shoe was stained with blood from the beating—castoff from the baton. Katie Madrone, 24, the ex-Army MP, had lost it. He'd seen her repressed anger as she swung, stark naked, again and again, her whole body into it slamming her weapon down on the man's face — the way she'd kept on hitting the intruder long after he was unconscious, had gotten to him, unnerved him.

The vicious attack had brought back all his own PTS feelings and fears. He'd screamed at Madrone to stop once the man's brains were spilling out of his skull. The intruder was obviously dead, but she'd refused until he'd grabbed her and picked her up, his arms wrapped around her tiny waist.

He'd understood exactly what she had been feeling, understood her blood rage. He knew it was ugly, yes. But that rage was what kept them alive. Surviving. War horror, it crept into your brain and re-wired it, setting up the rage and mapping new regions ready for instant and violent expression. Instant killing.

He put the magazine back in its place carefully and replayed the last few hours. They seemed surreal. He'd found Bharti Kumar's iPhone charger in a drawer and charged her iPhone, password blocked, putting it on airplane mode so no "kill signal" could be sent to delete its memory, as the SFPD criminalists had trained him to do. Once the phone was charged, Marvin had ticked the phone's security by using the emergency call feature and applying a hack he'd learned from his last partner. They got through.

Bharti's phone stored a series of texts from India, the most recent only a few minutes old. The same number had been calling her. The messages were all in Hindi.

O'Higgins called the number back in India, using his own phone. He spoke to someone who identified himself as Bharti Kumar's brother. O'Higgins explained that the man's sister was dead, and that he was investigating her murder. Kumar's brother, frantic and speaking in English, had refused to believe his sister was dead, and hung up on him.

He'd taken Kumar's phone with him to the bar at Kokkari, something he should not have done. They'd gone to Madrone's place and made love; it had been frantic, almost violent. He'd fallen asleep and woken to see Madrone stark naked, swinging her

Smith & Wesson 16" police baton, battering an intruder who was holding Kumar's cell phone in his free hand.

O'Higgins first instinct, jumping up from the bed, was to protect Kumar's phone. When it was over, while they were waiting for the police to come, he checked. The phone was intact, but the man had managed to take it off airplane mode, leaving it susceptible to a kill signal. Whoever sent him, the man had come for Kumar's phone. Whoever sent the man had succeeded. The phone's memory had been wiped clean.

"She killed him. I tried to stop it once it was obvious he was unconscious. But she wouldn't stop beating him with the baton," Michael said.

Schneider looked at him. His world was so strange to her that he could tell she was incapable of understanding how someone could be so violent— a woman, especially. In the doctor's world, women didn't kill people. In her world, everyone got along. In her world, everyone was safe, and treated with respect. In her world, everyone mowed their lawns. Her world had more in common with the bullshit glossy magazines, with their photos of perfect beaches and swell couples. There was no such place, he thought, looking at her. Or at least, not for people like him and Madrone.

"This young woman you'd gone out with — this was a date?" Schneider asked.

"Yes. I tried to stop her, but she — she was out of control. He had a gun. He was going to shoot me. She'd gone to pee. And he must have missed her. The door to the bathroom was half open, but he walked right by her. She sat there peeing and heard him breaking into the apartment. She had a baton stashed in the hall by the front door for protection. I think she wanted him to break in. She must have heard him hacking the front door — she's a cop. But I think she — I think she let him walk right by her so she could —"

"You did what you could," the doctor said.

"Yes. But she wasn't having it. I was yelling at her to stop. She beat his brains out."

"You're upset," the doctor said, looking at him carefully.

It was true, and it was obvious. But it had taken the doctor saying it for him to realize just how upset he was. It was as if her words had woken him from a dream. The office carpet, the walls, the artwork, all came into focus. He'd run here, after leaving Madrone's apartment, the scene of the crime already taped off, the crime scene log book being constructed by patrol, the early-morning passersby curious to watch the cops work. It was all so familiar to him. Like a boy running home, he'd come here, almost instinctively.

"Look, I came to tell you that you have to tell my superiors that I'm okay. That there's nothing wrong with me. They're going to contact you. They have access to my medical records. But now — after this morning —"

"I don't understand," the doctor said.

"You have to tell SFPD that I'm fit for duty. I have to work. They might think I'm crazy."

They looked at each other. Her face had an expression he'd never seen before. It was the face not of a clinician, in control, but rather of a frightened young woman before someone she was afraid of. She was staring at his shirt cuff, which was soaked in blood. He'd brushed against the blood on the floor of Madrone's cramped apartment as he'd hurried to dress, the police knocking furiously at the door while the dead man's skull leaked into a dirty carpet.

"Are you all right?"

"Yes."

"I can't say I understand your world," the doctor said. It was not a professional remark.

Something was frightening, he realized, about the way he was sitting there — his shirt soiled, without a tie, the look on his face communicating the awful violence he'd witnessed. A woman had beaten someone to death in the most brutal fashion. It was all taking on a ferocious reality that the doctor wanted no part of. She was repulsed, he realized. In her world, women didn't beat people to death with steel batons.

"Will you tell them I'm okay, fit for duty?"

"You can't just show up here, you understand that?" the doctor said, trying to get her bearings and perhaps her authority back.

"Yes. I'm sorry," he said. "It won't happen again. I need your help."

"You mean you want what you want. I agree, you're ready to be back at work."

"What do you mean?"

"I mean, you were trying to be normal. Isn't that what we talked about last session? You were attracted to someone, and you acted on it. That's called normal behavior where I come from. The violence has nothing to do with that. You took a step. And it's the one you should take. It's life, with all its warts."

"Okay?" He'd misjudged all of her looks. She wasn't disgusted with him. She'd only been trying to appreciate what had happened to him, and been taking it in. The fact that she thought his sexual adventure had been positive shocked him. He'd wanted to be censured.

"I think that's a good sign," she said. "You're trying. It means we're making progress."

"It didn't go as intended."

"No. It didn't," she said.

"My daughter wants to come home. She called and left a message. She's worried about me."

"How do you feel about that?"

"I'm not ready to take on a teenager. Not right now."

"Have you told your daughter how you feel?" the doctor asked.

"No. I've been busy." He gave her a thin smile. "Trying to get better and all."

"I've got to go," the doctor said. "I have an appointment."

"You'll tell SFPD I'm okay, then?"

"I'm going to tell them that you are fit for work, Detective. Okay?"

"It's all I have now. Work. Thank you."

"What about your daughter? You have her. She needs you."

"That's not fair."

"To whom? I think you're trying to get better. I believe that's true. But you can't shut your daughter out of your life because she's not convenient. Now you have to leave, Michael." It was one of the few times she'd called him by his first name.

"Okay," he said.

A young woman stood in the doorway, maybe twenty, if that, her hair shaved on her right side. A laptop bristling with stickers was in her hands. She was looking at them as if she'd caught them at something intimate.

"Should I —?" the attractive young woman said. She started to turn away.

"No, come in," the doctor said. "Come in, Karen."

O'Higgins left, walking past the dark-haired freaky girl, who was looking at him. He realized the girl might not be a patient. It occurred to him, as he walked toward the elevator, that his psychiatrist might be a lesbian. It took him by surprise.

***

Asha lay in the hospital bed, not knowing where she would go. The news that her daughters were being flown back to India, without her being able to see them, seemed impossible. Surreal, like the rest of the last 48 hours.

She looked around her. They'd brought another woman, very elderly, into her hospital room. The woman was asleep and seemed barely alive. Asha stared at the old woman, envying her unconsciousness.

Her cell phone rang, on her lap. She saw it was Nirad.

"I'm taking the girls to India, to our house in Delhi, Asha. They'll leave today. They'll be safe in India," Nirad said over the phone.

"I don't understand," Asha said. "Can't I go, too?"

"I'm afraid not. The police are asking us both to stay and help with their investigation here."

"No," she said. "I can't allow it."

"It's decided," her father-in-law said.

"I would like to talk to the girls. Put them on please, Nirad," she said.

"I'm afraid that's not possible. They're en route to the plane now." He fell silent, and she wasn't sure he'd not hung up on her.

"Why are you doing this?" she said.

"I'm doing it for the girls' protection. This could be political, the murders," Nirad said. "How are you feeling?" She could tell he was angry with her, and didn't mean it.

"I'd like to go home. To — the house. Can you send someone for me? I came in an ambulance. I've no car. I'm not even sure exactly where I am," she said, and it was true.

"I'm afraid they've not released the house. Yet. I've the lawyers on it," her father-in-law said.

She realized with horror that he'd not answered her question about someone coming to fetch her.

"Perhaps it's best if you stay at the hospital," he said. "You need to prepare yourself — you know what you must do."

"What happened to Rishi? Who would do such a thing?"

He'd hung up. She held the phone in both her hands. You know what you must do. She knew what he meant, and it frightened her. Sati.

She was sure that everything that had happened in the last forty-eight hours was a nightmare. At any moment she would wake from it, roll over and feel her husband's sleeping body. A guru, a good friend of her mother's and a much respected pandit, had once told her that her sattva guna, one of the three fundamental life forces, was dominant. This sattva guna force would make her prone to complex dreaming, which could carry her away. He told her that she might even have "God-realization" in a dream and be forever changed by it.

The sweet moment where she touched her husband's shoulder, felt his body, didn't arrive. Instead the morning lingered in a horribly prolonged way, with only random visits from nurses and the pedestrian sounds of busy hospital corridors.

The doctor on the ward, the old kind one who had been so angry with the detectives for upsetting her again, showed her a Western-style breathing technique designed to alleviate panic attacks. He'd come in and held her hand and told her everything would be all right. She'd rung the call bell and asked to see a doctor after speaking to her father-in-law on the phone. She felt a renewed sense of helplessness and panic, made worse with the realization that she was completely alone, and in a strange country without any family.

And now her father-in-law wanted her to commit suicide, because that was what good Hindu widows were supposed to do.

As soon as the old doctor left her room she pronounced the AUM mantra, without thinking about it consciously. It took shape in her throat first, then on her lips. She sat on the edge of the bed waiting to be told she could leave, repeating it and repeating it. She began to hear music on top of the sound of her mantra; it was Beethoven's Moonlight Sonata. She could see her mother playing it in the living room of their family home in India. Suddenly she was there, standing behind her mother as she played the piece.

"I've lost my husband."

Her mother stopped playing and looked up from the keyboard. "I know," she said.

"I'm alone."

"I know, my child."

"Help me, Mother!"

Her mother began to play the piece that she so loved when she was a child. "Listen," her mother said. The volume increased, and it was as if Asha had her ears up against the piano. She heard the notes with exquisite distinction —the sound of the piano's hammers tapping the wires, sounds within sounds, all of them at once: Beethoven, the AUM mantra, her mother's humming, the sounds of the keys, the sounds of the hospital ward, the sounds of her heart, the sounds of her children playing with Bharti upstairs in the new house. She heard peals of laughter that at moments became, and matched in intensity, the sound of her mother's playing.

But the piece, the piece she knew so well, was going to end. It was going to end in a way she hated, and in a way that even as a child she dreaded. It had Beethoven's awful definition of finality. End. A shapeless black ending sent across all time— twice, a kind of signal, mortality's sigh. One note repeated in the most awful yet starkly beautiful way. The way of all genius is to destroy us, a professor at Cambridge had once said to her.

She looked up at the ceiling and screamed as Beethoven's final two notes of the sonata—so famous—were played by her mother's educated brown fingers pressing on the keyboard, three thousand miles away. Twice in harmony, the last chord with all endings and all beginnings written in time forever. To destroy us and make us whole all at once.

She screamed, thinking it would stop the music, but she continued to hear it, and finally the second chord fell and she was looking at her husband's body lying in the elevator. She heard the motor. The elevator that she'd never liked, soundless. It took Rishi away. The door closed and she was with her mother again, her mother's back to her. The sonata's last moment hung in the air as her mother played, as if her mother were an Indian goddess. Her hands pressed into the keys. The entire universe, all things known and unknown, spoken and unspoken, left to cotton and wire touching.

It was the detective's voice that broke over the disharmony of sounds moving in her head, swamping her mind, her screaming at her mother. A new sound/voice fought with the sound of her scream.

"Mrs. Chaundhry? Mrs. Chaundhry. It's Detective O'Higgins."

She threw her arms around him, thinking he was her father. She'd seen her father come into their living room. Frightened, she was sure it was him. Her father would make it all right again, as he had when she was a child. Everything would be all right. She would wake up. It would be all right. But it was, she realized finally, only the policeman.

CHAPTER 14

O'Higgins drove Asha Chaundhry to the Clift Hotel on Geary Street, not wanting her to have to take a taxi alone from the hospital. She told him in the car that the Clift was where she, Rishi and her girls had stayed when they'd first arrived in San Francisco. She didn't know where else to go, if she couldn't go home.

Geary Street's sidewalks were chock-a-block with pedestrians. He realized, pulling up to the Clift Hotel's doors, that he had a strong urge to protect Asha Chaundhry. She slipped out of the car without saying anything. He knew he should just pull away and leave her there, and not heed the incredible attraction, as if she was some larger planet pulling him into her orbit. He sat and watched her enter the expensive hotel. She looked so fragile, he thought. People seemed like giants on the street in comparison. He watched her disappear.

He'd intended to interview Asha Chaundhry at the hospital, a second time, with Marvin, but it seemed too cruel to interview her when she was having what seemed to be a psychological breakdown. It was something he understood all too well.

He'd texted Marvin that he was postponing the interview and that Asha Chaundhry had been discharged from the hospital.

Marvin texted him back immediately: WHY WAIT?

His phone rang after he didn't answer the text. It was Marvin.

"What the hell is going on, Mike?"

He told Marvin that he'd been attacked, and that the nanny's phone had been wiped clean.

"Someone was willing to kill me, and Madrone, to get that phone," he said.

"A kill signal? Didn't you have the damn airplane mode on?"

"Yes. But he managed to turn the phone on."

"So they sent someone to get the phone. They tracked the phone with the airplane mode on? Maybe they used the IMEI number," Marvin said, trying to make sense of what had happened. "What the fuck is going on?"

"Someone got to it, that's what's going on."

"They tried to kill you? Jesus," Marvin said. "Who is doing this shit? They could have used the IMEI number, but they'd still need a carrier's help. And they needed to know Kumar's IMEI number. I couldn't find one, and I'm the police. This is some Big Brother shit."

"Well, it's someone who hires killers, someone sophisticated enough to track cell phones when they're turned off," O'Higgins said. "Sounds like a government to me."

"That would have to be a carrier. It's the only way, if the airplane mode was on. And they needed a police report saying the phone had been stolen — from the person who owned the damn phone," Marvin said.

"Yeah. Like I said, a government. Spooks could do it. Who knows what they can do," O'Higgins said, not wanting to talk on the phone about it. "I don't think we should talk about it like this — you understand?"

"Okay. But you've got to bring Asha Chaundhry in for an interview, Mike."

"Okay. I will, just not immediately. She's in a bad way, Marvin."

"Are you listening to me, Mike? We need to question her. We need to tie her to a story."

"Yeah. I know. We will."

"Today," Marvin said.

"Okay. Okay. Later today, then. Tonight."

"Are you okay, man? Were you hurt last night?"

"No. I'm fine. The other guy has a serious condition, though." It was their running joke, referring to death as a "serious condition." Marvin didn't laugh. "I'm fine, man."

"Tonight," Marvin repeated.

"Okay, tonight."

He parked the car in a red zone and followed Asha into the hotel, drawn to her not as a policeman, but as something else that he couldn't quite explain. Had it been simply a sexual attraction, as it was with Madrone, he could easily have left her there. It was something else, something more powerful, and something that he couldn't explain. He'd never felt anything like it before. It was as if he were being drawn toward a light in a dark room.

He walked up behind her as Asha explained to a well-dressed young woman at the hotel's desk, who remembered her, that she wanted to take the same suite her husband and she had before. The attractive Asian clerk asked her about her daughters. Asha said nothing. She explained that she would have her luggage sent along soon. The clerk at the desk looked at Asha, and then at O'Higgins, who stood beside Asha. The clerk realized, without being told anything, that something was terribly wrong.

O'Higgins thought he would leave her at the elevator doors, but didn't. Instead he rode with her to the top floor and followed her down the hallway to the grand suite of rooms.

"Do you want me to come in?" he said.

"Yes," she said without turning around, slipping a white room card into the door's electronic lock and opening it.

He walked in behind her, apprehensive about his motives. It was a huge suite with views of the City that were just now clearing, white bits of cloud-scud flying like flags over the teal colored bay and a metal-grey downtown, all of it saying "Big West Coast city."

"I lost my wife," he said. "I know what it feels like."

She went to a kind of wet bar and plugged in her phone, which she had held in her hands the entire way over. The phone's charging cord looped around the wrist of her left hand. The cord, her phone and her purse, which he'd brought her from the scene, were the only things she had left from her former life.

"It's almost a year ago now," he said.

She turned and looked at him. She seemed tiny, her face drawn. She had no makeup on and her hair, pulled back in a ponytail, looked oily. Her long black hair was the first thing he had noticed about her that day on the ferry, how beautiful it was, how luxurious it seemed.

"You must do puja, Detective. We can do it together," she said. Her tone was earnest but had a frayed, tired quality from the sedatives. She put down her cell phone, making sure it was plugged in. It seemed, looking at her, that everything depended on her phone charging. Her entire future hung in the balance, as if she would get news that her husband were alive and that the last 48 hours had been just a horrible nightmare. Rishi would call her any minute to reassure her.

O'Higgins too sometimes felt as if someone would wake him,

perhaps Jennifer herself, and tell him he'd overslept. She would slide into the bed and lie next to him and his nightmare would be over.

"What's that — puja?" he asked.

"Prayer. You must pray and I must pray," she said. "There are gods. Do you believe in God, Detective?"

"I should go. I will have to —"

"No — please! Don't leave me alone," she said. She said it quickly and spontaneously, as if she realized she might spend the rest of her life alone. "My mother is to call me. She's gone to see the guru. He will have a mantra for me." She walked toward him. "I will ask her to tell the guru you need a mantra, too. For your suffering. Please, stay."

"I — okay. A little while."

She went into the bathroom and closed the door, leaving him standing in the suite's living room. The hotel suite was like an apartment; it was that big. When she came out she had a vermillion colored spot drawn on the center of her forehead, just above her eyebrows.

"What is that, the mark? What's it mean?" he asked. He was still standing, feeling like someone waiting for a plane to arrive. He felt he held a ticket to somewhere important, and he was ready to leave everyone and everything behind to start his life over.

"It's a bindi. Mother said I was to wear it immediately. It will help me, she said, with what's coming."

"Help?"

"Yes. It will help strengthen the power of my third eye. I will need my third eye. I'll watch my girls with it. And they too will feel my power. It's the power you feel when you look at the moon.

The energy."

"What's coming? I don't understand."

"Madness. Madness will come to test me. Test my strength. But you've come to help me. You are the god Ganesh, and will help me. My mother too will help me through the test," she said. "We're not alone, Detective."

"I'm not — I'm not a god. You need a doctor, Asha — Mrs. Chaundhry. You need a psychiatrist. It helps. It helped me. I know how you feel. It hurts, I know. You get — confused. Afraid. I was afraid. It's a kind of fear." It was the first time he was able to articulate what he felt since his wife's death. Before it had been a pain that he couldn't explain even to himself.

"Yes. Yes, you are. I can tell. It's coming from your face. You want to be kind to me and you want to love me. I can see it. You were sent to help me and to help my girls."

He didn't know what to say. It occurred to him that Asha Chaundhry had gone mad in some classic sense of the word, lost touch with reality. But something about her eyes seemed sane and very brave. He'd seen the look in Iraq and recognized it as the look of a warrior going into battle. They might die, but they were tired of being bullied by the fear of death.

"Did you kill your husband?" he asked.

He didn't want to feel this debt to her, or whatever he was feeling. She'd done something to him that day on the ferry. Her kindness had been special. Something had flowed through her and touched him, the moment she'd laid a hand on his shoulder. Her touch had helped him stop feeling the pain, if only for an instant. In that brief moment he'd been able to gather up his strength for the first time, to feel the undamaged inner self that jumped, alive, when she'd touched him. I need to repay that debt.

"No. Of course not. I loved my husband."

"Do you know who might have wanted to kill him?"

"No."

"Did you know he was involved with the American government?"

"Yes. I knew. He told me. My brother told me. My brother told me it was dangerous, what Rishi was doing for the Americans. That he would have powerful enemies. That they were his father's enemies, too."

"You knew? Was your husband a spy?"

"I think so. Yes. He never said, exactly," she said. "We must do puja now, Detective."

She'd had him stop at an Indian market, explaining that she needed something. She got out and came back to the car on Turk Street with a paper bag. It was incense. "We burn it," she said, "while we do puja."

She motioned for him to sit by her on the floor. He wanted to leave. The whole thing was bizarre: the incense, her calling him a god, her acceptance of suffering as if it were some kind of disease she could fight off.

"You must do puja with me, Detective." She lit the incense stick and placed it in a small brass holder she'd bought, placing the holder on the coffee table in front of them. A tail of smoke lifted from the lit brown stick of incense.

"Where's your phone?" he asked.

"On the counter. Why?"

"I want to turn it off."

"No. My mother is going to call me. She went to speak to the guru, Pandit Tata. He's known me since I was a child."

"Who is the carrier?" he asked. "Your phone? Who provides

service?"

"BSNL, I think. I would imagine. It's an Indian company," she said. "The family is a major stockholder. My husband said we get the service for free. They gave us phones before we came to the States."

"And your nanny's phone?"

"All of the family's phones are BSNL phones. Bharti's phone, too. That was all arranged by my husband back in India, before we came to the States."

"Bharti Kumar is dead," he said. "She was murdered by the same person, or persons, who murdered your husband."

"Bharti? Yes. I understand." Asha's phone buzzed as a text hit it. He looked across to the stark white marble counter. She rushed to the phone and read the text.

"It's my mother. She loves me, Detective. We must do puja. Please, sit down, next to me. We must do it together, you and I."

He started to smell the Blue Pearl incense, sweet and cloying. Asha sat on the rug and started to mumble a mantra, looking at some point in the distance. It was a well-known Hindu mantra, but it sounded like nonsense to him, and frightening. Gibberish.

"Mrs. Chaundhry. Asha. I need your help! Do you understand? Stop it. It won't help. None of this — bullshit. Not incense, not God. Nothing will bring them back. Nothing. They're dead, do you understand? Your husband and Bharti Kumar are dead."

She glanced up at him, but continued to mumble her mantra.

The bindi on her forehead was crude looking. It had been done with lipstick, he realized. It looked absurd. Why did she believe anything could help her? Had he gotten any real help for his suffering? Even his visits to the psychiatrist, had they really made him feel better? Had they stopped the pain of existence, or his feelings of guilt?

He went across the suite's living room to her iPhone and looked at the message. The text message she'd just received was in Hindi, unintelligible to him. He ran through her contacts, found Bharti Kumar's cell number and punched it into his iPhone. He found Asha's number in Settings and dialed it into his contacts. He put the phone down, angry and frustrated. He wanted to take her phone with him, but he couldn't, not without her permission. He had no desire to be cruel to her, or to anyone. The calculated cruelty he'd summoned in war, as a Marine officer doing his duty, was unimaginable to him now. He put her phone down.

He left, walking out into the hallway and toward the elevator, past an alcove burdened with Room Service carts and maids' trolleys piled with fresh towels, all of the activity having appeared since they came down the hall. For some inexplicable reason he began to trot, as if he were running away from something that was pursuing him—the fear that, like Asha Chaundhry, he was going mad. That the madness was closing in on him and he would soon be just a hollow shell, unrecognizable, killed off—left just a soulless, violent idiot.

***

"Nirad Chaundhry will be here soon. We have to return the house to the family. That's an order," Marvin said.

"Why did the Gilberts change their story, Marvin, huh?" Michael asked.

"I don't know, man. I want to interview Asha Chaundhry," Marvin said. "Today. It's time to lock her into a story."

"Who sent the kill signal to Bharti Kumar's phone, Marvin?"

"Who shot JFK, Mike, huh? I don't know who sent the kill signal, all right?"

"What's the rush with turning over the scene, Marvin?"

"Stop it, Mike. You know why as well as I do. Nirad Chaundhry is a billionaire. He has a big-time law firm calling the DA twice a day, hounding him for a decision. They're tired of the calls. The bodies are gone and the criminalists have done their work. End of story. They get the house back."

"She thinks I'm Ganesh," O'Higgins said. "Asha Chaundhry."

"Who?"

"Some kind of Indian elephant god." Curious, he'd downloaded a picture of Ganesh on his phone. He showed it to Marvin.

"Looks like you, all right. Especially the ears."

"Very funny. You think she's our girl. You think Asha Chaundhry came in here and killed her husband and nanny in a jealous rage? That's what you think happened?"

"No robbery. Where's the forced entry? The place was locked up when patrol cleared the house. They checked. We checked. There is no forced entry. They have an expensive alarm system. No alarm went off."

"So what? Someone could have had a key."

"Okay. Who?"

"Probably a lot of people. Contractors, for one. They just did a big project. Think of all the workers who might have had access to this place." He saw the coroner's number flash on his cell phone and took the call.

"Kumar was pregnant, Mike," Millikin, the coroner's investigator, said. "I just heard from the medical officer. She thought you should know. She's still working on her."

Michael ended the call and told Marvin the news.

"Okay, now you have a good reason for Asha Chaundhry to commit murder," Marvin said.

"I want to pretend that Kumar's phone wasn't wiped clean," Michael said.

"Why?"

"Just a feeling. If someone was willing to kill me to make sure the phone's memory was deleted, we should find out why."

"So, book Kumar's phone into evidence," Marvin said.

A limousine pulled up out front. They could see it from the foyer where they were standing.

"I said they could have the house back at four," Marvin said. "And they're right on time."

"Meet me at the Clift Hotel at six, tonight," Michael said. "Now leave. I want to speak to Nirad—informally."

"What do you mean, informally?" Marvin said.

"I want to worry him."

"Worry him?"

"Yeah. Get under his skin," O'Higgins said.

"You have to give him the house back, Mike."

"I will. We are. You're leaving. I had something I left upstairs."

"Yeah. Really? Have you lost your fucking mind?" Marvin slipped on his raincoat and watched O'Higgins walk up the elegant oriental carpeted stairway. He thought of stopping him, but he felt angry that Kumar had been pregnant, and that a baby who'd never known the world had also lost its life so horribly.

Fuck Nirad Chaundhry, he thought, and left.

"I understood that the house was being returned to us," Nirad said. An attractive young Indian woman, well-dressed, was with him. They both walked into Rishi's office. Nirad was wearing a grey suit and looked very elegant, his hair cut since they'd met. The young woman was in a pants suit. She was pretty and thin, not too different, Michael thought, from Kumar.

"Yes. I was just looking for my raincoat. I left it here, somewhere," O'Higgins said.

Nirad looked back at the girl and said something in Hindi. She initiated a call on her phone and walked out into the hallway with a rock-hard look on her pretty face.

"If you don't mind, Detective, we've work to do. It's been over two days since we could access my son's office." Chaundhry leaned on his cane with both hands.

"We found Bharti Kumar's iPhone," O'Higgins said.

"I see. I'm sure it will be useful," Chaundhry said.

He had been watching Chaundhry's face intently since he'd stepped into the office, and saw in his sideways glance a micro expression that connoted fear, which he had been hoping to see.

"We have a remarkable crime lab. The people working there are experts at cloning phones. Retrieving data. Kumar's password was her birthdate. Apparently they've already gotten into her phone. It's common for people to use weak passwords," O'Higgins said.

The young Indian woman came back into the room. "Someone would like to speak to you, Detective," she said, and handed O'Higgins her cell phone.

"Detective, this is Kathy Price, one of Mr. Chaundhry's lawyers. I understood the police would be out of the house by 4:00 p.m. That was our agreement with the District Attorney's office. Any further intrusion would be seen as harassment of my client, Mr. Chaundhry."

"Of course. I've misplaced my coat," O'Higgins said. "Simply trying to find it. The house is his." He handed the phone back to the girl. Something about her was soldier-like, he realized. Spook?

"It may be in the nanny's room." He saw Chaundhry roll his eyes. "I'll see. Could have been. I've been in there, criminalists too, all morning. Hair is what we found. Everyone drops hair. It's crazy how much we shed every day," O'Higgins said. He walked out of the office and went up the stairs toward the third floor.

He walked into Bharti Kumar's bedroom. It was chilling, still, as if he might see the girl's body in the shower stall. He heard Chaundhry come down the hall, his cane making a distinctive sound.

Chaundhry walked into the room behind him, without his assistant. "She was from the Punjab. A nice girl. Very simple girl, really. I find girls like that delightful. Don't you, Detective? Untouched by pretenses. It's too bad what happened. I've told her parents. I sent them some money. They're poor village people. They were very grateful. It's the least we could do. I promised them if they had other daughters, they could send them to me and we would put them to work. A job can change a person's life, in India."

O'Higgins turned around to face Chaundhry. Suspects always wanted to know more. That was the interview technique he used to pull them out of their protective shell. He'd offer to tell them what he knew and they wanted to believe him, even if it was a lie. They desperately wanted to know what he knew. Rich or poor, stupid or Berkeley PhDs, they all wanted to know what he knew.

"The scene tells a story. Did you know that? To the trained eye," O'Higgins said. "The truth is just waiting for us to reveal it. To print it. To capture it and bring it to the lab. And there it will sit until someone pulls up a chair and looks at it under a microscope. Truth. 'This is what happened.'

"Cast off? That's blood that flies from the weapon. I have some on my shoe — it's from another scene. Someone tried to kill me. Tried to get a piece of evidence. But we were lucky. He wasn't. He was beaten to death. It was horrible, face obliterated," O'Higgins said. "I'm guessing he was a professional."

"I don't see your coat, Detective. Perhaps you left it downstairs? You really must let us get to our work now."

"Maybe I left it in there. In the bathroom? I might have. People are careless, aren't they? Leave things. In a hurry, and they just aren't thinking straight. I'll look and see. It might be in there."

O'Higgins walked into the bathroom. The shower stall's glass walls were dirty and dry, showing the fingerprint powder's residue.

"It's right here. My coat. I left it here. What do you think happened, Nirad?"

"I've no idea. I suppose Asha came in and confronted the girl about the affair."

"She brought a knife, I suppose? Went to the downstairs closet and took it out of the box?" O'Higgins reached for the shower door and opened it. "She walked in here, you think, and confronted Ms. Kumar in the shower?" He turned around and looked at Chaundhry, who was standing in the bathroom doorway.

"I suppose," Nirad said. "Yes."

"She was pregnant, did you know that? Ms. Kumar."

"No. Of course not. How would I know that?"

"Yes. We just heard. Well, I've found my coat. House is officially yours, then," O'Higgins said, and left.

CHAPTER 15

18 months before the murders

It was five in the morning. The Bay's waters glistened and shimmered as the dawn seemed to come up from beneath it, sent up from the depths. It was so lovely that O'Higgins was transfixed by the scene: the Berkeley hills, the distant stark megalopolis called Oakland to the southeast, the Bay creeping along the Marin coastline, the midnight blue sky unifying it all, making it a whole landscape that was part of his DNA.

He looked out the big picture window of their living room. He was barefoot wearing just pajama bottoms. He stood and looked at the Richmond Bridge being lit by the dawn, tarnishing its steel-rib structure and rendering it from dawn's gloom. A few early-morning cars, their taillights glowing, moved across the bridge heading for Richmond. The sketchy-looking lights signaled the beginning of a new day.

It was so good to be alive, he thought. He'd survived war and here he was standing on the floor of this house, with a good job, a wife and a daughter who loved him. He felt as if it was all meant to be. The dead he'd left back in Iraq were somehow meant to be; the living, their comrades in arms, went on living.

The victims of crime, whom he met after they died, the sky, the soon-to-be sun; they were all part of life. The moment he would start the engine to his boat and they —the three of them — would leave the dock, pull out in to the thick mercury-like water of San Francisco Bay was the moment he looked forward to. The smell of the saltwater, the look on his wife's pretty face while she stood in the tiny cabin lighting the stove.

He'd lived, and there was a reason, and it was called God. God had saved him from death. He was sure of it, standing there welcoming the sun. God had wanted him to live, to marry, to have a child and keep it all going. Not a biblical staid God, but something else, more real, reflected on the surface of the water.

There was no fog, which he took as a good sign as he planned to take out his new sailboat, a 1958 40-foot, all-wood Lapworth, designed by a famous California boat builder. He was excited. He loved to sail, and he loved having his wife and daughter with him. He was full of energy and looking forward to the day that was starting out special. He'd named the new sailboat after his wife— Jen.

He went into their kitchen and made coffee, leaving Jennifer and Rebecca to sleep a little longer. He heard the heater kick on. He had two texts on his iPhone, but he ignored them. One was from a mother whose son had been beaten to death in a road rage incident. The suspect had disappeared, abandoning a car he'd stolen. The suspect was Salvadoran; his girlfriend told them he was a gang member, and had fled back to El Salvador. They had little hope of catching him. The mother was distraught, unable to cope with her son's loss. She was a single mother, and alone. He'd befriended the woman, and kept in touch.

He fixed coffee and hot milk, and went to the living room again to look out on the quickly vanishing dawn. Traffic was light on the 101 freeway running south, as it was a Sunday. It was just

5:49 a.m. He wanted to be out of the house by 7:00 a.m., and be on the water by 7:30.

He heard his wife get up. She went to the coffee pot, got a cup and walked out into the living room. She was wearing a t-shirt and a pair of his boxers and looked so alive and sexy. She came up and put her arms around him. Getting on tip-toes, she kissed him on the neck, still half asleep.

"What time do we have to leave, skipper? Your mates are a lazy bunch."

"Seven," he said. "I love you. I really do."

She looked at him then. Something was still girlish about her, all her impish fey quality captured in the smile of her freckled Okie-girl-from-San-Bernardino's face.

"Likewise, Detective." She slipped out of his arms and went to wake their daughter. They left on time. All the time in the car he'd been talking about the boat and how well made she was. His daughter took a selfie of the three of them standing in front of the new boat. The photo's time stamp was seven-fifteen, exactly.

***

Mrs. Asha Chaundhry had showered and dressed. She was wearing a bindi on her forehead but it didn't detract from her beauty, a beauty that even now seemed indelible. It was the kind of female beauty, Marvin thought, that pulled you toward her. He'd known a few other women who possessed it. He felt it himself as he'd turned on the recording device, hidden from her. It was what he'd once heard described as the "Catherine Deneuve effect."

She was being recorded surreptitiously. Asha Chaundhry seemed eager to talk to the two detectives who had come to the Clift Hotel to interview her. Marvin noticed she was wearing a gold sari and it struck him as odd, her Indian garb. She seemed too modern for it. He also saw finally why his partner felt differently about this particular young woman. It was obvious his partner was attracted to her, and Marvin accepted it as part of life. Had his partner fallen in love with her he wondered. That would be crazy, but it was a crazy world. He'd thought it crazy that Jennifer O'Higgins, a woman he truly cared for, had died because of some stupid freak accident—one broken bolt. It had tested his faith in God, shaken it. Why? When so many horrible people live on.

"When was the last time you saw your husband yesterday, Mrs. Chaundhry?" Marvin asked.

"I saw him at about four, maybe a little after. In his office. He'd come back while I was out at my Pilates class. He'd texted me that he'd come home and was in his office working."

"Your husband texted you? He was in the house with you?"

"Yes. But it's a big house. We often text each other. It's simpler to find him," Asha said.

"Where had he been, your husband?" Marvin said.

The three of them were sitting in the living room with views of the City. They had decided that Marvin would ask all the questions, with the intention of building a timeline that they could tie Asha Chaundhry to.

"He'd flown to Gilroy in the morning. The car service came at about eight-thirty and picked him up after breakfast and took him to the heliport."

"When was the last time you saw your father-in-law?"

"At breakfast. Thursday. The same day."

"The day your husband — the day it happened?" Marvin said.

"Yes. The three of us had breakfast together. My father-in-law took a cab to his lawyer's office, immediately after breakfast."

"Bharti Kumar, when did you see her last?" Marvin said.

"About the time I went in to find my husband and tell him I had to run to the store. The girls were at the Gilberts, across the street. I'm sure Bharti was in her room because I noticed her door was closed when I went up to make sure the maids had cleaned my father-in-law's room. The guest room he's using is across from Bharti's room. The other two guest rooms aren't quite ready."

"Maids?" Marvin asked. It was the first they'd heard of maids.

"We have two. They come in during the day. I always check to make sure things have been left tidy, in their right place. My father-in-law is very particular about that type of thing."

"But when was the last time you actually saw Bharti Kumar?" Marvin said.

"I suppose it was when I brought the girls back from school, and before Bharti took them over for their play date. I left for my Pilates class at about quarter to three. The play date was scheduled for three, after the girls came home from school. So I saw Bharti then, just before three o'clock."

"You have a maid service every day?" Marvin said.

"Yes. We asked the Gilberts who they used. They came highly recommended, two Latin girls. Maria — I can't remember, Gloria. Yes, Gloria is the other girl. I have their number on my phone."

"They were there, in the house, that day?" Marvin said.

"Yes. They come in every morning around nine and leave by two or three. It's better if they come regularly, with the children. It's a big house — you know. And Rishi doesn't want them there in the afternoons because he usually works in the office before dinner, and didn't want to be bothered with housecleaners."

"Was anyone else there at the house that you know of? Workmen? Contractors? Do you have a gardener?"

"No one was there except Bharti and myself, and of course my husband. We do have a gardener. He's Basque. But he never comes inside. My husband speaks to him. I've not met him yet. Rishi found him. I've only waved to him."

"Do they do the laundry, the maids?" Marvin said.

"No. Bharti does it. In the machines. We have two sets of machines. One downstairs behind the kitchen, and one upstairs on the third floor."

"The bed linens? Who does those?" Marvin said, reaching for the pot of coffee room service had brought in. He poured a cup, looking up at Asha while he did. She made eye contact, which surprised him. She seemed unfazed by the question, unafraid of it.

"Yes. The maids strip the beds once a week and make them up. Bharti makes sure the laundry is folded while the girls are at school. It's one of her duties. That, and to help me in the kitchen—tidy up after meals. Will this help you?" Asha Chaundhry looked at Michael, expecting him to say something.

All Marvin's questions were designed to lock her into a timeline, O'Higgins knew. Marvin was careful to intersperse the timeline questions so as not to tip his hand.

She turned back to Marvin.

"You were home after 4:00 p.m.? Is that correct?" Marvin said.

"Yes. Until I went out to the supermarket in the Marina around five. The horrible Safeway. I was gone perhaps half an hour. Parking is always difficult at that time of the day. The Safeway parking lot was full. I had to find a place to park nearby. It's what took me so long. But I had to go out. I'd forgotten the coconut milk, and it —"

"Why did you go? Why not send Ms. Kumar?" Marvin asked.

"Bharti can't drive. We have been talking about getting her lessons. I wish she could. Have you told her parents yet? I — I looked for her parents' number in India but — I didn't have it. It's at the house, on my husband's phone, I think." Asha said. "Someone has to call them."

"We've notified the Indian Consulate. And Mr. Chaundhry, senior. I believe he's contacted Ms. Kumar's family in India," Marvin said. "How long were you out of the house at the Safeway?"

"No more than forty-five minutes at most," Asha said. "It had to be after 5:30 by the time I got back. I know because I heard it on the BBC World Service, the satellite radio in the car. They gave the time— 17:30 GMT. The radio presenter gave the time when I turned on the car. I always translate from GMT. I've been doing it since I went to school in England. I did it then as I was coming home, because I knew the girls were due home from their play date at five."

"You are sure it was after five thirty when you got home?"

"A few minutes later. Five-forty, perhaps. It took me a few minutes to drive from the Marina up the hill. There was horrible traffic."

"When you came into the house, where did you go?" Marvin asked.

"I went straight into the kitchen and texted Bharti to say I was home. She was to pick up the girls at five, so I thought they were already home and upstairs in the playroom, or en route from the Gilberts' house. Sometimes it's hard for Bharti to get them rounded up."

"And did Ms. Kumar text you back?"

"No."

"Did you think anything was wrong when you didn't hear back from her?"

"No. Sometimes, especially if she's with the girls, she might not be holding her phone. I knew she'd text me soon, or she'd simply walk into the house with the girls."

"So what did you do?"

"I got on with preparing dinner — baingan bartha was the dish I was cooking. I had everything ready, you see. Everything was set. I'd just forgotten the — but when Bharti didn't text me back, and I didn't hear the girls come in, I went out into the foyer to see if I could hear them playing upstairs. I noticed the elevator door was ajar. I walked down the hall and called Bharti's name, thinking she might answer. I thought the girls were playing in the elevator and that was why the door was ajar. I don't remember much after that — after calling Bharti's name and walking toward the elevator."

"You saw your husband's body in the elevator then?" Marvin said.

Asha shook her head up and down. "I didn't believe it was Rishi, not at first. I thought it might be — I don't know what I thought. The police came then. I don't remember exactly. I got into the elevator and they took me out."

"You got into the elevator?"

"Yes. I held Rishi. I tried to pick him up — but I couldn't — I kept trying. Then the police came."

"Okay. Let's take a break," Michael said. It's the first time he'd spoken since they'd walked in the hotel suite. He gave Marvin a look that said lay off.

"It's all right. My mother said I was to tell everything to you. We must find who killed Rishi and Bharti. I understand that. I want to help," Asha said.

"Did you have any reason to believe that Bharti Kumar was having an affair with your husband?" Marvin said, ignoring his partner's call for a timeout.

"No. That's ridiculous — what are you saying?"

"So there was no indication that your husband might be — cheating on you with Ms. Kumar?"

"No. That's absurd. She was just a girl." Asha looked at Michael for help, sensing that he was protective of her.

"Your father-in-law suggested that Ms. Kumar and your husband were having an affair," Michael said. "That's why we're asking the question. I'm sorry."

"He's ¬— He's wrong. That's ridiculous."

"Did you know that Bharti Kumar was pregnant?" Marvin said.

"No."

"Did you go upstairs while the girls were at the Gilberts and harm Ms. Kumar? Is that what happened? You discovered they were having an affair and you decided to confront her?" Marvin said. "Things got out of hand. You two argued."

"No!"

"Did you catch the two? Is that what happened? Were they — did you catch them in an intimate situation while they thought you were out of the house?" Marvin said.

"No." She looked at O'Higgins for help.

"Did you argue with your husband and then stab him because he was having an affair with a very attractive young girl who he employed, and who he could pressure into having sex with him whenever he liked?" Marvin said.

"No."

"No what, Mrs. Chaundhry?" Marvin felt his neck muscles tighten. He was angry, he realized, because his partner was putting them both in jeopardy by his attitude toward the woman who might have committed the murders. It was the first time he felt betrayed. All eyes were on them. The Chronicle had run a front-page article about the "society killings." The story had also been covered by the New York Times, as well as in several European and Indian papers. Both his name, and his partner's name were cited as the lead detectives in the Chronicle's story. The heat was on.

"No. I didn't kill my husband. I didn't kill Bharti," Asha said in a quiet voice.

"Did you go into the bathroom and see Ms. Kumar's body yesterday?"

"No. I never saw Bharti after I left the house for Pilates class."

"Did you go into the third-floor bathroom of your home and stab Ms. Kumar after killing your husband, and while your children were across the street at the Gilbert residence?"

"No!"

"Were you jealous of Bharti Kumar? Perhaps she was the one pursuing your husband? That's possible, isn't it? Your husband was a very wealthy man, an attractive man. Any young girl would be tempted, I suppose," Marvin said.

He'd found that pushing people at the right time broke them. Not always, but sometimes, and because they wanted to break. Marvin thought that if he pushed Asha Chaundhry, in just the right way, she would break and confess. He believed she was probably the one who'd killed both victims. He believed that she'd killed her husband. He wasn't sure why, but he did. It was the simplest explanation for the two killings. And it was usually the simplest explanation, he'd learnt, after so many years in homicide that was the explanation for the crime.

"Stop it. Please," Asha said. "Please, stop it!" She began to shake. She reached across the table and Marvin Lee witnessed the unthinkable. His partner took her hand and held it.

We're fucked now for sure, Marvin thought, turning off the recorder. He was being pulled into a conspiracy and he didn't like it. It was crazy.

"My daughter is coming home this weekend for a visit. Tonight. You can't be here." Michael said. He was standing in the doorway of his place in San Rafael. Madrone had called him and asked to see him. "She wouldn't understand."

"You want me to leave?" Madrone said.

"No," he said. He got out of the doorway and she walked by him. "Are you okay? I'm sorry I didn't call," Michael said.

"Wrist was tweaked, that's all," Madrone said.

His neighbor saw the two of them standing in the doorway as she pulled out of her driveway and gave Michael a surprised look from the street. She'd been very friendly with his wife. He closed the front door.

"I just didn't hear him," Michael said. "Did you? Breaking into your apartment?"

"No, not really. He walked right by the bathroom. I was taking a pee. It was dark. I think he was scared and focused on you in the bedroom. He was looking for something. I watched him from the hallway. I was going to shoot him, but decided I might miss and hit you, or the bullet would go through a wall and kill someone. I keep the baton by the toilet. It's the one I had in Iraq. I live alone, so — I stash weapons around the place."

"What is it … I mean what do you want?"

"I want to be with you. Sex. I guess. If I'm being honest. I like you. Hey, I don't beat someone like that, unless I like you," she said and smiled.

He smiled back. It was the kind of humor he'd heard over there. He'd missed that about Madrone, her battlefield humor. She'd seemed squared away, balanced. But he'd met a lot of vets who appeared to be "squared away," and most definitely were not.

"How old is she? Your daughter?" Madrone asked.

"Sixteen."

"Uh-oh," Madrone said.

"Yeah. Well. I do the best I can. I don't know if I'm ready for a — a relationship."

"Well, I'm not asking you to marry me," Madrone said. "Nice place. I've got to be at work at six."

"My partner just screamed at me and called me an asshole," Michael said. "I don't know if I'm ready for —"

"I said I've got to leave in — four hours," she said. She took off her raincoat and threw it on the couch. "You should clean the place up — I mean, if your daughter is coming over."

Madrone crossed the room and kissed him. He put his arms around her waist and tried not to feel ashamed of himself. But he wanted her, the closeness of a woman's body again. The feel of it in his arms. He'd missed that more than he'd realized.

She helped him clean up the house a little before she left. He let her sort the piles of mail. He watched while he did the dishes. She was quiet while she went about it, as if she'd lived there. He admitted when she'd left that he liked the feel of her in the house. It seemed a different place with a woman in it again.

He took his daughter out to Marinitas, her favorite Mexican restaurant in San Anselmo. They had a long talk about where she might go to college. She was leaning on him again, asking his advice. They talked about her coming home from Sacramento. He said he was still not ready. He wanted to be honest, he said. She reached across the table and held his hand. She said she understood and she would wait for him to get better, and then she would come home and everything would be all right again. She'd changed too, he noticed. She seemed more grown up than when she'd left for Sacramento.

They drove home. Despite what he'd said, he told her she should come home if she wanted to. They made plans and had a laugh about his changing his mind. It was their first real laugh together since the accident. A friend rang his daughter on her phone; a boy, he imagined. She took the call but winked at him.

It all seemed normal again in the flash of an eye. He felt his wife's presence in the car. It was palpable. He turned and looked into the back seat, and saw her. She was smiling. His daughter didn't notice. He never told anyone about seeing his wife. He knew what it had to mean about his state of mind. But she'd been with them in the car on the way back to the house. It had been comforting to feel her presence again, the three of them back together again as they drove down the tree-lined streets.

CHAPTER 16

Detective O'Higgins sat behind the wheel of his Ford on the half-empty parking lot of the Target store on Geary Blvd. The store was closing for the night. Bedraggled raincoat-wearing shoppers filed out, mostly Asians, clutching red and white Target bags. A strong wind was blowing straight up Geary from Ocean Beach, knocking into people on the parking lot and forcing them to lean and hurry to their cars.

Asha Chaundhry had called his cell phone. She asked him to meet one of her Indian girlfriends, saying the woman wanted to talk to him about the case, but in private, and anonymously. He'd agreed to meet the woman at the Geary Street Target's parking lot, saying she should look for his white four-door Ford.

But it wasn't a woman who pulled up next to his car two hours later. It was a young Indian man who looked almost like a teenager; he appeared that young to O'Higgins. The well-dressed young Indian opened the Ford's passenger-side door and looked in at him.

"I'm Asha's brother. Neel Roa. Thanks for meeting with me, Detective. I'm afraid I had Asha lie to you. It was my idea. I will explain."

"Okay," Michael said. "I can see you're not a girl." He waved the kid into the car.

Roa slipped into the passenger seat of the Ford and closed the door, fighting the wind that wanted to keep it open. The young man was tall, thin and wearing a dark suit, white shirt, and tie his hair like his sister's, coal black, and very thick, was combed straight back.

"You have to help us. Asha is in danger, Detective. Anything could happen to her now."

"Danger from who?" Michael said, annoyed that he'd been lied to.

"Nirad Chaundhry," Roa said.

"Nirad Chaundhry? Her father-in-law?"

"Yes."

"You look like your sister."

The kid leaned over, offering his hand to shake. Michael took it. "Asha says that you are a kind man. My sister needs your help, Detective. She didn't kill Rishi. I swear to you."

"What about the nanny?" Michael said. The question was defensive, designed to allow him a moment to sort out what the kid wanted and to get the upper hand.

"My sister didn't kill anyone. You have to believe that," Roa said.

"I don't really have to believe anything right now. Your sister is a person of interest, as is her father-in-law, and that's all she is. The investigation is ongoing," O'Higgins said, using cop lingo to stop the kid from speaking to him as if he were convinced of Asha's being innocent.

"Nirad Chaundhry is a powerful man, Detective. A very powerful man in India," Roa said. "You wouldn't understand. My country is very — you wouldn't understand what it means when you're that rich in India. There is no law for Nirad."

"Why would Nirad Chaundhry want to hurt your sister, if

she's innocent?"

"I'm not sure yet. But he's taken my nieces to India without asking Asha's permission. He just did it. And he is telling everyone at home—including important people in the government—that my sister murdered Rishi. People are turning against Asha. People in high places. They believe Chaundhry's lies," Roa said.

"Were you at the house, the day of the killings?" Michael asked.

"No. I was in New York," Roa said. "I've come here to try and help my sister as best I can. But I can't — how can I say this — I can't be seen helping her. That's why I wanted to speak to you in person. My helping you has to remain a secret."

"Why?"

"I'm an Indian government employee. That's all I can say."

"I don't need your help. What I need to know is who murdered Bharti Kumar and Rishi Chaundhry," O'Higgins said.

"I can help you find out what you want to know about the murders. I'm an Indian government employee. That's all I can say. But if you tell anyone about meeting with me, I'm afraid that it will get me dismissed, and perhaps worse. It has to be a secret."

"What are you trying to say? Nirad Chaundhry is guilty of killing his son?"

"This is what I came to tell you: the Chaundhry Company is working on an important project for the US government. The Chaundhry plant here in Silicon Valley is not what people think. It is not a production plant for motherboards at all. It's in part a research facility. The Chaundhry Company is cooperating with the US's Argonne National Laboratory on a joint Indian/US government project that is top secret."

"What's this got to do with the murders?"

"Maybe nothing, but I thought you should know that the US government is going to protect Nirad, and so will the Indian government. No matter what Nirad might have done, including murder."

"Protect him?"

"Yes. I think they will. I think my sister might be a convenient scapegoat for the killings."

"Did Chaundhry send someone to try and take Kumar's cell phone from me?"

"Yes.

Nirad Chaundhry wants you and your partner Marvin Lee off the case. So does the Indian government — and probably your government as well. You have no idea what you and your partner are facing," Roa said.

"How do you know all this?" Michael said.

"I just do. You have to believe me," Roa said.

"Do you work for Indian intelligence?"

"I can't answer that. I can say I'm posted to India's New York consulate, and I'm a diplomat. That's all I can say. But I do know the Indian government, at the highest level, ordered the Research and Analysis Wing —RAW— to take Kumar's phone from you. And there are other RAW officers, here now, in San Francisco, trying to disrupt your investigation."

"Indian intelligence sent someone to steal Kumar's cell phone from the police? Why?"

"Obviously there must be something on that cell phone they don't want you to find. I heard they were unsuccessful, and you have the phone. If that is true, you are in danger. They will try again."

"Well, they didn't succeed. We have the phone and it's safe,"

Michael said. It was a lie, but only Marvin knew that the phone's memory had been wiped clean.

"Then you can expect them to try again to kill the nanny's phone, and they will succeed. And they will ask for help from the US government."

"What do you mean?"

"Just that. They will ask US intelligence to step in if they're not successful in stopping you. They will want that phone killed. Do you understand? They're not afraid of the local police."

"Okay," Michael said. "Well, I'm not afraid of them. How's that sound?"

"It sounds foolish, frankly, but I'm glad. I'll try and help you all I can. But you must keep our meeting a secret. I have to know if I can trust you. I've no one else to help me protect my sister."

"I've no reason to tell anyone we met, if that's what you're worried about. You've nothing to do with the case as far as we're concerned," Michael said.

"Take this. It's a phone NSA or the Indian government won't expect you to use. They're listening to your phone now—yours and your partner's phones. NSA and RAW. You should know that. This phone I'm giving you should be impossible for them to hack into, I hope. I'll call you on this phone when I know more. Do we have a deal, Detective? You'll need my help, you have to believe me."

"Okay. Why not." The appeal of a fight with anyone was something he'd been spoiling for. He felt a strange relief in the idea of being a soldier again. He didn't care about the odds. Formidable odds only made him feel better. Would they kill him? They'd be doing me a favor.

Roa handed him what looked like a normal old-school Blackberry, albeit very used looking. “Good luck. I’ll do what I can to find out what they’re planning,” he said.

“Listen — I found some strange kind of wafers in an envelope on Rishi Chaundhry’s desk. They were in a Lockheed Grumman envelope. The wafers were clear and felt like glass, but I couldn’t break one, or even bend it,” Michael said.

“Diamonds,” Roa said.

“Diamonds?”

“Yes. Synthetic diamonds. That’s what they’re working on, for computer applications. Diamond chip technology. That’s all I know. That’s what they’re working on with the people at Argonne Labs.”

Michael looked at him. He’d not mentioned the envelope to anyone, including his partner, mostly because he’d not thought the wafers of importance to the investigation. He’d put the envelope back on Rishi Chaundhry’s desk where he’d found it.

Roa got out of the car and turned to him before he closed the door.

“The Indian official who asked to be let into the Chaundhry house, the night of the murders, is a RAW officer. He’s a dangerous man—Colonel Ankur Das.”

“There’s one thing, Roa,” Michael said. “I’ll have to tell my partner what you’ve told me. Everything.”

Asha’s brother nodded quickly. He closed the car door. Michael turned off his recorder, having taped the entire conversation. He sat for several moments thinking about what he’d agreed to. Marvin might not approve or stand for cooperating with Asha’s brother.

The rain that had obscured the Ford’s windshield turned the night-time headlights into shimmering, striated lines, running helter-skelter across the Ford's windshield. Roa's car, sporting a rental company sticker, disappeared, turning right toward Geary Street from the parking lot.

O'Higgins started the Ford and pulled out of the almost empty parking lot into the night. He did something he'd not done since Iraq: he took his weapon and laid it on the seat next to him. It felt better that way. He had the nanny's phone in the glove box. He'd told Marvin he wasn't turning it into the crime lab yet, knowing they would write a report saying the phone was useless to the investigation, and that report might be leaked.

His phone rang as he pulled out onto Geary Street. It was Madrone. He took the call. She told him that there would be an inquiry into the man she'd killed. He could tell she was frightened. She could lose her job if she was judged to have used excessive force.

***

The lobby of the Clift Hotel, with its famous Redwood Room, was full of young hipsters looking for a good time. It was late, past midnight. O'Higgins didn't want to go home to an empty house. His daughter was moving back at the end of the week, but until then he would be alone there. So he'd come instead to the Clift Hotel to be close to Asha Chaundhry, who was on his mind all the time.

He felt restless. He wanted to see her and ask her about her brother, ask her about Nirad. He wanted to ask her point-blank again if she had murdered her husband and her nanny. Not asking as a policeman, but as someone who cared about her. It was not right, that wanting to be near her, but he did. It was all unexplainable. He'd never felt like this before. The woman was some kind of lighthouse, her strong beam coming around and around his dark place, flashing a powerful light.

He would have to play the tape recording of Roa's conversation for Marvin, but he didn't want to do it yet. Marvin was already angry, and he could only imagine what he would say after hearing it. O'Higgins had crossed the line, and he could lose his job.

He'd parked right in front of the hotel, flashing his badge at the gaggle of bellboys who were watching young girls on Geary Street. The night was alive with young people bar-hopping and enjoying night life. He couldn't imagine what that was like anymore, that sense of freedom. The kids passing his car made him feel old. He'd had their carefree optimism before going to war, and been robbed of it.

He walked into the hotel lobby and into its famous bar. The Redwood Room's lights were designed to create a boudoir make-out atmosphere for a perfect date. It was pleasant, the yellowish pools of intimate lamp-light bathing young couples' faces. It all seemed so innocent and comforting. He and Jennifer had come here when they'd dated. It seemed a thousand years ago.

He ordered a brandy neat from an over-tattooed bartender who looked like he belonged in a perfume commercial and sat nursing the drink, processing the last few days.

A text came in from his daughter, saying that she'd decided to stay. Her aunt—his sister— was to have picked her up and taken her back to Sacramento. He texted her back that it was okay, and to go to bed. They would sort it out in the morning. He was glad that their separation was ending. Maybe the worst of it was behind him, he thought, killing his drink and getting up mindlessly. He went out to the lobby and got into an elevator with a mixed couple who were going, quite obviously, to play boom-boom.

Asha Chaundhry, out of her head on something, had danced around him in the demi-light twirling like a dervish in a red sari, very stoned. She'd opened the door barefoot; the grand hotel room behind her was filled with lit candles. Indian sitar music was playing on a CD player. He could smell the sweet pungent smell of dope—hash, mixing in with the smell of incense. It smelled good.

She was drunk, or high, he couldn't tell which. Probably both, he decided. He'd come back to the hotel because he'd wanted to talk to her. He'd wanted to tell her he'd seen her brother, and, against his best judgment, he was entering their conspiracy. He believed that Nirad Chaundhry was an uber-wealthy asshole who probably had the Indian government in his back pocket. He didn't like him.

He had a strange desire to tell Asha he would protect her. He wanted to be in her presence, it might be as simple as that. Did he want to make love to her? Probably.

What was it about her, Asha Chaundhry, that was pulling at him? He didn't know, and he couldn't explain it. But he felt it. It would be palliative, like the no-strings sex he'd had with Madrone. Only, unlike sex-ecstasy, with an end to its grip, this feeling was incoherent, and not exactly physical, although it felt physical as well. It was a sense of merging, of being overwhelmed by some force that was greater than his selfhood. It seemed to have no end. He'd felt it since the moment he'd first seen Asha on the ferry, and it was only getting more powerful. The murders were only circumstantial to it.

He'd not expected to find her this way, out of her mind. He'd wanted her sober and motherly. Instead she was barefoot, her hair down, smiling in a drunken stupid, lost way. The bindi was still painted on her forehead, smudged slightly, bigger than he'd seen it earlier.

She led him into the candlelit living room, sat on the floor and motioned for him to sit across from her. Between them was a bong with its bowl filled with hash. She lifted a Bic lighter and lit the bowl's contents, sucking on the bong's mouthpiece. The hash, lit red, produced lots of smoke. She blew the hit out into his face and said in a sing-song way:

"There is a cobra in my house and its diamond hooded head is the darkest blue.

It is. It is. It is dear Vishnu only you— you my lord. It is you.

And when the Cobra moves through the house, along the hall's dark seam

While Monsoon winds whistle fierce …

The deadly house-snake sings:

"I'll dinner soon"

But I am not afraid God Vishnu because it is you. It is only you."

"Asha, stop it," he said. "Please. I want to talk."

"About what, ferry man? You're the ferry man." She stared at him, sitting with the pipe in her two hands. Several hash rocks were on the coffee table. Someone, perhaps one of her friends, had brought her the drugs—to help her?

"I saw your brother," he said.

"Are you going to help me?" Her eyes were bloodshot. Her face looked thinner and she looked younger. Like one of the girls downstairs, he thought, challenged by her own beauty. Was that all it was? He wanted her despite everything. Was he a monster?

"What's wrong with you?" he said.

"The guru called and said it was all right. That I would lose my mind, and I was to let it happen. Let it be lost."

"What are you talking about?"

"My mother's guru. Don't you understand?"

"No. No, I don't," he said.

"My brother told me you have a secret. Is it true? About an accident?"

He looked at her sitting on the floor, smelt the raw dope and saw the pools that were her eyes. They seemed huge. He remembered the silences of Angkor Wat in the morning, recalled Jennifer moving down a stone temple corridor wearing blue jeans and a yellow tank top, a lone monkey watching her as she approached it.

"Yes."

"So, you understand this madness then? It's forced on us," she said.

"Yes. Helpless. You feel helpless," he said.

"Yes. Helpless." She reached for his hand and held it. Then put his index finger on her bindi and pressed it onto her forehead, exactly on the mark.

"This is the Command Chakra — do you understand? It should be red turmeric, but I don't have turmeric here."

"No. I don't understand."

"It doesn't matter. But you can feel that energy. Madness's energy. Chakra energy? The Guru says we should not avoid it, madness. That we have to let it come. To be the helplessness. To be the madness — to be the anger. They all have to play out, they have to. Do you understand? What would we be if they didn't play out? Nothing. We would be nothing. Not alive. I saw you on the boat, and you had it coming out of here." She touched his third-eye spot and held her thumb against it. "That's why you were stuttering and looking so frightened that day. Rishi said it might be madness. See, my husband saw it too — your madness."

"Stop it," he said. He grabbed her wrist, offended that they'd talked about him that way.

"Nirad killed his son—why? This is madness. It's real, all around us. There is madness. Do you understand that? The world," Asha said. She took a hit of the pipe. He saw the square looking piece of gold colored hash in the bowl. Its edges turned red-orange and flamed as she sucked on the pipe.

"Is your brother an Indian intelligence officer?"

"Yes. And my father too, once. They're working hard to help me. Will you help me?"

"Yes," he said.

There was a knock on the door and a well-dressed young man walked into the room.

"Detective, I want you to meet Robert — Robert Thomas."

The men looked at each other, both sensing a rival.

"How do you do. I ran into Asha on the street, trying to buy drugs," Thomas said. "You must be O'Higgins, the detective who called me."

"It's true," she said. "Thomas helped me. I needed this, oblivion — it's the world, you see, it makes us mad. I know you'll help me. Both of you."

CHAPTER 17

O'Higgins got out of bed. The hashish he'd smoked with Asha Chaundhry had knocked him out and he'd not needed a Valium to fall asleep. He'd slept well, without the horrible dreams he'd been having since the accident. Dreams where he was always searching for his wife, still wearing his life jacket.

He went to the kitchen and made coffee, surprised by his drug taking and by the fact that he'd enjoyed being seriously zoned out, sitting on the floor of Asha Chaundhry's hotel suite and staring out at the City's night lights, listening to Asha repeat a mantra over and over. They were both crazy. It was obvious, and he woke up accepting the fact. All his trips to see his psychiatrist weren't effecting a cure.

Okay, I'm nuts, he'd thought, lying in bed. He wanted to make love to Asha Chaundhry. He couldn't escape the feeling of physical attraction, nor could he explain it exactly as it was far more intense than just physical lust the way it was with Madrone.

He noticed, as he passed in the hallway, that his daughter's bedroom door was closed and he remembered that she'd stayed overnight. It felt good to know she was home again. He went down to the family room, opened the wall safe and took out Bharti Kumar's iPhone, bringing it upstairs with him to the kitchen. He brewed a pot of coffee. It was just after seven in the morning.

A text from Marvin hit his cell phone as he went to the kitchen table with his coffee cup.

I'll come to your crib this AM.

OK, he texted back immediately.

He would have to play Marvin the tape of his conversation with Asha's brother, and he had no idea how Marvin would react. But it was time for them to touch base on the physical evidence and on the coroner's autopsy reports. He intended to interview Nirad Chaundhry again, allowing Chaundhry, to believe that Bharti Kumar's phone was still intact and a real threat to him.

He heard his daughter get up and move around the house. When she finally came downstairs, she was wearing brown yoga pants and a T-shirt that had belonged to her mother. She seemed to be even skinner than usual, and it worried him. Her arms looked incredibly thin.

"Good morning," he said.

"Hey, Dad. Late night?"

He didn't answer. "I'm glad you decided to stay," he said instead.

"Yeah. Sacramento is okay, but — it's kinda boring. The cousins are cool. But not much to do there, really."

"What about school?" he said.

"I want to go to Marin Academy, if they'll have me. Kate is there." His daughter had been a good student before the accident, but since, she'd been slipping, spending more time dancing than studying. Marin Academy was the county's premier private high school, and expensive. They had debated sending her, but they couldn't afford it and have a savings account for her college. Their wealthy friends in the neighborhood had sent their children, afraid of the public high school, which was predominantly third world and full of the children of immigrants, half of them non-English speaking.

"Sure. Okay. You want me to call them?" he asked. He went to the refrigerator and pulled out some frozen waffles. His daughter liked them.

"It's expensive, I know. Can we, like, afford it?" She poured a cup of coffee and sat across from him, holding her cup in both hands the way her mother used to.

"Yeah, we can," he said.

His wife had left a life insurance policy, one of the perquisites of her job at Cal. He'd intended to use the two-hundred and fifty thousand dollars she'd left for his daughter's college. But the Marin Academy where a lot of her friends were going, and very near their house, was a good school. He wanted her to be happy, right now, more than anything else. And he felt guilty for sending her away. He owed her this.

"Okay, I'll go there and see about enrolling, what it takes. I mean, if you call about the money. I want to try out for the SF ballet school, too. They have try-outs next week." They heard the waffles pop up. "Excellent," she said. "Waffles!"

"I need your help," he said, picking two waffles out of the toaster.

"Okay."

"That kid you knew, the propeller head. The tall Iranian kid," he said, finding a plate. "These are for you. I want you to eat them. Alex?"

"Yeah," she said.

"I want to see him. Can you get him to call me?" he asked.

"Sure. He's working at the Apple store in Corte Madera now."

"How much do you weigh?" he said, plating the waffles.

"Ninety-seven and change," Rebecca said. She was lying. She

weighed ninety pounds the last time she'd checked, weeks ago.

"I want you to gain some weight, okay? Didn't you eat while you were at your aunt's?" He put the plate in front of her.

"Yeah ..." She looked down at her coffee cup, avoiding his question.

He knew a lot of ballerinas fought to lose weight because the "look" the ballet companies wanted was of wafer-thin, long-necked girls. His daughter had the look they wanted but she, like so many dancers, fell prey to eating disorders, trying to appear more than perfect.

He got syrup from the cupboard and made a show of putting her breakfast on the kitchen table. "I'm getting butter out, too. Please use lots of it. It's good. You'll love it."

"Yuck! Animal secretions ... A guy came by last night looking for you," his daughter said. "He was wearing a turban thing. Big guy."

He stopped pouring a second cup of coffee and looked up.

"He said he'd come back. He knew my name. He said 'You must be Rebecca?' He left a card. I put it out by the front door. He was kind of creepy. Asked me where I was going to school."

He finished pouring his coffee without saying anything, playing it off. He reached into the refrigerator, got the butter dish out, walked it over to the table and set it down in front of her.

"Eat your breakfast, will you please. Then call Alex for me. See if I can stop by his place." He watched as she poured only a little line of syrup on her waffles. When she was little she would drown them. He wished she would do that now. He bit his tongue, not wanting to fight with her on her first day back home.

They couldn't talk right away because Rebecca had come in and sat with Marvin. Marvin had known his daughter since she was a little girl, and the two had always been close. Rebecca had spent weekends at Marvin's house, as Marvin's two daughters were the same age. It was the first time that Rebecca had allowed herself to be natural with Marvin. Both, after the accident, had felt awkward, not knowing what to say to each other. He enjoyed seeing them together, with their small talk and jokes. And he knew that if something ever happened to him, Marvin would make sure his daughter was all right.

When Rebecca left to see about the Marin Academy, he'd played Marvin the recording of his conversation with Neel Roa from the night before.

"I'm going to load Kumar's phone with some bullshit to show Nirad Chaundhry. So he thinks Kumar's phone is still working and intact."

Marvin looked at him. The nanny's iPhone sat on the coffee table between them.

"That should be over at the crime lab," Marvin said.

"Yeah. Well, if her cell was wiped clean, I didn't see the point."

"What's wrong with you, man? Really? Are you losing your shit, completely?"

"Nothing is wrong with me. I think that Asha's brother is telling the truth. I think we need his help or we're going to get played. You can see who we're up against now. The Indian government. And maybe the CIA, too."

"It's illegal to include him in our investigation, and will destroy our case if you're found out. You're the police. He could even be a suspect. Have you thought of that? You're conspiring with a suspect's brother, for Christ's sakes," Marvin said.

"It's not illegal. Not really. He says he was in New York City the day of the murders. You heard him. I've not told Roa anything, and I'm not going to. But if he wants to call me to talk. What's wrong with that?" O'Higgins said.

"You believe him? This Roa guy," Marvin said.

"Yes, I do. Nirad Chaundhry is an asshole. You saw how he acted. He was scared when we questioned him. He didn't act normal from the get go. And why did he send his grandkids back to India? What did they know?"

"You're digging a deep hole here, Mike. You see that, don't you? This whole investigation is going off the rails, man."

"There's something else. Here, look at this." O'Higgins slid a business card across the coffee table. "It's a guy named Das. The same Consulate guy who demanded we let him enter the Chaundhry house the night of the murders. He came here. Rebecca talked to him. He knew her name, Marvin."

"Shiiit." Marvin picked up the business card and looked at it. The coin finally dropped: the Indian Consulate was targeting them.

"I've got to know if you're in or out about Neel Roa. Are you cool with it, yes or no? If you're not, I'll swear you didn't know anything about it, if it blows up on me. You have my word," O'Higgins said.

"Rebecca. My kids? Have you thought about that? Maybe it would be best if the FBI did take over. All we have to do is play this tape for them. That's obstruction of justice," Marvin said. "Their killing of the nanny's iPhone. Attacking a police officer. All of it."

"I don't trust the FBI. For all we know they'll do a grassy knoll and stitch up Asha Chaundhry. And how can we ever prove Indian spooks are working for Nirad Chaundhry? Neel Roa isn't going to come forward. He can't," Michael said. He looked at his partner. "I don't trust anyone else but us. Not on this. I believe Roa. And besides, the FBI could fold under pressure from Washington. Why wouldn't they? You know what they're like when the big political dogs get off the porch. They'll go along — and we'll be fucked and fucked over.

"We are the only ones who can win this," he continued. "We're just the local cops doing our job. They can't stop us investigating a murder."

"They can stop the DA from prosecuting whoever we arrest," Marvin said. "What about Rebecca? What about my kids?" Marvin said. "What am I supposed to do if they come after them?"

"I'm going to tell Rebecca to go stay with my brother in Bolinas for a week or two, until we get by this. I think we can make an arrest soon. Can you send your kids to your mother-in-law's?"

"I guess. But it's crazy. Jesus, Mike. Why should we care so damn much?"

"We can't let this rich bastard run the table, Marvin. We can't. I didn't serve in Iraq to let foreigners push us around here at home. And Nirad Chaundhry is trying to fix this case so an innocent woman goes down for something she didn't do."

"How do you know Asha Chaundhry didn't do it? You still don't know that she didn't. We don't know who did it yet, Mike. That's the truth, isn't it?"

"If it turns out Asha Chaundhry committed these murders, we'll arrest her. I promise you."

"Yeah, okay. You got to tell me the truth, first. Are you having an affair with Asha Chaundhry? Did you hook up with her, after you met her on the ferry? Is that what this is about, Mike? Have you slept with her? Just tell me the truth, man."

"No. And if you're thinking that I was the one to kill her husband—no, I didn't kill her husband, either."

"Where were you that day? The day of the murders. Before we got the call?"

"Here. And the pistol range at Point Richmond in the morning. They have cameras. And I paid with my credit card."

"Did anyone see you? Did anyone visit you here in the afternoon?"

"No. From about eleven on, I was here — yeah, someone did see me. The UPS guy saw me. He came to the door around 3:30 or so."

"Fire up your computer and show me the range charge and we're good," Marvin said.

"You're evil, Marvin."

"Just do it, man. You're acting so crazy I don't know any more about you. Really. I got other news for you: the judge gave us the green light to look at the neighbor's bank account for probable cause. I just got a call from Wells Fargo's legal department. Paul Gilbert got a wire transfer from a German bank for a hundred and fifty thousand dollars—just ten hours after the murders."

"No shit."

"Yeah. Now, show me your credit card charge, you jackass."

While they were looking up O'Higgins' credit card account online, the coroner's investigator Millikin called and told O'Higgins that not only had Bharti Kumar been pregnant when she was killed, but her wounds were too deep to have been caused by a conventional knife, like the ones they'd found in Rishi's office. She'd been "run through almost" in several locations, the investigator said.

"And now we don't have a murder weapon either then," O'Higgins said, putting down his phone.

***

He'd come home that afternoon from a meeting with the District Attorney, who said that she'd gotten complaints from the Indian Embassy in Washington, as well as from the US State Department, both accusing O'Higgins and Lee of harassing Nirad Chaundhry.

The DA herself wanted an explanation. All of the accounts she cited had been completely false, including one of a Ford, like his, parking in front of the Chaundhry mansion with someone who looked like him — "a tall white man" — behind the wheel. All lies.

She also had claims of calls to Nirad Chaundhry's offices and cell phone, recorded by Nirad, of someone telling him to confess or "We'll get it out of you one way or another." The person making the threats said he was "a friend of the detectives." The accusations were being taken seriously.

He'd had to assure the DA that he had not done anything wrong, and that Chaundhry was making these accounts up to get him and Marvin off the case. They were just doing their job. After hearing the facts, she'd assured both of them that they had her support. O'Higgins didn't believe her. He thought she was only pretending to support them for the benefit of the SFPD's brass, whose support she needed if she was to run again.

He'd called Chaundhry's lawyer and set up a meeting with Nirad. He'd walked in with Kumar's iPhone and asked Nirad if there was anything incriminating on the phone that he should know about. The look in Chaundhry's eyes turned murderous. He'd gotten up and walked out of the conference room without saying another word.

"I want you to stay out at the beach, at your uncle's. I can't explain. Not right now. I'm sorry, but it's for your own good," O'Higgins said. His words sounded mean even to him. They drove fast, west toward the turn off for Dogtown where Sir Francis Drake split and became Highway 1 in West Marin. He'd told his daughter, when they'd gotten in the car, only that they were going to Bolinas to drop something off at her uncle's house.

He'd dreaded asking her to stay in Bolinas for a few days. He knew it would look like he didn't want her at home with him. She couldn't help but think that he was pushing her away a second time. But he knew he had to do it for her own good. He felt that Nirad Chaundhry's government was going to come after him, try to hurt him, or even his daughter. He'd seen how the US spooks worked in Iraq, and it was usually bloody and effective. He expected the same from the Indian intelligence service.

"But I don't understand," Rebecca said. "I just got home. I thought you wanted me to come home?" She was upset. He'd waited until they were half way to Bolinas to tell her he wanted her to spend a few days out at the beach.

"I called Marin Academy. It's all set up. You start in a week," he said. He'd made a point of not telling her about Marin Academy until now, because he knew that she would be pleased and that might make up for her being sent to Bolinas.

"I don't want to go to Uncle Andrew's right now," she said.

"You have to go," he said.

"Why? It doesn't make any sense."

"Because I'm asking you to, all right?"

"Do you have a girlfriend? I found hair … in the bathroom. It wasn't Mom's, and it wasn't mine. Long blond hair. Is that it? Do you have a girlfriend? Are you just going to forget me and Mom? Is that it? Let me out!" Rebecca said.

He pulled the car over in Lagunitas by the post office. It was cloudy. The south side of the road was deep in shadows, the road there lined by old redwood trees. The hills were obscured in part by fog, pushing in from the coast only a few miles away.

"No."

"Whose hair is it?" Rebecca said.

"A woman I've met," he said.

"A woman. You saw someone there — in Mom's house. Did you fuck her?" Rebecca said.

"I have to try and have a normal life, Rebecca. It's been almost a year — it just happened. It's someone from work. I — I don't have to explain it to you."

"That's why you sent me off, isn't it? So you could fuck girls?"

"No, it's not why. I was depressed—okay. I've been seeing a psychiatrist. I didn't want you to be around me like that. I felt guilty that I couldn't be a real father to you. I felt guilty that I had to see a doctor. I didn't want you to know because I thought you'd think less of me. That everyone would think I was crazy. I knew your aunt June's house would be normal. I wanted things to be normal for you."

A horse trailer passed them driving too fast, the trailer swaying disappearing finally into the fog.

"Are you crazy? Sending me away now for no reason is crazy."

"There is a reason," he said.

"What is it, then? I want to know."

He reached for her hand, but she pulled away and got out of the car and ran back down Sir Francis Drake. He swore under his breath, watching her in the rear view mirror.

"Shit."

CHAPTER 18

It was 12:15 noon on Friday. He'd been determined to make his appointment with Dr. Schneider.

"Have you had symptoms, since I saw you? Has the agoraphobia gotten any better?" Dr. Schneider asked. She seemed different, more intense, less clinical, as if they were friends who had a past rather than doctor and patient.

"No large bodies of water in Pacific Heights. I'm acting in a self-destructive way, though. I can say that," O'Higgins said. "I don't know about the other. It might be better, or it might be worse."

Dr. Schneider gave him a puzzled look.

He explained that Pacific Heights was where he'd caught the double murders. She said she'd read about the case of the Indian family in the press, and that it sounded truly horrific.

"You were ready to discuss the accident. What happened that day?" She was fired up again, and wanted him to face that day.

"Not today," O'Higgins said blandly, stealing her urgency.

Their relationship was changing. He'd come in, hat in hand, those first few times as The Patient who was ill and somewhat intimidated by the doctor's fresh-faced, medical-voodoo aura. He felt different today about everything. Nothing looked the same. She appeared to be just what she was: a young doctor trying her best to confront an angry male psychology. Good luck with that.

He'd taken his daughter, after a terrific fight, to stay at his brother's place in Bolinas. The confession that he had another woman in his life was, he realized, a confession about their life going forward, and how it would be different. It signaled that they would both have to leave Jennifer's death behind them, no matter how painful and difficult, for good, and search for life.

Nothing they could do to themselves as punishment was going to change that, or bring her back. It was live now, fully in the present, with all that it implied, or wither away and die spiritually themselves. As soon as he confessed his affair, he understood that he was reaching for life again. It was clear now he'd turned the corner, all the things that had been wrong with him were a result of his not wanting to live. And now, surprisingly, he realized he did want to live.

He and his daughter had ridden in silence after his pronouncement past Dogtown on the road toward Bolinas, the tree tops—pines and redwoods— glimmering green tips in the fog; the road cast at times in deep winter shadows—the winding black asphalt wet from fog. The afternoon hooded by a dark winter sky.

As they drove in silence, he thought of outings taken long ago to nearby Limantour Beach, when Rebecca was just a baby and he was still a patrol officer. Jennifer would carry their daughter papoose style, wearing cutoffs and barefoot, her hair up. They would walk down the beach for miles to the north toward Point Reyes, picnicking in the dunes at the estuary, far from everyone, in a spot where it was said Sir Francis Drake had first come ashore in North America.

It had seemed a holy place to him. It was starkly beautiful, sand and sky, great piles of driftwood bleached by the sun. The beach lonely and ancient feeling, and yet they were so young it seemed, even then, odd to think that they too would grow older, that the baby would grow up to be a young woman. Jennifer seemed almost like a teenager herself at the time. She'd been in her early twenties when they had Rebecca.

Later, when Rebecca was older, he would walk her down to the surf and let her play in the tidal rush, naked, in what looked like a painting that might be called "Humans On A Beach". All of that sacred-feeling past seemed like an impossible dream now. He remembered turning back and seeing his wife sunbathing, her top off, her Okie-white freckled skin almost completely hidden in the low grass-dotted dunes, his daughter's joyful screams, sandpipers in flocks walking arrogantly along the edge of the surf, all lifting off at once in a burst, as a wave broke and rushed at them. Happiness. Joy. Nature.

Jennifer would watch them playing at the water's edge, her knees drawn up, smiling. He had to leave the memory there on that ancient lonely beach, as beautiful and wonderful as it had been. It was just that now: only a memory and ephemeral as life itself, like water on sand. He'd turned toward his daughter, wanting to speak to her and tell her that they only had the future. That they had to get along in order to build it together. But she was angry, and wouldn't look at him. She played a game on her cell phone the rest of the way to his brother's house.

He had constructed a trap for Nirad Chaundhry and was waiting to spring it on him, knowing that the trap would, most likely put him and Marvin in danger. He didn't care. On the way to his doctor's appointment he realized that he was inured to consequences. Life and death were all the same to him. Life required taking chances. He realized that when he told Rebecca the truth about his affair with Madrone.

What he wanted was to arrest Nirad Chaundhry for murder. If he was completely honest, he wanted to sleep with Asha, too. Since he'd sat with her on the floor of her hotel suite, watching her chant, he'd wanted to draw her to his side, to comfort her, to explain to her everything he'd learned about death and its wake. By sleeping with her, he fantasized, in physical union they would burn up all their pain on some kind of sex-altar. It was crazy, and drug-induced at the time, but the feelings had lingered, the wanting. He was not proud of it, given the circumstances. But it was true, nonetheless. The truth, no matter how difficult, sets you free, the doctor had said once.

"I'm working a strange case," he told the doctor.

"Okay, you want to talk about it?"

"I've decided to spit into the establishment's eye," he said. "That's dangerous."

"What does that mean, Michael?"

"There's been a murder — no, two murders, and the person who is probably responsible is above the law. Or seems to be, anyway. And I don't want to accept that. It's stupid. Everyone around me wants to accept it. But I don't. It offends me. It's personal."

"Why is that?" Schneider said.

"I'm not sure, exactly. It makes me feel alive, I think. Fighting. When I was over there, I felt very alive. After the accident I felt just the opposite. I felt numb. For months now I've felt numb. I slept with this woman I met, and that broke the ice. Helped me feel something again."

"By over there, you mean Iraq?"

"Yes. Iraq. The war. Killing. Soldiering. I was good at it. Too good."

"Aren't you supposed to go after the bad guys?" she said. "You're a policeman."

"When they're poor, but when they're rich and connected, it's different. Completely different. This guy. The guy I'm after, he's as connected as it gets. What I'm doing is probably career suicide."

"Then why do it? Everyone has a right to stop suicide, career or otherwise. Don't take that call," Schneider said.

He realized she meant it. From a medical point of view, sacrifice was a kind of illness. He'd never thought of knuckling under to corruption as healthy, but he saw how society was moving that way, inch by inch. Descending toward something horrible, slowly every day. He saw how psychiatry could make the case that sacrifice was futile and harmful to the individual and therefore dangerous, like sex.

It was the first time he felt the doctor was not following him, not really getting it. This was an existential fight, deeper than living contentedly inside a corrupt society, accepting its norms. He'd thrown down the gauntlet because he wanted to live, not be numb to his emotions, and this meant consciously living, being aware of what he wanted no matter how shocking or perverted it would seem to outsiders. He was going to climb out of his funk hole where he'd been hiding from life. He understood this, but she did not. Was she simply there, in her capacity as a doctor, to allow people to conform to the majority's POV?

Was conformity the necessary component of mental health? Conversely, was non-conformity a sign of mental illness? Was it that stark a choice? Was this the upshot of all his doctor's fancy medical education? Were Freud and his ilk simply the crossing guards for what turned into German society's Fascist death spiral? Was the human subconscious, itself, to blame for Hitler? For

Stalin? For the 20th century's impressive record of mass slaughter and programmed genocide—or was it something else? How could it not be all our collective fault?

"I may have permanently damaged the relationship with my daughter. We had a terrible fight yesterday," he said.

"You didn't answer my question," Schneider said.

"That's because you don't understand what I was trying to say, and we only have an hour here. I'm sorry, but I need to discuss my daughter today and —"

"What don't I understand about career suicide? Help me," the doctor said, not letting it go.

"That it might be very good for my mental health. My anger feels good. I'm angry at this guy, and I should be. He's an asshole. And he's a killer."

"I assumed you wanted to keep your job. You've told me that it was important to you, being a police detective."

"I said it was important to me, yes. I saw it as a life preserver. I wanted to latch onto it, hold on to it. It's true. I'm not so sure now. I live in the moment. Isn't that what we've been going for? Leaving the past behind?"

"So, as far as your happiness goes, you don't have to commit career suicide. That's all I'm saying. Whatever this man has done, it's your job on the line is what I'm hearing," the doctor said.

"I'm a soldier. I fought for things I believed in, things that are important to me and make me feel like what I did over there has value and stood for something. That all the lives lost were not wasted. Otherwise, what did we achieve there?"

"I'm trying to be practical, Michael. That's all I'm trying to do here," Schneider said.

"Are you afraid that I'll lose my medical benefits? I mean,

we know that without a job I'm out the coverage, and you're out a patient who can afford the hundred and twenty-five bucks an hour."

"That's not fair. You seem to want to pick a fight. I'm here to help you. I've no desire to fight. This is not about me. This is about you losing your job, according to you. For what, exactly? It's not clear to me why you're putting yourself in harm's way."

"My daughter may not forgive me for having a girlfriend. She wants to pretend that nothing has changed. She won't accept her mother's death. She's worse than I am, I think. I didn't realize that until yesterday."

"Maybe she should see someone. I can recommend someone."

"Yeah — maybe you're right." And he meant it.

"Is there a reason she had to go to your brother's place?"

"Yes."

"What is it?"

"I'm afraid someone might want to hurt her."

"Your daughter?"

"Yes."

They looked at each other. He realized that he was out of her reach. He was heading somewhere new and he would have to leave her, and everything the doctor represented, behind if he was going to get well. He'd stepped through a door. He and his anger, together, fighting for his life.

"Have you — are you able to tell —"

"Who, the police?" he said.

After his session with Schneider, he met with Rene Fields at a nearby Starbucks. She said that they'd found no prints on the knife they'd discovered, and after a second test, no traces of blood either. They discussed the coroner's report in detail. People next to them stared when O'Higgins made a stabbing motion in the air.

"What makes a wound like that?" he asked. "The girl's wounds? The coroner said Kumar was 'run through' which I take to mean the blade was long, like a sword."

"Has to be something thin then, but knife-like, by the look of the wounds," Rene said. "How are you doing, Michael? You and Rebecca?"

"Holding up. Things are back on track now. It was rough. I won't lie — so it was some kind of weapon, like maybe a sword, for wounds like that? You agree?"

"But swords have wider blades, don't they?" Rene said. "These were narrower wounds, like a boning knife. Narrower, even. And it was at least sixteen inches long, it seems from the report. Perhaps longer."

"I suppose. We turned the place over. No swords, or other edge weapons — just the ornamental daggers we found and the kitchen knives, which you said were all clean. And they don't fit the wounds, anyway."

"He could have taken it with him, the weapon — Nirad Chaundhry," Rene asked. "Left the house with it?"

"Nirad wasn't seen carrying anything at all when he left the house. A neighbor saw him cross the street and walk to the Gilberts' place. The neighbor, a woman, said he was acting normally and she certainly would have mentioned seeing an obvious weapon, given what happened. She didn't. Her interview was in patrol's report from that night. I reviewed all the interviews. No one else saw anything unusual. The woman didn't recall exactly what time she saw Chaundhry, unfortunately. She was walking her dog and didn't think much of it."

"So, we have no murder weapon at present?" Rene said.

"Right," he said. "Nothing that seems to fit Kumar's sword-like wounds."

"So was the same weapon used then on Rishi Chaundhry?" Rene said.

"Probably, is my guess. Rishi Chaundhry's wounds didn't match the width of the dagger we suspected either. I double-checked. The coroner has Rishi Chaundhry's neck wounds at about 24.5 millimeters, and whatever was used traversed his throat and nearly came out the other side of his neck. The dagger you tested broadens too quickly. It goes to 50 millimeters plus, at the hilt. So it couldn't have been the weapon used on either victim."

He drove down Broadway toward the Chaundhry mansion. The sky was clear and clean after the storm that had hung over the Bay Area seemingly for days now. He was parking the car when Marvin called him.

"Where are you?"

"On Broadway. At the Chaundhry place," O'Higgins said.

"She's confessed. Asha Chaundhry. She walked into Bryant Street an hour ago. Told someone she was there to confess to our murders."

"What?"

"She says she did it. Both of them. She caught her husband with Kumar the night before. I'm on my way to Bryant now. She's there at Homicide now. Mike — are you there? Mike? What are you doing at the Chaundhry place? We turned the scene back to the family."

"Okay. Yeah, I'm on my way. I'll be right there." He ended the call and looked at his watch. It was quarter to four. He got out of the car and went up the stairs. He could see lights on in the house.

He walked on toward the front door, feeling in a trance. He rang the bell. He didn't believe she'd killed anyone. She was lying. But why?

A young Latin woman, about twenty, dressed in jeans and wearing blue rubber gloves, opened the door.

"I'm Detective O'Higgins. SFPD." He flashed his badge and walked by her.

"Mr. Chaundhry is expected back shortly. We're cleaning," she said.

He walked by her, putting his wallet back. He looked at her jeans. They were rolled up and she was barefoot. "In the hallway. Mr. Chaundhry called us and told us it was okay to clean. That we could come in and start cleaning up."

"That's okay," he said. "You're fine."

He looked around and saw the big landscape painting across from him. To his left was an antique umbrella stand with an assortment of umbrellas and what looked like a cane with a decorative head. He walked to the stand and moved the umbrellas and cane around, looking for a murder weapon they might have overlooked. He stared down into the bottom of the polished brass umbrella stand but saw nothing.

"Go ahead, I won't be long," he said.

The young woman looked at him a moment, then turned away and went back down the hallway. She'd been cleaning the elevator. As he approached he could see another cleaning woman, on her knees, with a brush scrubbing Asha's bloody shoe prints from the hardwood floor. Most of her shoe prints had been cleaned, and were gone.

He imagined Asha walking crazily in the hallway. Why hadn't she gone upstairs? Because she was telling the truth … She got here only moments before patrol arrived and after Nirad called 911. Why did he call it in? Why not just leave the house? He had to establish an alibi.

He didn't know why he'd come back to the house. He didn't know what he was looking for either, other than the murder weapon itself; someone would have removed it by now. Something like that. It would have been obvious, yet they'd not found it. Why? The only explanation was that the killer had hidden it and it was here in the house somewhere. It had to be here. He would be in trouble for coming back into the house without a justification, but he didn't care. Let Nirad scream to the DA about it.

It was cold in the house, the heat having been off for days, dank. He walked into the cavernous kitchen and snapped on the lights. He looked at the stove and decided to open it. He saw two withered eggplants lying on a Pyrex dish, their purplish skins burnt. He remembered Madrone telling him they'd smelt something burning when they first arrived and while struggling with Asha, who was hysterical. Someone turned off the stove. Asha? Or had patrol? Would she have cooked dinner if she'd just stabbed her husband and Kumar to death?

He closed the oven door and turned to face the kitchen, with its huge granite bar separating the kitchen from a long chef's table. On the opposite wall were a collection of posters of the Red Fort in Delhi.

I was cooking Rishi's favorite, Bengin Bartha, Asha had told them during their first interview.

He turned back to look at the stove top. A pot held what looked like congealed tomatoes. A small coconut milk carton stood by the stove where she'd left it. A Safeway bag was sitting on the white Carrara marble countertop next to it. He peered inside the bag, lifted a bottle of wine and saw a receipt in the bag. It had stuck, folded in two, to the bottom of the bottle and they'd missed it. It was a Safeway receipt for three items: coconut milk, a bottle of wine, and parsley, time stamped 5:25 PM the day of the murders.

The children would have been due back from their play date with the Gilberts by then. Kumar should have picked them up, but she didn't — why? So Kumar was dead by five, or before? And before Asha got back from the store?

He took a photo of the receipt with his phone. She'd paid with a credit card, so a record on a bank statement would confirm the time.

He saw an immersion blender still plugged in. Who cooks dinner for someone they intend to murder? Maybe for the girls? No — He turned on the lights over a large chef's table. It had been set with six place settings. Doesn't make any sense. She had a window of time to kill them both before the girls were due back, no denying it.

"No." He said it out loud, walking toward the chef's table that was frozen in time. White dinner plates sat in brown wicker chargers; clean flatware lay on folded linen napkins. The table linen was spotless. Someone had taken pains to set the table.

Had Kumar set the table? Would a woman like Asha actually stay in the house with her daughters if she'd caught her husband with another woman? Would Rishi Chaundhry have sex with his nanny when he knew his wife was only going to the store and his children—old enough to know something was going on between Kumar and their father—were due back home by five? It was all preposterous. Asha didn't do it, because she didn't have time. The call from Nirad to 911 had come in at 5:30 when Asha Chaundhry was at the supermarket using her credit card. She signed something. They'll have that signature too ... She was here cooking dinner ... She left for the market knowing Kumar would pick up the girls and before Nirad came home. What happened between the time she left and the time she returned?

He walked by the two maids, who were grim faced and quietly working to clean the elevator. He went down the hall into Rishi's office, and tapped on the computer that was still on. The screen lit up and showed the spreadsheet he'd been working on. He looked at the Excel sheet's title, went into File Manager and began to look for it, but the file system seemed chaotic and the Hindi file names were impossible for him to read.

He clicked back to the open file, and, as if Jennifer who so often helped him with his computer, were standing next to him, helping him, he quickly inserted the sheet's file path in a header. With that information he went back and searched again, and found the file in File Manager. The file had been last updated and saved at 4:51 p.m. on the day of the murder.

Holy shit. Rishi Chaundhry was here on his computer working before he was killed. It was exactly what Asha had told them. She was telling the truth. He was alive when she left for the Safeway.

"She didn't do it. He was alive when she left." He spoke out loud again. "God damn it!" He leaned in and looked at the Excel file's time stamp carefully, then slammed his hand down on the desk. His intuition had been right. She didn't kill him. And she didn't kill Kumar either.

He was careful to grab a screen shot of the file's time stamp before he left, emailing it to himself from Rishi's computer. He called Towler and told him what he'd found, and that he and Marvin still needed access to the scene. Then he called Fields and told her to take Rishi's computer from the house.

Both maids, on their knees, their rubber gloves bloodstained, looked up at him as he walked by. He told them they'd have to leave, that the police weren't finished with the scene. He called for a patrol officer to stand guard and to keep the family, including Nirad Chaundhry and his employees, out of the house under any circumstances. He got a call almost immediately from Chaundhry's lawyer, but didn't take it.

CHAPTER 19

"Why did you come here today?" Marvin said. The two detectives and Asha Chaundhry were sitting in one of Homicide Division's interview rooms on Bryant Street. The walls were dirty, the furniture shabby. The hallways of SFPD's headquarters held a sense that all of it would be abandoned soon, for the new headquarters and a new era.

A strong smell of men's cologne in the interview room added to the room's claustrophobic atmosphere. It was a room where people were broken down, a room where lies were manufactured and guilty faces hidden in a last resort—deals finally made. The room's bare bones furniture—just table and chairs— spoke to the room's history of profound human suffering.

"I want to confess — confess to killing my husband and Bharti Kumar," Asha said.

She was dressed conservatively. She'd not worn a sari to the interview. And the bindi she'd worn the day before was gone, too, Michael noticed. She looked child-like and frightened, as if someone were about to burst through the door. The two detectives sat across from her and seemed like giants compared to the slight young woman sitting across from them in an all their suited and very male glory.

"Would you like something, Mrs. Chaundhry? Coffee?

Soda?" Marvin asked.

"No thank you," she said.

"You say you killed them both? That's what you came to tell us?" Marvin asked. "You want to confess, is that correct?"

"Yes. Both," Asha said quickly. She didn't look at either one of them. Marvin tapped his pen on the laminate tabletop.

"We have a receipt from your purchase at the Marina Safeway that has a 5:27 PM time on it, the day of the murders," O'Higgins said. "The receipt was found in your kitchen. It listed three items: a bottle of wine, coconut milk and parsley. All three items were sitting in a paper bag in the kitchen. You were at the Safeway, weren't you? Ms. Kumar didn't have a driver's license, or a car. Your neighbor, Mrs. Gilbert, said Ms. Kumar didn't drive. You were at the Safeway. Someone called 911 at 5:42 from a number that we believe belongs to Nirad Chaundhry's cell phone. The recording of the call to 911 is of a man's voice. Please explain how you could have killed your husband and Bharti Kumar?"

"I did it before I left the house," Asha said. "I killed them before I left." She looked down at the table.

"Why?" Marvin said. "Why did you kill them?"

"Because Rishi was having an affair with Bharti. I was angry. I caught them. Nirad told you. He's right. I killed them."

"How long had you known about the affair?" Marvin asked.

"I don't remember. Several days — no, several weeks," Asha said.

"Which is it?" O'Higgins asked.

Asha looked up. She'd been avoiding making eye contact with either detective. "I suppose it was days," she said.

"So everything you told us, before, was a lie? Is that what you're saying?" O'Higgins said.

"Yes. I lied to you. Yes," she said.

"I don't believe you," O'Higgins said.

"I killed them," she said. "It's the truth. I swear it."

"How did you do it?" Marvin asked.

"I stabbed them — with a knife," Asha said.

"What knife? Where is it now?" Marvin said.

"A kitchen knife. I put it back in the knife block, in the kitchen."

"Which knife?" Marvin said.

"I don't remember. I was in a state. I don't remember which knife."

"Okay," Marvin said. "Who did you kill first?"

"Bharti. Bharti first, then Rishi," she said.

"So tell us then, exactly, what happened," Marvin said. "You walked into Ms. Kumar's bedroom and — explain to us exactly what you did."

"I — I heard the water and knew she was in the shower," Asha said.

"Which hand did you hold the knife in?" Marvin asked.

"I don't remember."

"You don't remember which hand you held the knife in?" Marvin said.

"My right hand. Yes. My right hand," Asha said.

"Show me how you held it," Marvin said.

"Show you? I don't understand."

"Yes. Show us exactly how you held the knife. At your side? In front of you? Was it hidden?

"No, it wasn't hidden," Asha said. "I had it out in front of me."

"So you came into Ms. Kumar's bedroom, prepared to stab the girl to death? Is that what you're saying? Holding the knife out so Ms. Kumar could see it?" Marvin said.

"Yes. Yes, that's what I'm saying," she said.

"Go on. Tell us what you did next," Marvin said. He unbuttoned his jacket and wrote something on the yellow legal pad in front of him.

"I came into the bathroom and — I — I stabbed Bharti. I killed her."

"No," Marvin said. "I want to hear what you did exactly. How you stabbed her."

"What do you mean?" She looked at Marvin, then at O'Higgins. "I don't understand. I'm confessing to this — isn't that enough?"

"I want you to tell us what happened—exactly. What did Ms. Kumar do when she saw you with the knife?" Marvin said.

"She — she was frightened," Asha said.

"Did she call out for help? Did she scream? Did she beg you not to kill her? What did she do?" Marvin said.

"I don't remember," Asha said. "I killed Bharti. That's enough. I'm confessing."

"You don't remember? You say you murdered Ms. Kumar in the bathroom with a kitchen knife because the girl was having an affair with your husband. But you don't remember anything about how you did it?"

"I was — I was out of my mind. With jealousy."

"Okay. You were angry. Is that what you're telling us?" Marvin said.

"Yes. Of course."

"But certainly you remember what happened in the bathroom after you walked in? Did Ms. Kumar scream? Did she beg you not to kill her? What happened?" Marvin said, pressing her, a look of disbelief on his face.

"She was getting out of the shower. I stabbed her. She fell and I left."

"So you stabbed her and she fell down. How did you stab her? Show me. Here—pretend this is the knife." Marvin rolled his ballpoint pen across the desk, obviously not believing her "Go on. Show us how you stabbed Bharti Kumar to death in the bathroom before you murdered your husband in cold blood and then went to the Safeway to buy some coconut milk for dinner."

Asha stared down at the pen as it rolled toward her. She didn't pick it up.

"Go on, show us, Mrs. Chaundhry. Please, stand up and show us." Marvin said, standing up and moving away from the interview table. "Let's pretend I'm Ms. Kumar. I just came out of the shower and I see you. Where am I exactly? In the shower stall? Out of the shower stall? What do I do? Where am I exactly when you stabbed me? How many times did you stab me? Did you look me in the eye when you stabbed me?

"Show me how you stabbed Bharti Kumar to death with a kitchen knife you say you took from the kitchen and carried up the stairs. Or was it the elevator you took to the third floor? Elevator or stairs? Which was it?"

"She just stood there. Bharti —" Asha picked up the pen. "I don't remember." She started to sob and let the pen fall from her hand.

Marvin looked at O'Higgins. They both knew she was lying, and the confession a fantasy.

"Okay, if you can't remember how exactly you murdered a girl you said was like a daughter to you, what about your husband? You must remember that, certainly? Tell us about how you murdered Rishi. Go on, describe it to us. Were you in the elevator with him? Was he in the elevator when you found him?"

"Yes. Yes, he was in the elevator."

"And you had already killed Ms. Kumar. Is that right?"

"Yes."

"So you left the bathroom with the knife you used to kill Ms. Kumar?"

"Yes. Yes!"

O'Higgins watched tears stream down Asha's face.

"And you did what exactly?" Marvin said.

"I — I got in the elevator and I rode it down."

"Down where?"

"To the first floor. To Rishi's office."

"You're in the elevator? Not you and your husband?"

"Yes."

"How did your husband get into the elevator?"

"I don't remember." She looked up at them. "I'm confessing to killing them both. That's what I want to say. I want to speak to a lawyer," Asha said.

"Why are you lying to us?" Marvin said.

"I'm not lying," she said. "You have to believe me. I killed them both."

"Yes, I think you are lying, or you could explain to us how you did it. How many times did you stab Ms. Kumar, then? How did you manage to not leave any blood, anywhere in Ms. Kumar's bedroom? Did you change your clothes? You must have, after stabbing two people to death? Where are those clothes now? In the house? Certainly you must have changed clothes, Asha, bloody clothes? You couldn't have gone to Safeway like that, correct? They must have been blood-stained? After stabbing two people? How is it you managed to not leave a trace of blood anywhere? None in your bedroom, none in the kitchen? None on the knives in the kitchen. None in the Land Rover. Yes we looked at the Land Rover. No blood found. None around the kitchen sink, in any of the bathrooms? Did you clean the knife? You must have cleaned it? But where? In the kitchen sink?

"Why would you go to the Safeway to pick up a bottle of wine and some coconut milk after brutally killing Rishi and your nanny when you knew your daughters were due home and could have walked into the house? What if they'd come home on their own? No, I don't believe you," Marvin said. "The question is, why are you lying to us? Why? Do you believe her, Detective?"

"No. I don't," O'Higgins said.

"You have to believe me. I killed them," Asha said.

"I'm afraid we don't have to believe you," Marvin said. "That's not how this works. We deal with facts, and the facts say otherwise."

"Did your father-in law put you up to this, Asha? Is that what this is about?" O'Higgins said.

"I want to see my daughters. Do you understand? I don't want them to be near him —he's a monster. Why can't you understand?" Asha said. "I killed them. Both! Why can't you believe me?"

"Come on. I'll drive you back to the hotel," O'Higgins said, standing up. "We don't have time for this nonsense."

They sat in O'Higgins' Ford, parked in front of the Clift Hotel in silence. One of the three doormen had asked them to move on. O'Higgins had flashed his badge and they were left alone, making it hard for airport vans and limos to unload. Asha had not wanted to get out of the car. Twice she'd grabbed for the handle but had not pulled the door open. He could tell she wanted to talk and was building up to it. He turned the engine off and turned his cell phone over and over waiting for her to say something.

"Are you going to get out, Asha?"

She shook her head no.

He was calling her by her first name now, no pretense. No playing the official role of police detective and suspect.

"I don't want to be alone," she said. "I can't stand it. The silence —"

He understood what she meant. After the accident he couldn't even sit still for more than a few minutes or he would immediately go back to those first moments, floating in the ice cold water, his daughter next to him — the sound of the buoy clanking, his screaming his wife's name over and over. The cold quickly making his frantic screams stop altogether, the cold making it impossible to even swim. The fear of sharks …

A continuous crush of tourists passed them and seemed surreal, all the different types of fun-seekers mixed in with the occasional baggy-pants-wearing gangsters from Turk Street's open air drug market, a no-man's land that tourists avoided, or missed all together, only five blocks south of where they were sitting, and a world away from the elegant hotel.

"Who is this Thomas?" O'Higgins said finally.

"Just a friend," she said. "I don't have any now. My Indian girlfriends haven't returned my calls. Nobody wants to see me. They all think I did it. It's absurd. They're afraid of the publicity. And what people are saying back home in India."

"So you admit that you were lying to us."

"Yes. Yes. I was lying. Is that what you want to hear? That I'm pathetic, Detective. Does that make you feel good? I lied. Yes!"

"No, it doesn't make me feel good. But we need the truth. Did Nirad ask you to lie to us?" he said.

She turned and looked at him. She seemed completely shattered, as if she were held together by only her pain and loss. He wanted to grab her and hold her, protect her.

"He said that if I confessed to what I'd done he would bring the girls back and I could see them again. He said he would get me a lawyer. I could plead temporary insanity — He won't let my mother see the girls. He's got them — The Indian prime minister is a personal friend of his. There's nothing I can do to stop him. He won't even let me talk to them. He said he would keep my parents from even visiting them. He has all the power. Do you understand? He's like a god in India."

"You should stay away from Robert Thomas," O'Higgins said.

"Why?"

"Because. He vibes weird. And he's been a person of interest in other murder cases. Nothing was ever proven. But his name has come up before. He was the one who was texting you all the time, wasn't he?"

"Yes. I was wrong about him, maybe. I have no one here. I've no money either. All my credit cards were Chaundhry Company cards, and they've been shut down. Nirad, again, I suppose. I tried contacting the company, but no one will explain why— I can't pay the bill here. I have no money. I don't know what to do. Robert paid my hotel bill. He paid my hotel bill. He used his own credit card. Do you understand, Detective? They were going to ask me to leave the hotel. I can't go home either. I don't think I can face that place," she said.

"Do you want to go back to the house, back to Broadway?"

O'Higgins said.

"No. Maybe, I don't know. Yes, if you could get my girls back for me, Detective. Can you? They're children — how is it possible? How can he steal my daughters from me? Is it sex you want? I've seen you look at me. I'll do anything."

He didn't answer her, in part because she'd surprised him. He'd thought he'd kept his desire tucked away, out of sight. It shocked him that she'd known it was there all along.

"I spoke to Neel again. He called," he said. "He's trying, on his end, to help —"

"I'm sorry for suggesting — I didn't mean — what I just said."

He shook his head as if he'd not heard her ugly offer. "Neel said that your father-in-law is working with my government. Do you know what they were doing, with the Americans?"

"Rishi told me they weren't building a normal computer chip. In the new factory. It was secret, what they were doing. He was very proud of it. They are using a new technology. He showed me once. One of the chips. The new chips are going to be made of synthetic diamonds. I wasn't supposed to say anything to Nirad about knowing about the new technology. It was a company secret. The new chips will change everything. Something about heat."

"I saw some, I think, in Rishi's office."

"Yes. He'd been working on this technology for a few years in India, with the Americans. They don't conduct heat. The idea was developed in the family's research laboratories, and then here in America. He said this new technology would make the Chaundhry Company the most important tech company in the world, and the richest. That's why Rishi was working so hard. It was a terrific strain because of the secrecy, and the Americans insisting he build the plant here. They threatened — if the company didn't decide to build here, in the States, that they would interfere with the Chaundhry businesses and end Nirad's chances of being Prime Minister of India. They made it very clear there was no choice in the matter. They were told to build here. The Americans wanted Nirad to be Prime Minister. He's done everything they've asked of him.

"Nirad didn't think I knew anything about it. We even had monitors—Indian Intelligence people and American—watching us night and day. The Americans are afraid the Chinese want to steal the technology, Rishi said. The minders were there that day on the ferry. I was annoyed because we couldn't even go on a simple family outing without being bothered by the security people. It made me uncomfortable. I wanted to be free of them. The girls were embarrassed at school because of the minders."

"Where were they, your security, the day of the murders?" he said.

"They must have been outside the house. They were there, parked night and day. Someone followed me to the Safeway. They always followed me. Anytime I went anywhere, someone was following me. But someone was parked in front of the house night and day since we arrived, first here at the hotel, and then at the house. Rishi said the FBI was part of it, guarding us."

"So you're saying they would have seen everyone and anyone coming in or out of the house that afternoon?" he asked.

"Yes. They know if anyone broke in. They know who came and went. They even made sure that the house wasn't bugged before we moved in, and would sweep it while the contractors were in the house."

"And now?"

"No one. I'm alone. Since the murders, I've seen no one. They've all disappeared."

"You're sure?" O'Higgins said.

"Yes."

"The big guy, the one who wears the turban?"

"His name is Colonel Das. I saw him at the house several times. Rishi told me he was an Indian intelligence officer and in charge of our security. Will you help me, Detective? Please?"

"Did Nirad kill Rishi and Kumar?"

"I don't know. That's the truth. I saw Rishi before I left for the market. He'd gotten home around three or so. He was in his office working, we spoke. I told him I'd be right back. Oh my God. It seems impossible. All of it. Nirad wasn't there when I left, but I suppose he could have been. I don't know."

"When did you see Ms. Kumar last?"

"She helped me set the table, and helped me start dinner before I left for my class. Getting things ready. She washed the eggplants. It was Bharti who noticed that I'd forgotten the coconut milk, and that I'd better get some. She called me and left a message."

"What time? I need a time, when you saw Bharti last."

"She'd walked the girls over to the neighbors at three and come back. I saw her just before she took them. She went upstairs and straightened out the children's playroom on the second floor. I noticed she'd finished setting the table for dinner while I was away at Pilates."

"The neighbors, the Gilberts — did they know Nirad before you moved next door?"

"No."

"You're sure?"

"Positive. Impossible. We didn't meet the Gilberts until a week after we arrived. We had a housewarming and invited all the neighbors before Christmas. Nirad, as far as I know, doesn't know them even now. He was in India when we had the house-warming party. I never saw him speak to any of the neighbors," she said.

"He does now," O'Higgins said.

CHAPTER 20

They met at Lefty O'Doul's on Geary Street. The San Francisco institution was a throwback to a time before the City was invaded by New Yorkers and their tall soulless buildings and their big-money, people-squashing high-rise plans for the City.

The restaurant had paneled walls and "carving stations" with hunks of rare roast beef under warming lights, glowing reddish yellow. Chinese cooks wore tall white chef hats, their faces bathed in the warm light, carving portions of meat in silence. It was as if time had stood still and men outside still wore fedoras, women wore white gloves, and Dashiell Hammett might walk through the doors. More than anything it was a man's place, even today.

"These are from her phone? The nanny's phone?" Marvin asked. They were sitting in a booth in the back.

"Yes," O'Higgins said.

"Well — now what?" Marvin said.

"Look at them. They change everything."

"Are you sure you want me to? It's not going to make a difference now," Marvin said.

"What does that mean?"

"It means this case is a problem. We need a suspect. The DA told Towler we've botched it. We don't have a suspect. We can't find the nanny's phone, because you didn't tell anyone we found it. The DA wants us removed. And they're thinking of putting you out to pasture, amigo. The DA is saying you're a nut job who couldn't find your ass in the dark. They found out you're seeing a head doctor. They want to interview her. They want the department to explain why you, someone with obvious psychological issues, was assigned this high-profile case. The Indian government wants to see you patrolling Wal-Mart for Bozo Security. How's that sound?"

"Fucked up, I guess," O'Higgins said, indifferent. "Now can I show you these?" Since the accident the idea of being threatened seemed almost comical.

"Fire away, white boy."

"Okay, a kid, a friend of Rebecca's, pulled these off of Kumar's phone's iCloud backup. Here you go." He rolled through a series of photos that his daughter's propeller-head friend had somehow managed to get off Bharti Kumar's backup files, automatically stored on her iCloud service, which she was most likely unaware of having activated. They were all photos sent in the body of emails. All of them were "selfies" of Nirad Chaundhry and Kumar having sex. All were disgustingly pornographic. They'd all been sent to her from the same email address. Some showed Kumar in bondage and were especially hard to look at, as the girl looked frightened and cowed.

"No shit. Wow," Marvin said, looking down at the iPad on the table.

"So we have a connection between Nirad and Kumar. It was Nirad who was having the affair, and my guess it wasn't really consensual," O'Higgins said.

"You mean he got what he wanted when he wanted it. Okay, I've seen enough." Marvin stopped scrolling through the photos and pushed the iPad back at him.

"Yeah. Probably it was going on before Asha and Rishi came to the States. Asha said that Nirad's wife had chosen Kumar to help Asha. I don't believe it. I think Nirad chose her, and told her to keep her mouth shut. I think it had been going on for years."

"So now what?" Marvin said.

"We question Nirad about these photos," O'Higgins said.

"No, I don't think you heard me. They're taking us off the case any minute now. This guy Chaundhry has important friends. Don't you understand? This is not a joke, Mike. He's got the spooks calling the DA. He's got the US State Department calling the DA. The DA got a call from the fucking Indian Prime Minister's office, no less. Nirad Chaundhry is an untouchable.

Has the coin dropped yet, Mike? 'Cause it should have by now. I got two kids in private school who cost me a fortune. I got a pension. I got eight years and I can go to Cancun and sit on the beach and watch Mexican girls with tight butts walk by. Are you getting the picture?"

"Marvin. We can get this asshole."

"Yeah. How are you going to do that, Mike? You can't prove he killed the girl, much less his son. So he's fucking the nanny—that's not proof he killed her, last time I checked. But I know you will piss him off with these photos. You need to prove the asshole killed Kumar and killed his own son, and you need a motive. You don't have one the DA will prosecute a billionaire on."

"This is the motive! The affair. Rishi finds out. My guess is Kumar finally goes to Rishi and asks him to make it stop. Rishi confronts his father, maybe Kumar knows she's pregnant and tells Nirad, who goes off and kills them both because he can do anything he wants. Maybe Rishi threatens to tell the press, if his father doesn't leave the girl alone. Threatens to ruin his father's chances of being the next Prime Minister of India. You've seen the guy. He's a volcano. He goes off on both of them. Okay, he's connected; I get it. Come on, man. Help me get this fucking guy. I don't care who he is — we can do it. He's a killer. It's as simple as that."

"No, see, we can't. Give me Kumar's phone and I'll lose it. It won't ever be found. That's your only chance at getting out of this, Mike. I want you to go tell Towler you can't do this anymore. You're not well. You'll get a half pension. There's State disability. Rebecca can go to college. Give me that fucking phone! We never found it. Who knows what happened to it."

"No."

"Why, Mike? Why? What's going to happen to Rebecca? Huh? Tell me that. This guy is going to come after you, and he won't be alone. He's bringing a lot of friends. Don't be a hero. They're all dead now. There's only Big Money, and it will bury you. That's what's going to happen."

"I don't know. I saw people die Marvin, Didn't they die for something? Bad deaths, eighteen-year-old kids. They had to die for something. Didn't they? I don't care anymore. I'm just going from day to day. I don't care what they do to me. They can do what they want."

"You can't set the world right, Mike. You can't. All you can do is duck. Take it from a black man. I know the rules. 'Them that's got the gold, makes all the fucking rules.' That's the way it is, man. That's the way it's always been. Get next to it. You don't understand the rules of this game.

"Now, I'll tell you why I'm here. We're going to bring Robert Thomas in for the murders. Both. He was seen hanging around the place the day of the murders. The Indian consular staff took photos."

"Who saw him?" O'Higgins said.

"Indian security people were watching the house. Indian spooks from the Consulate, obviously. They won't say why. They've got photos of Thomas, and say that they were taken the day of the murders. They've passed them to the DA."

"He didn't do it," O'Higgins said.

"You know that for a fact? You were the one who found all his fucking texts on Asha Chaundhry's phone, right? From this guy Thomas? Now let's go. Let's bring him in for questioning," Marvin said. "You might even be able to keep your job."

"What about these photos? Nirad had a motive, Marvin."

"What about them? Remember we didn't find Kumar's phone. You stay employed. Let them decide who did it. We arrest this guy for the killings, and we look like we're doing our job. Let the DA do the rest. End of the case. We move on and chase some Mexican gang bangers. That's the best deal we can get."

"You mean play along with what Chaundhry and the government want?"

"That's exactly what I mean. They're going to decide who to prosecute for this, and they're going to do it quickly. Don't you get it? They want the newspapers and all the media to go away. That's how you do it. Charge someone, and the media goes away. You know that. This guy Thomas, or the wife, but somebody has to take that perp walk, and soon. You don't want it to be Asha. I get it. You've sprung on the chick — so then, it's got to be this guy Thomas. Take it or leave it. You're running out of cards and time. Do it for Rebecca, man. Jesus Christ, don't be so fucking naive!"

O'Higgins' cell phone rang. He saw it was Towler and took the call. Towler said he wanted to be present when they brought

Robert Thomas in for questioning. He congratulated them for their fast work on the case.

***

“We’ve arrested the wrong man,” O’Higgins said.

“What do you mean?” Dr. Schneider said.

“I mean someone who didn’t do the crime has been arrested,” O’Higgins said.

“For the murders on Broadway?”

“Yes. But everyone is happy. The DA is happy. My immediate superior is very happy.”

“I don’t understand,” Schneider said.

“It’s called the justice system,” O’Higgins said.

“How are you? You seem upset, Michael.”

“Okay.”

They sat for a moment in silence. He saw in his mind’s eye the look on Robert Thomas’ face when they handcuffed him in the interrogation room on Bryant Street. It was a strange look that he still couldn’t place: fear coupled with something else, confusion probably. Thomas admitted to stalking the house, and that had been enough. He swore he’d not been there the day of the murders, but the photos taken by “Indian Consulate staff” were conveniently time- and date-stamped, putting him at the scene at five o’clock on the afternoon of the murders. No one questioned the photos’ authenticity. Or whether the Indian government might be protecting Nirad Chaundhry.

“Do you want to talk about that day? The day of the accident?” Dr. Schneider said.

He got up and left. It was the first time he’d walked out during an appointment.

***

He didn't have the heart to show her the photos. He simply told Asha he had proof that Nirad and Kumar were involved sexually, and left it at that. He'd driven directly from Schneider's office to the Clift Hotel. It was getting harder and harder to stay away from Asha Chaundhry. When he was away from her, he would dwell on her. Touching her. He wanted her to leave the States now, before Thomas was charged, because he knew it wouldn't stick and that she would be next. Robert Thomas might only be a placeholder until Nirad could get what he really wanted. He wanted Asha in prison. That was obvious. Exactly why wasn't clear.

"Did you know about Nirad and Kumar? Tell me the truth, Asha."

"No. When Nirad came, he wanted the room across from Bharti. I wondered then, because we had a larger guestroom. But I didn't — perhaps I should have said something to her. To Bharti. I'd caught him looking at her in India in a way that — in a way I understood wasn't right."

"Did Rishi know?"

"No."

"How can you be sure?"

"I just know. He would have told me. He liked Bharti—he treated her like a daughter. He wouldn't have put up with it if he'd known what was going on under his roof. I'm sure of that. Rishi was kind. It was his nature. He was nothing like his father."

"Do you think Nirad would kill the girl if she was pregnant?"

"Yes."

They looked at each other. He'd come to the Clift Hotel to tell her that she should go to India before the case against Thomas fell apart. He was sure that Thomas was telling the truth, and his lawyer—a very competent one—would get the charges dropped, soon. Thomas had told them that he was with his employee at his gallery the afternoon of the murders, and he could prove it.

"You've got to leave," Michael said.

"What will happen to Robert?"

"Nothing. They won't be able to keep him for long. He's gotten a good lawyer. The photos are from a month before, he claims. He'll prove he wasn't there and they'll have to let him go. You should leave for India. Now," he said.

"Nirad won't send my daughters to my parents' house. I begged him. He blames me somehow for what happened to Rishi and Bharti. Neel called and said that you are in danger. Neel is frightened he'll lose his government job because of what's happened."

O'Higgins stood looking at her. She was wearing the bindi on her forehead again. She was in Western clothes, jeans and a white blouse, and was barefoot. She'd lost weight and looked like a waif. He could smell the incense in the suite, burning somewhere in the hotel room.

"Do you have Bharti's phone? Is that what Neel means? Why you're in danger?"

"Yes. Nirad wants the emails he sent Kumar," he said.

"Why would he do that? Take photos?" she said.

He shrugged. "It's common even for billionaires to take photos like that. I've seen hundreds. Men just do it."

"What are you going to do?" she said.

"I don't know."

"Do you want me?" she said.

"What do you mean?"

"You know what I mean. Do you want me?"

"Yes," he said. "Yes, I do."

She took him by the hand and led him down the hallway. The smell of the incense got stronger as she walked toward the bedroom. It was thick, a kind of fug in the air. He heard a cell phone ring as they kissed. It was as if he'd been waiting for her since the moment he'd seen her on the ferry. It was all very wrong, and he could have cared less. He wanted her. He wanted to make love to her, to be shut off from the world with her alone.

"Are you going to love me — the way you loved your wife?"

He didn't answer. He unbuttoned her shirt. Something was starkly beautiful about her brown skin, incredibly warm when he touched her breasts.

"It was Rishi's shirt."

"I don't care," he said. "They're dead. They're both dead, and there is nothing we can do about it." As he unbuttoned her shirt, he realized that she wanted him too, and he was surprised.

He fell asleep afterwards and dreamt he was at Limantour Beach. It was a beautiful blue summer day. The air was warm. He was looking at his footsteps in the wet sand being slowly washed away by the surf, impressions that were deep, but softened by the foamy tide and polished away wave after wave. Birds followed along behind him. He turned and saw his wife, naked, she waved to him standing in ankle deep water motioning for him to come join her. She smiled. It was summertime because the air was warm and the sky stark blue and clear. He waved back and then woke up in Asha Chaundhry's bed.

"Are you sorry?" she said. She'd been watching him sleep. Her black hair was beautiful and thick. He reached out and touched it. Put his fingers in it. Touched her face and her lips.

"No," he said.

"Can you help me get my girls back?"

"Yes."

"How?"

He got out of bed and looked for his clothes, gathering them up. He didn't feel like talking. And he had no practical answers. He was up against a fucking billionaire, probably about to be unemployed, and he was half crazy. What were the odds?

He had a sudden desire for silence, a restful quiet that he'd not had since his wife died. Surcease, peacefulness, a great pause as if he'd been put on a raft and left drifting, but toward something. If he could just figure it out; piece his broken crazy life back together.

He walked out of the room and dressed in the big living room, looking out at the city at night and all that it harbored, all that it promised during his life: his childhood, his adolescence, his father and mother and sisters and brother, all of them there in the lights, the last night at home before going to war. The morning he met his wife in the Starbucks, and saw a look in her interested eyes. It all seemed so strange, and could only be explained by a great silence.

He looked out at the city, tying his tie. Life's textbook was coded, and never would explain anything. Gibberish. Nothing but one page of strange markings after the next. He found his Glock sitting on the wet bar. He tucked it into the pancake holster, the one he'd carried since he had made detective.

He picked up his phone and checked it. He had text messages from his daughter and one from Marvin, saying they'd been pulled off the case. He turned and looked at Asha standing in the hallway.

CHAPTER 21

"Is Rebecca with you guys?" O'Higgins said on the phone.

"No. You have a week off. Towler wants you to take it. So we'll be up again next week. It's okay. They are still looking at Thomas," Marvin said. "He got some fancy Montgomery Street lawyer and made bail. But we're good."

"I can't find Rebecca. She texted me — she was starting at Marin Academy today, but she's not answering my texts." Marvin had never heard that kind of panic in O'Higgins' voice.

"Call her again," Marvin said.

"I've called her three times. She doesn't answer. It just goes to voice mail."

"Do you still have it — the phone?" Marvin said, afraid to mention Kumar's name.

"Yeah," O'Higgins said.

"God damn it, Mike!"

"You better come over here, Marvin." O'Higgins hung up. A text had hit his phone.

GIVE IT TO US AND NOTHING WILL HAPPEN TO R.

He stared at the message, as if he wasn't reading it correctly. He read it three times. He was out of body for a moment, frightened and watching himself look at his phone. He saw what he was wearing, and saw his hand shaking. He'd never felt like that before, never so afraid, even in combat. He'd been anxious in combat, but this was a bone-crushing fear, and he had to stand back from it in a bizarre, out-of-body way.

"Dad, what's wrong?" Rebecca had come in the front door as he was looking down at his phone.

"Where were you!?" he said, startled.

"I was at school. Started today. You sent them money, remember? What's wrong?"

"Nothing." He needed to be sure he wasn't imagining her.

"Something's wrong, don't lie to me," Rebecca said. "You're pale."

"What time is it?" he asked.

"Twelve thirty. I came home to eat lunch. The SF ballet called. They want me to audition for their school — are you going to tell me what's wrong?" She closed the front door and crossed the room.

"How is it, the school? Marin Academy?" He tried to get his bearings.

"Cool. They don't take any shit there. People are different. Classes are quiet. It's a lot different from where I was in Sacramento. I like it. No stoners allowed, thank God."

"You want me to make you some lunch?" he said, trying to sound normal. His voice sounded strange from the shock of seeing her. He turned off his phone. Would they come here to his house?

"Okay. I was going to have soup, Amy's. Why aren't you at work?"

"We closed a case. I'm off for a few days."

"You look awful," she said. "Are you sick or what?"

"Give me your phone," he said.

"Excuse me?"

"I can't explain right now, but — please give it to me," he said. They were probably using it to track her, he realized.

"No."

"God damn it, Rebecca, give me your phone!"

"No," she said. "Have you gone crazy?"

"No. I can't explain, but — I need it."

"No. I'm not giving you my phone. You're acting weird. I'm going to call Aunt June and have her talk to you."

He didn't know what to say. He couldn't tell her the truth without scaring her. But if he lied? He was trapped without an answer or a direction. They were going to go after her if he didn't give them what they wanted. His choices were stark, and his daughter's life was at stake.

"I'll fix the soup," he said, looking at her. She was too thin, and looked like her mother more and more every day. She would be a beautiful woman soon, all the awkwardness of adolescence gone and replaced by a ballerina. A woman. Protect her. He saw the future in front of her. It would be glorious, his sister in New York would help her — she would get beyond the accident, she would fall in love and have her own family someday.

"You aren't going to tell me what's wrong?" she said. "Why are you acting so weird?"

"I love you," he said. "You know that. Right?"

"Yes. But don't act weird on me, okay? Please. I — I don't want to leave again. I want to be here, at home. I want things to be normal again. That's what I want. So you have to cooperate. I don't care if you have a girlfriend. I get it. That's why you didn't come home last night. You're a man and they want … you know. I get that. But I want us to be a family again, you and I — I come home, and you tell me to eat and pick up my room and come home by midnight and I act like a shitty teenage girl — normal. Okay? Like if … like if Mom was going to come through that door. Like that. I want it to feel like that. Okay?"

"Okay," he said.

"I'll make lunch, then. You want some?" She put her arms around him like she used to when she was a little girl. The distance between them dissolved, as if they had been lost in a wilderness and stepped out of it to find each other again.

"Do you remember Limantour?" he said.

"Of course. It was mom's favorite place in the whole world, I think."

"We should go, you and I, for a walk. Like we used to," he said.

"Yeah, I'd like that." She let him go. She was weeping. He started to cry, too. They'd not touched since the day of the accident, he realized. When they'd been on their rescuer's boat, cold and in shock, the horror of what happened closing them both down.

"You miss Mom?" she asked.

"Yeah, every second. It just doesn't go away," he said.

"Why is it so hard?" she said.

"I don't know," he said. "It just is."

"Is that what love is? Just pain? I don't get it."

"No," he said. "No, it's not. It's Limantour, when we were there together, the three of us. Just hold onto that from now on. We had that and we always will. It's forever," he said.

"But we don't have Mom," Rebecca said. "That's the hard part. Memories only hurt you."

Marvin came in the front door while they were eating lunch. He and Marvin looked at each other. Marvin could tell, immediately, that he'd not told Rebecca anything.

"Can a black man get a cup of coffee with you Irish bastards?"

"Uncle Marvin, if something happens to Dad — I mean if something happens at work — you know — would you —? Could I go live with you guys? I need a back-up plan," Rebecca said. "I don't want to go back to Sacramento. And I can't stand Bolinas. I love Uncle Andy, but I can't live out there with all those hippies."

"Yeah," Marvin said, not blinking. "You'll have to share a room, though. And everyone has a curfew. And my wife will want you to go to church. Now can I have that cup of coffee?"

"I can't tell her," O'Higgins said.

"Why not?" Marvin said.

"Because she's fragile right now. I can't drag her out of here. I just can't. If I do that now I might never get her back. She hates Bolinas. She wants to be here at home. And I want her here with me."

"What are you going to do, then?" Marvin said.

"Give them Kumar's fucking phone, ASAP," Michael said.

"Good. Thank God. Finally you're making some damn sense."

"I slept with Asha Chaundhry, Marvin. It just happened — last night."

"Am I supposed to be surprised? Isn't that what you wanted to happen?"

"I guess. I think I'm in love with her. Asha," O'Higgins said.

"Okay. Why not."

"I give them the damn phone and we catch another case, and it's all okay," Michael said, as if he were trying to convince himself. He texted the number back.

Limantour State Beach—4:00 PM. It's yours.

Their answer came back almost immediately:

Bring Asha.

Michael slid his phone across the table at Marvin, who stopped it, keeping it from sliding off.

"I don't get it," Marvin said, reading their message.

"They're going to kill her," Michael said.

"What?"

"I think so. Both of us, maybe," Michael said.

"Why?"

"Takes care of a lot of problems for Nirad, doesn't it? Asha was a 'loose woman.' The detective and her were having an affair? They know it somehow. What happened yesterday? It's perfect for them. I led them to their solution, really, what Nirad wanted. He's smart. That's why guys like him run the fucking world. I was stupid. I just wanted to be with her. Wanted her."

"You can't go then, Mike. Just tell them we'll leave the phone somewhere. Fuck them," Marvin said.

"I have to go. Its Rebecca's life we're talking about. I have to go. They win. Don't they? About Rebecca — will you take care of her? Funny she asked. She must have felt something was really wrong when she came in."

"Mike —"

"I'm asking you the same goddamn question she just did. Do I have your word?"

"Yes. You have my word. We'll take care of her."

"There's a life insurance policy. We had two. There's enough money to see her through. College, and all that. And her new school," Michael said. "Keep the house for her. She'll need a house when she has her own family."

"Mike, come on! We can figure this out," Marvin said. He looked frightened, realizing what was at stake.

"It's one o'clock. I've got to go." He called Asha, said he had to see her, and hung up.

Marvin was giving him a strange look. He understood there was no law now. The rich people of the world were running the show, and there was nothing two cops could do to stop it. The world was in a free-for-all, greed at the center of it.

"Jennifer loved you. Did you know that? I've been meaning to tell you. I wanted you to know that," Michael said. "I mean, if she knew that Rebecca was going to — you know. She would be very happy with that."

"Mike. I get it. All of it, man. I really get it. God damn it—I do."

The phone he'd been carrying in his pocket from Neel Roa rang. O'Higgins took it out and answered.

***

He told Asha the truth in the car, and said that she could get out if she wanted to. She didn't have to go with him. They drove Van Ness Avenue toward the Golden Gate Bridge. It was the last day of March. The winter clung to the City like an old shrew, stubborn, loud, its wind blowing up from Monterey Bay, ice cold. He used to like to sail in March because of the winds and the difficulty of sailing in winter. Wintertime offered a sense of wild freedom that summer's idyllic skies never gave.

"No, I'll go of course," she said. She was wearing riding boots and had tucked her pants into the tops, and a black turtleneck. She looked beautiful, young and without flaws, a kind of womanly perfection, he'd thought when she got into the car.

"Why are you doing this?" he said.

"He's going to take the girls to my mothers. He promised. So I have to go with you. We made a deal."

"Do they know about us?"

"Yes. Everything," Asha said.

"Is that why — is that what made you. Last night. Is that why you made love to me?"

"No. They didn't have to make me. They just wanted us to be together. Photos. I was attracted to you the moment I saw you." She turned in her seat and looked at him so he would see she was telling the truth. "On the ferry. That first day — I was ashamed of it. It had never happened before like that. I loved Rishi, you have to believe me. I did," she said. She turned back and looked out the window.

They were approaching the Golden Gate Bridge. He'd looked west and saw the spot where he thought they'd capsized. At the same instant he remembered what she'd felt like. The smell of Asha's body mixed with the sweet smell of Blue Jasmine incense. Her small breaths in the dark as they made love, the way she'd held his neck, the wonderful feel of her sculpted against him. He'd felt completely alive in her arms.

"But they —?"

"They took photos of us. That was the deal. I'm sorry. I betrayed you, if that's what you're asking. But I had no choice at all, do you understand? None, Michael. Nirad is a monster, and I couldn't have my girls in the same house. It is unthinkable." She spoke without looking at him. They passed Vista Point on the north end of the bridge and headed up the hill toward Sausalito.

He looked out and saw Alcatraz cloistered in cloud scud. A hulking container ship, looking impressive and unstoppable, was passing under the bridge. It was heading out to sea and would pass the North Tower where it all started. All of it seemed to have started there — his long journey — where the Bay met the ocean.

They passed the throng of cars heading into Sausalito. He swung his Ford into the fast lane, punching the throttle. He felt the cold water of the ocean again, his wife's hand gripping his tightly. The moment when he spotted Rebecca's red coat in the fog as he swam toward her. How red it looked, how grateful he was she had put it on.

"I understand," he said finally.

They drove in silence, then all the way to the turn off at Sir Francis Drake Boulevard that they would take them out to West Marin. They left the fog behind. The Marin hills were as green as he'd ever seen them.

"Where are we going?" she said.

"Limantour Beach," he said.

"Is that near Tomales Bay?"

"Yes, just west. Near Point Reyes. You'll see the bay. We'll drive by it," he said.

"I always wanted to go," Asha said. "But then everything happened to us."

***

Dr. Schneider had called him that morning and asked him to stop by. He thought of not going, but decided at the last moment he owed the doctor that.

"Are you going to tell me, Michael? I have to end our working together. But I want to hear what happened that day," Dr. Schneider said.

"Why?" he said.

"I just need to know. I can't explain why, exactly. Maybe it's because I — I don't think I can help people. I don't think I'm any good at it, really."

"So you'll do what?" O'Higgins said, surprised. They took

their usual places, sitting where they'd always sat, aware that it would be their last session together.

"I don't know," she said. "I wanted you to get over something. I thought that your wife's death, as hard as it was for you, was — how can I say this? That it was just a moment in life's continuum, something that you could pass by finally, and then go on with your life. I didn't get it. Loss, what it means; that it changes you forever, that it marks you. I didn't understand that. Nothing in my training taught me that simple thing about life. Now I understand. It bashes you, there's dents and nothing can make things perfect again. That's why I can't go on with this, pretending somehow that I can fix people. Change anything.

"Something's happened?" O'Higgins said. He saw it on her face. Something indelible was now printed there, marked in her eyes, he recognized a life-scar expression.

"I lost a patient. She killed herself. I blame myself," She said.

"That's not your fault," he said.

"Maybe … You were my first patient. I was so sure of myself when you walked in here, so sure I could help you — but I didn't understand. I think you did, from the very beginning. Somehow you knew It couldn't be fixed. Perhaps only forgotten." She was wearing jeans, and she'd boxed up things. The painting of the geese was gone from the wall. Papers on the floor, medical reference books stacked up by the door. It was obvious she was closing down her practice.

"I want to tell you what happened that day. Out there. I've kept it a secret from everyone because it was too much," he said, ready to tell her. It was a story he was finally ready to tell.

"Why now?"

"Maybe you did help me. I think you did. A lot of things. I

came here, that first day, to tell you what happened to us. From the first session. I wanted to tell someone, but I wasn't ready to."

Schneider reached for his hand and across the divide that had separated them for months. The two club chairs were only a few feet away from each other, but a universe apart until she touched his hand.

"Okay, tell me now. I want to hear it. I need to hear it," she said.

He looked at her. Her expression was one he'd never seen before, something lost about it. The doctor, too, was struggling to hang on to something now.

The water was ice cold and a shock. The shock forced him to involuntarily inhale saltwater. He saw the sail under him, pearl white covered by water. He was looking for Rebecca. He was holding Jennifer's hand. She'd fallen in a moment after he had. They'd landed near each other and were lying on the boat's sail, inches above the ocean, until the torn keel came up out of the water and they were thrown into the freezing water.

He pulled the inflation ring on his wife's life jacket. It immediately inflated around her.

"Where is she?" Jennifer was trying to control her breath, but like him she'd swallowed salt water from the involuntary cold water's shock and was coughing. The sailboat's hull was sinking, disappearing, the red line he'd painted across the waterline that summer vanishing. He saw it covered and then the broken keel rise up again, dirty and ugly.

He saw something maybe twenty yards away, a shark's fin. The look of it evil and frightening. He turned away looking for Rebecca, but still couldn't see her.

"There she is, there!" He got the words out. Waves were

breaking over the hull as it sank, foaming over it, but he'd caught a glimpse of Rebecca floating in the water, wearing his red jacket, just off to their right.

He started to swim and felt the strange tug of his life jacket holding his head up. Jennifer held his hand, trying to go with him toward where they saw the red jacket bobbing in the foamy grey, the waves pushing Rebecca away from them. He saw their daughter's shoulders lift near the disappearing hull, the last of its broken-open wood hull finally covered over by the ocean.

"Get her, Michael, God please!" Jennifer said.

"Dad! Dad!"

The boat's emergency life raft, designed to employ once it was submerged, popped up suddenly making a terrific noise. Its hydro-static release having worked as intended. He knew he had a decision to make between getting Jennifer to the life raft, and to safety, or swimming towards his daughter who he knew wasn't wearing a life vest and would be carried away by the current quickly.

He hesitated a moment, the taste of salt water in his mouth. He looked for Jennifer in the chop while the life raft finished inflating, building itself; its canopy mushrooming up now. It looked huge.

"And what happened?" Schneider said. She was still holding his hand and she was crying, but it was as if he was back in the ice cold water, the waves hitting him in the face, the cold making it harder and harder for him to swim. A terrible numbness had come over his arms and legs. The hull moved up, reappearing like some kind of weird Moby Dick, like a living creature fighting to live. The broken keel nearly hit him.

He saw Jennifer behind him now, she was looking at him,

Her face locked between the yellow life jacket's bulk. He felt helpless but instinctively moved off towards his daughter, swimming as best he could.

"When I got to Rebecca, Jen was gone. I never could tell anyone about seeing the shark. I knew what had happened. I had to make a choice between the two of them you see."

It was moments before Schneider could speak, as if he'd punched her in the stomach. "Does anyone else know? Rebecca?"

"No, And I'll never tell her. It's our secret—I guess. Thank you, Doctor," he said. "You're wrong, you did help, you see. I had someone to tell it to, my story ... Don't give up on my kind." He got up and left the office, not looking back closing the door behind him.

The doctor sat there for a long time, her life hanging in the balance, her years of medical school and her youth holding her up as she finally walked across the office to her desk.

They never spoke or saw each other again. But she realized she'd helped him despite feeling horribly inadequate in the face of her patient's suicide. She'd made a difference to the detective's life. Her feeling of hopelessness left her as quickly as it had begun because she believed him. She decided to go on, that it was important.

They often thought about one another the detective and the doctor, almost as if they'd been lovers. The detective was her first patient and she'd learned a great deal. She kept all the notes about him at her home in a bookcase, by a window that had a view of the Golden Gate and the Pacific Ocean beyond it. For some reason she'd written at the end of O'Higgin's notes: There is no science that will ever change the nature of life, which is to suffer.

I do what I can to help. She accepted the fact that there was no escape. No Brave-New-World Soma. No mind-numbing drug. No conversation with white-coated shamans, even, could alter that horrible truth about life.

CHAPTER 22

They drove through Fairfax, full of aging hippies, mountain-bike shops and redwood fences hung with weather beaten and sad-looking Tibetan prayer flags. O'Higgins drove over White's Hill, heading due west toward an iron bar of fog in the distance. The populated end of Marin County was well behind them now. Here the old California took shape, looking the way it had been before any white men ever saw it. The hillsides were clean, oak-studded, greenish with flinty rock outcroppings scattered across fields, ancient.

O'Higgins looked up on the ridge where he had hunted deer as a boy with his high school friends. A huge oak tree stood near the ridgeline west of White's Hill, massive. He recognized the spot where he'd fired his first shot from a long rifle, his shoulder pressed into the wooden stock of his .30.30.

The buck had been making his way to the shade of the tree and stood a good sixty yards in front of him. The animal was taken down after the first shot. Its death came stumbling and terrible at the end of a long hot summer afternoon in late August. The tall Johnson grass smelled of star thistles, and the ocean. He and his friends had run down into a golden-grass ravine toward the kill. It was a good clean heart shot, his hands steady—his first shot. Cocking again, he'd waited for the animal to get up, finally lowering the hammer, the deer not moving and a second shot unnecessary. Later, and during the war, he'd thought about that first shot often, how it would help and hurt him.

The oak tree was craggy now, twenty years later, but still a solitary and living reminder of his youth, of his high school days. They'd been good, even idyllic. It was a time of innocence, as it was with all youth, he imagined. He was glad to see the landmark still signaling something about world-time always going on, stopping for no one.

He wondered what would happen to his daughter. What kind of world would she become a woman in? Would she be a mother? A wife? Certainly. A career as a dancer, perhaps? He was optimistic for her happiness. He knew she had that one thing people need to succeed: she was committed to her dreams, selfish about them and brave. Without bravery, he knew, nothing could be had of life.

He understood, from the moment he turned on the car and pulled away from his house, he might not be there for her. He'd driven through San Rafael toward the freeway looking at everything. All the magnificent details that were so familiar and been so ordinary had appeared different as he drove through town. They seemed important—the homeless guy and the businessman. Everything seemed to stand out as if he were on some kind of mind-expanding psychedelic. Death didn't frighten him.

"You shouldn't come," O'Higgins said, speaking again after a long silence. He sped up as the battered Ford headed down into the San Geronimo Valley and toward the ocean. The valley's hillsides were dark, almost steel blue, the redwood trees dismal and beautiful, a kingdom of fog and Redwood trees. Their trunks were black from the rain.

He'd crept along the ridge line here, hunting past abandoned summer shacks from the 1920s, their roofs mossy green, his rifle's barrel wet from the fog. He'd enjoyed the loneliness of the Coast Range as a young man. It was different from any place else, singular with its views of the Pacific, its redwood trees magnificent and lonely in their grandeur. Often he would take his rifle and hunt alone, stopping to eat lunch under a redwood, the food—sandwiches made in haste— tasting good, the loneliness of place revealing something about himself. He was bookish, with the short rifle he loved between his legs as he ate.

"You should go home, to India. To your girls," he said finally.

"The US authorities won't let me. It's too late, anyway. Rishi is gone and I have to do sati."

"What's that?" O'Higgins said.

"Do you like Tomales Bay?" Asha said, not answering his question.

"Yes. I sailed there a lot when my wife was alive."

She turned to him. He hit the heater and let the hot air blow in, not finishing his sentence. He had the desire to make love to her again, to take her up some fog-bound fire road and escape their awful predicament, disappear in the cold mists like high-school kids. Why should they accept death?

"I saw a painting of the bay in Richard's gallery one day. I must have been thinking of you. No, it was before we met; but I must have felt something. That you were near? Do you think the person you really are meant for — that you can feel them, that they might be close by?" she said.

"I don't understand," he said.

"I had a fantasy about meeting the painter. Robert thought, perhaps, I was reacting to him and that's why he fixated on me —

but I was thinking of someone who I could share something that was deep inside. I can't explain," she said. "The thing that was truly me, something beyond the good Indian girl, the A student. The Cambridge graduate. I never showed it to Rishi, really. Not really. I don't know why. I thought maybe he would be put off by it. But I think that's the person you're meant to be with; it's the person you want to show your real self to, and you know it when you're making love to them because you show it then, I think. I felt it with you last night.

"I was meant to come here, and I was meant to meet you. I'm sure of it. That's what the guru told my mother. I told my mother I'd fallen in love with someone, and she wasn't shocked — I mean, shocked because it was too close to Rishi's death, of course. But my mother is a blessed person and she understood that love could happen that way, despite tragedy, or because of it. Maybe only an artist could understand that. What is this place? Where are we?"

"Lagunitas," he said. "I lived here, when I got back from Iraq."

"It's — dreary," she said, and smiled.

"Yeah. Lot of redwood trees in the fog." he smiled back. Were they really traveling toward their death?

"Was it difficult, when you got back?" she asked.

"Yeah. But I liked it out here. It was always wet and foggy. After Iraq, I wanted to feel the cold again."

She reached over and touched his thigh. He felt her touch go through him the way he had with his wife. Electric. Sexual, compelling and something else that was indescribable, as if the universe itself had reached out and touched him.

She smiled again at him. It was a girlish smile, and authentic as if they were on a first date and hadn't a care in the world.

"It looks cold. Like Scotland," she said. "And it's like the Lake Country, too."

"The house I rented, if you could call it that, was a summer place. Old. No heat. I would light the potbelly stove and read and try and figure it all out. What I would do next. I decided to be a cop sitting by the stove reading Hemingway and Jack London. Sounds trite, but it's true," he said.

He remembered the decision that would lead him to Jennifer and to Rebecca. The sides of the stove had turned orange. The potbelly stove was full of coal he'd buy on the cheap in San Rafael, by the train tracks. It was about two in the morning and he could not sleep. The big summer house felt empty and ice cold if he stepped away from the stove.

"Do you think I was wrong, sleeping with you?" Asha said.

"No. I'm glad it happened, really. That's the truth," he said.

"Even if I deceived you about — about Nirad. What he wanted. You have a right to hate me."

"So what? I didn't tell you the truth, either. That I was — pursuing you selfishly. Since the ferry, maybe. When I saw you, I felt something powerful. I wanted you then," he said.

"It's all so strange, isn't it? I mean, that we ended up falling in love. Or that I will do sati today."

"What's that? And tell me this time." He took his eyes off the road and looked at her.

"It's what Indian widows do," she said. "Good Hindu widows."

She turned and faced him. They were heading toward Samuel P. Taylor State Park. They'd entered a part of the valley that was very narrow, dark on the west side, with Samuel P. Taylor Creek to their right. The two-lane country road seemed made to fit between the hulking redwoods. The fog had seeped up the road from Bolinas, lying in all the low spots, covering the sky in places, making mysteries in the trees.

"It's a kind of sacrifice," she said. "Traditional. But I'm a traditional Indian woman."

"But you don't have to do it," he said, "whatever it is."

"Where are we now?" she asked.

"Samuel P. Taylor State Park."

"There's a creek, isn't that the American word for it? It's beautiful."

"There's steelhead in there now. They swim up from the ocean every year. We aren't far from the ocean. Only a few miles, really. Tomales Bay is close, too."

"Pull over, for just a moment, I want to see. Please, can we? Please."

O'Higgins pulled over into the campground. He showed his badge, and the young female ranger at the entrance booth waved him through. The campground was empty because of a storm the night before, so they had the place to themselves. He stopped the car. She got out immediately. It was raining very slightly, the way it had been the night of the murder — so lightly you could barely see it, but you could feel it on your face.

He watched her. She walked toward the swollen creek. He knew the place. He'd taken girlfriends here in high school before it was gated; and before the State had made it a park with rules and rangers and asphalt parking lots and uniforms. The windshield started to fill up with tiny rain dots and obscure the scene.

He got the full sense of time as he slid out of the car. The movement of it: time as some kind of magic. The high school locker room after football practice, noisy and happy. His Irish and Italian-looking pals pulling their rifles out of the trunk of his old Mustang, getting ready to hunt. The girls he'd brought wide-eyed to this place, college's marijuana clouds and library hallways, a painting of a blue-period "Saltimbanque" by Picasso that he liked for unknown reasons. Signing up for the Marine Corps at the post office as soon as he graduated from college. The war. Finally walking into a random Starbucks and seeing Jennifer pretend to stare into her laptop as he walked by her, heading to the counter to order. He couldn't keep his eyes off her. He waited for his name to be called by a barista, trying not to stare at her.

"I don't want to bother you, but I think that guy over there is going to come over and ask you out, so I thought I'd better do it first. He looks creepy. Be ahead of the curve," he'd said, sitting next to Jennifer at the "bar" with its view of Valencia Street. He was in his patrol uniform bristling with radio and weapons, customers looking at him.

"You're a policeman," she'd said.

"Yes. It's not a costume."

He got a smile out of her. "My brother is a Hells Angel, so I know a lot about the police," she said. "They were always coming to our house."

He found out later it was true. Her brother was a career criminal and a biker.

"All good experiences, I hope," he'd said.

She laughed. "Okay, that's twice you've made me smile. That's a good sign."

They went out that night. It was easy to be with her from the moment they met. It was his wife who really cured him of his PTSD, not the group sessions at the VA. She took the disease on, went mano-a-mano with it and won by simply listening to him tell her about the war.

He looked at his phone. It was almost 3:30 in the afternoon. He had decided that morning he was going to fight them when he got there. He'd brought his Glock and the backup revolver. He didn't want to just let it happen, some anonymous bullet. Something about his training, something about his spirit, just would not let him surrender without a fight.

He closed the car door and walked to where Asha had found the wooden pedestrian bridge over the creek. He didn't know what sati was exactly, but he realized she was ready to die too, and it was shocking. Her embracing it that way; her acceptance of everything that had happened to her in the space of a week. How could she?

He thought again of running and taking her and Rebecca somewhere. They would be a family, a strange one, but a family. Her two little girls, too. Why the hell not? Why shouldn't he be happy as he'd once been?

He walked up behind her and held her around the waist. What should he do? Fight or die?

"I'm in love with you," he said. "I can't let this happen to us."

"We have to accept. The guru told me that life is all an illusion, everything. I believe that now. I didn't before. The world seemed so real to me. Maybe love, too? Is that one more illusion? Could it be? I thought I was in love with Rishi, but I wasn't, not the way I am with you. Not really. I just realized that now. But it wasn't my fault really. Perhaps it was — if we hadn't married, maybe —"

She stood looking down at the creek, which was chock-a-block with Steelhead trout, some battered from their journey from the ocean. Their speckled backs were beautiful in the dark, thick water that rushed around them, the water seeming not to move at all. For some it would be their last journey. Their home in the ocean was behind them, and death waited further along the creek at some spot that smelled of eucalyptus and fog where it would all end for them in silence. Would some kind of God be witness? Something, perhaps just a shimmer on the surface of the water when it ended.

"What is sati?" he said, still behind her, holding her tightly, leaning down, his cheek on hers.

"Suicide," she said. "Suicide."

***

Marvin Lee walked down the quay, lined with odd house-boats, and toward Gilbert's "office" in Sausalito's Gate Five. He'd called ahead. Paul Gilbert sounded affable on the phone, and was expecting him.

Marvin stopped to admire the view. The bay was like glass, its surface reflecting a dying winter. March's usual scud broke in spots. The clouds, here and there, were backlit by a weak sun. Spring was coming, he thought. You could tell about spring in the Bay Area by the great show of heavy cumulus clouds that patrolled the skies for a week or two, biblical looking, making it seem that Judgment Day had arrived until April's change.

Marvin adjusted his tie, looked down at his shoes that were shined and clean. It was important, he thought, to always look your best. It made him feel secure to look sharp.

Detective Marvin Lee's father had owned a pool hall and shoeshine parlor in West Oakland in the Seventies, called O-Town Pool. His mother had died from a heroin overdose when he was just six. She'd been a prostitute working the Powell Street "corridor," west of downtown Oakland. His dad's place had been a well-known underworld hangout: ex-Black Panthers, big time pimps, whom he'd admired because of their flash and cash and big cars, and drug dealers of every stripe and color.

His father had been a felon whom the LA mob used as a front, someone who would clean up their cash. Italians came from San Francisco with sacks of cash on a regular basis, leaving the money on a pool table next to them while they caught a game, or a blow job in the "cigar room."

The Italians were nice to him, called him kid, showed him their weapons and gave him sips of beer. The Italians, often dark-complected themselves, were not racist; he'd felt that about them instinctively, and liked them because of it.

Marvin looked down the quay. The man he was going to meet was not any different, he decided. He was just another hustler. Yes, he was white and, no doubt, came from some tony suburb where kids rode their expensive bikes down leafy streets. But he was no different from the men and women he'd known as a boy.

He leaned over and spit in the water and decided he would do exactly what he and O'Higgins had discussed with Neel Roa. Fuck this guy.

He considered O'Higgins a brother, and had no problem with what he was going to do. His psychology had a dark side that made it easier. This dark side had always troubled him, even frightened him. It had driven him to church, to try to scare that part of him into obedience. He'd fought "the other" since he was a boy, but it was easy to call on when he needed it.

Marvin headed down the quay looking into the different kinds of rain-soaked houseboats as he passed, all of them so different and strange to a kid from Oakland. Who in God's name would want to live in a place like this?

"Nice office," Marvin said. The luxurious houseboat, brand new looking, had been converted into an office suite with a sunken living room that had views of Alcatraz. Paul Gilbert's chippy was making coffee. She was one of the hundreds of thousands of young women who were selling themselves in exchange for some sugar daddy paying off their student loans. Gilbert had found her on line on a site called Sugar D.

The girl was fine, with a hundred-dollar high ass, as far as Marvin could tell. She was working at the sink in the kitchen, wearing short shorts that did nothing but shout "Fuck me." She was a mixed race girl, her hair Afro-styled, kinky and reddish, her skin the color of coffee and milk. She was what the pimps in Oakland called a Bottom Girl, denoting their importance in a pimp's hierarchy of his stable of women. Bottom Girls were the last girls you'd get rid of. She was that fine, Marvin thought. He'd called Gilbert from the parking lot. He hadn't had time to hide the girl, which was what Marvin had planned on.

"Thank you," Gilbert said. He'd obviously just gotten laid, the kind of sex that left his face red, all the kinks out. He was as relaxed as a man his age ever got. He was fifty, so he was never completely relaxed, the way a younger man might get after sex. Nothing about Paul Gilbert was carefree, Marvin thought.

"Hey, honey," Marvin said. "Could you do us a favor?"

The girl walked out of the galley. She was blowing on a cup of coffee. She was even prettier from the front, her face freckled. Jesus, Marvin thought looking at her. Now that's a hard-on maker.

"Could you give us a moment?" Marvin said. He smiled. It wasn't his easy-going smile, it was another one he kept for street people designed to signal authority. It was this: You-chump-that's-who-I'm-talking-to smile.

"Excuse me," Gilbert said.

"Yeah, I need to speak to you and I think your friend will understand. Take a walk, honey," Marvin said.

"Paul?" The girl looked at her man as if to say, who is this nigger?

"Yeah, okay. Alicia, could you go maybe get my briefcase out of the car? This is Alicia. She helps me around the office," Gilbert said, expecting him to believe it. He actually did believe blacks were stupid.

"Okay, sure, baby," the girl said. The "baby" was for his benefit, Marvin thought. She looked at the big detective, perhaps letting him know that she was for hire, or perhaps that he was just another asshole in her life. He couldn't tell.

They'd spoken on the phone, Marvin questioning her about Gilbert. He'd made it clear to her who was the boss, speaking to her like a pimp in a bad mood. Neel Roa had found out about the girl and passed on her number. It was all part of Neel's game plan, designed to save his sister from Nirad and a murder sentence.

"What's this about, detective?" Gilbert said, watching the girl leave. He was trying to dress like a hipster when he was away from the ball and chain. The ex-banker was wearing a black hoodie with a loud design on its front, and blue jeans—no undershirt.

"It's about Nirad Chaundhry," Marvin said. He got up closer to Gilbert, the way he'd seen his father do to some guy who was late with the vig, as the Italians his father worked for ran a loan-shark business, too.

"I think we've told you everything we can about that awful day," Gilbert said, noticing that the detective had entered his personal space.

"You're going to have to do me a favor," Marvin said.

"I don't understand," Gilbert said.

"I want you to call the DA's office, after I've left here, and explain to them that Nirad Chaundhry sent you a large sum of money in order to keep quiet about his affair with Bharti Kumar."

"Now? I really don't understand," Gilbert said, smiling fatuously.

"Well, it doesn't really matter if you understand or not—asshole," Marvin said. "You're going to tell the DA that you received this large sum of money from Nirad Chaundhry to keep quiet about having seen photos of Nirad Chaundhry and Bharti Kumar that were mistakenly emailed to your wife's phone. They're on your wife's phone now. You are going to confess to blackmailing Mr. Nirad Chaundhry. You're also going to say you lied to the police about the time Mr. Nirad Chaundhry arrived at your home to pick up his grandchildren the day of the murders. You're going to tell the truth and say he arrived at 5:45."

"I will do no such thing," Gilbert said.

"You will do as you're told or we will drag your wife into this. And you will both be arrested for lying to police, which would make you both accomplices to murder. Do you want the mother of your children to go to jail, too?"

"I'll call the — police," Gilbert said.

He could see Gilbert was frightened, stunned that he was being threatened. He'd obviously never bumped up against the pointy-end of life. Like most people, he didn't understand that the police could lie like anyone else.

"Chaundhry won't like it," Gilbert said, the color draining from his face. "He might —"

"Blame you for this? He might," Marvin said. "Does your wife know what you do up in here?"

"No," Gilbert said.

"Okay, then," Marvin said. "Have a nice day."

It was strange. As soon as he'd walked off the houseboat, he dropped the cold hoodlum expression and became the "pleasant black man" and well-dressed police detective again, someone who would never cross the line. The kind man that his neighbors in the Marina District, knew and waved to while he walked the family's dog. The other guy was dangerous, brought up in a West Oakland pool hall during the COINTELPRO years. He put that person away as quickly as he'd taken him out. He belonged to the streets.

His father had disappeared one day in June 1970, with a man named Albert in a Lincoln Town car with a missing front fender. Had there been a problem with the count? No one knew. Was it the FBI, who'd he'd been informing for? He never knew what happened to his father. The pool hall was taken over by another black man, an ex-Oakland Raiders lineman with a thick neck and small porcine eyes, who walked in one day, handed Marvin a fifty-dollar bill and told him, "Shoot your last game boy, and then don't come back."

He'd gone to live with his grandmother after that in the Acorn Projects, some of the roughest projects in the country. It was his grandmother who had kept him from going bad, making sure he stayed in at night. She'd been a sweet church-going woman from Jamaica who never really understood America and kept to herself. When she'd died, he'd gone down to the "swings" and cried. It was one of the few times he ever cried about anything. He tried to pretend she was alive for months afterwards. He often dreamed about her. She had a kind face and had called him her "little man."

CHAPTER 23

The rough, serpentine, pothole-filled road to Limantour Beach ran up from Point Reyes Station and was bordered by craggy burnt-out ravines, steep and charred from a recent fire. Point Reyes was visible to the north as soon as they crested the mountain. A marine layer, diaphanous, sat over the fifteen-mile long beach below. The road felt empty, a far cry from the way it was in high summer.

"We came here as a family," O'Higgins said.

"They're waiting for us? Colonel Das?" Asha asked.

"Yes," he said. "They wanted you too. They want us both."

"I don't understand. Nirad said that if I came, that would be enough," Asha said. "He told me he would have the girls brought to my mother's. He promised me that."

"Did you kill Rishi?" O'Higgins said. "You can tell me if you did. It won't change how I feel about you."

"No. I've told you. I loved Rishi."

"Okay. I won't ever ask again. I never believed you did. What did he tell you? Nirad. About me."

"I was to prove that you and I were involved. He hates you. Something you said to him. I don't know what, but he wants to ruin you, personally. He's angry. That's the way he is. Vicious."

"Why does he want you here?" O'Higgins said.

"He wants me to do sati. He chose this place, I don't know

why. He said I must do sati here."

"Why would he want his grandchildren's —" O'Higgins said.

"Because it's what he believes Hindu wives are supposed to do. He's a Hindu fundamentalist. He believes wives should not continue on if their husbands die," she said. "I'm to leave a note. In the note I confess to killing Rishi. I left it at the hotel. If I do what Nirad says, he will send the girls to my mother's house. He gave me his word.

"You can't stop him. You must understand that. I have to do this, for my girls. They can't — they can't be around him. Live in his house."

"It's crazy," he said.

"Do you love me?"

"Yes. I told you," he said.

"If your wife was sitting here … and it was your daughter? Don't you think she would do it? Jennifer."

He didn't answer. He wanted to stop the car. He wanted to pull over and pretend again that it was all different. But he understood that love was a kind of insanity. It was as if someone opened up a door, and he saw through it. Love didn't make any sense, and yet it made all the sense in the world. You would kill for it, sacrifice yourself for it. It was the most human part of us.

"Tell me about the beach in summer," she said. "What was it like? Please."

"I can't."

"Please." She reached for his hand. "It's not your fault, Michael."

"It was always cool in the morning when we would get here. July, usually. When Jen was pregnant, she liked to feel the sand. Walk barefoot in the surf. We came a lot that summer she was pregnant. I was working nights." He turned and looked at her.

"What did she do — Jennifer?"

"Professor. Computer science. She was a prodigy. When she was a child, she tested off the charts. IQ. Her father was a factory worker. Mother was a waitress — they were Okies."

"Okies?"

"Poor whites from Bakersfield. They didn't know what to do with a child like that. They were afraid of her in some ways, I think."

"Okies," Asha said. "That's a funny name." He saw her smile.

They were driving off the mountain that separated Limantour from Point Reyes Station and Tomales Bay. The ocean massive spread out along the coast, and in front of it marshes with their fresh-water greenish-silver ponds. The scene looked like some fabulous plein-air painting.

"You don't have to go. I'll turn around," he said. "We'll call Neel."

"Neel knows. We spoke this morning I begged him to understand. Tell me more about that summer," she said. "When you and Jennifer came here."

"I wanted a boy. It was stupid, but I was hoping it was a boy," O'Higgins said. "Stupid."

"Why?"

"I don't know anymore. I can't remember. Maybe because of those boys I'd seen killed. My men — I don't know. Now I can't imagine the world without my daughter," he said.

***

It was late in the afternoon, but Jen didn't want to leave. He could see groups of people trooping off the beach that was now almost empty. The foam on the waves pushed up with each succeeding breaker. The tide coming in.

"What do you think our life will be like in ten years?" Jennifer asked.

"Busy," he said, joking.

"No, really. Will you still love me? I'll be old. I'll probably start to look like my mom." Jennifer said.

"Your mom is pretty," he said.

"Stop being so nice. You don't have to be."

"She is," he said.

"Don't you wonder — what it will be like? Our lives? If we'll have other kids. This kid, what she'll be like? If you and I will even be together?" She was wearing a maternity swimsuit and he thought she looked fetching. He'd loved the way she'd looked in it. Her pregnancy had never put him off.

"We should go," he said. "It's getting late."

"No. I don't want to. I don't want to go home yet. Will you still love me when I'm old? Guys are — they get tired of wives, don't they? Don't you guys talk about girls? Cute girls, girls who aren't fat? You can tell me," she said. "I want to know."

"What's wrong, baby?" he said.

"I'm … not sure. It's like I'm getting an error message, and I don't understand why," she said. "I keep searching 'Mother' and I get site not found. Just feel — strange. I feel good here by the ocean."

They didn't leave until after dark that night. She had the baby the following week. She was the best mother he'd thought he'd known. It was that night at the hospital waiting for fatherhood that he let the war finally go for good. The noise of it was the last to go. The noise of war was what people heard long after they came home. They couldn't explain it to those who weren't there and never heard it.

***

The big dirt parking lot at Limantour State Beach was nearly empty. From where he'd parked they couldn't see the beach, only the dunes that he knew separated him from the view of the ocean. A few horse trailers were parked at one end. The wind was blowing. He could see the Pampas grass on the dunes blowing wildly.

A new dark blue Lexus SUV pulled into the parking lot. He recognized Colonel Das behind the wheel. The big man got out of the car almost immediately, walked to the back of the Lexus and took out a plastic red jerry can. He looked their way, then walked toward them until he was standing beside O'Higgins' side of the car.

O'Higgins rolled down the window and handed the Colonel Kumar's iPhone. The Colonel took it and slipped it into his pants pocket without saying a word, then walked on down toward the beach. They could hear the wind blowing as O'Higgins rolled the window up. They watched the Colonel disappear over the top of the dunes, his black turban standing out.

"I wanted to marry since I was twelve or so," Asha said, watching the Colonel disappear over the hill. "Indian women — it is so important, marriage. The idea of it, of having a family, rich or poor, university women or slum dweller. It's all girls think about, being a wife and a mother. I don't think that will ever change."

"Do you trust him? Nirad? That he'll do what he says?" O'Higgins said.

"I have to. What choice do I have? I wish you — would you maybe, if you go to India someday. Would you go see them, my girls? Take your daughter. Is she pretty, your daughter?"

"Yes." He reached for her, and they held each other. It felt awkward and desperate.

"I never expected to fall in love with you," he said. It sounded strange, but it was true.

"It was fate. I believe in that," she said, holding him. "I'm sorry we didn't have more time."

"I don't want —"

She let go of him and put her finger on his lips. She took a ring off of her finger. It was a dark ruby ring, a big one.

"Give this to your daughter. Please. Tell her it's from me. A gift."

Asha got out of the car. He wanted to get out, but saw Jennifer standing in the grass, wearing her maternity swimsuit, and it frightened him.

"If it was Jennifer going," he said out loud. If it was Jennifer going to help Rebecca, would you stop her? Wouldn't you want her to go? Isn't that what Rishi would want? He watched Asha Chaundhry walk down the empty sand-colored parking lot, the wind blowing around her, the way it had on the ferry that first time he'd seen her.

"He believes wives should not live if their husbands die." Should I have lived? He felt paralyzed, as if he'd been wounded. He started the Ford's engine, heard the heater's fan start to blare. He didn't move for a moment, then he took off the parking brake and began to back up, at first slowly. Then he swung the wheel hard and headed across the dirt lot. He didn't want to understand what Asha was feeling, but he did understand. He'd felt it, too, for so long. It was Death's call and it was powerful.

He headed away from the beach. He heard the shouts of war again. He saw Nirad Chaundhry sitting with his lawyer, saw the smug look that crossed Nirad's face. He saw his daughter on the swing set in their back yard, Jennifer pushing her. He saw himself reloading during the battle of Fallujah when he'd gone mad. He saw the deer on White's Hill tumbling through the golden summer's grass, rolling, its body crushing the grass.

His Ford slowed when he got to the asphalt. He reached for the door. He was tired of death and its ways. Was it the rich, then, who had put him there in Fallujah? And was it a billionaire now who would get his way? Death, that was all the rich seemed to know, or create. He was tired of it.

"With these people, it seemed always to be about death," he said aloud.

The Ford's driver's-side door was open, the wind cold, the car's engine on. He climbed out, not bothering to turn off the ignition. He picked up the blue flashing police light and fixed the light to the top of the Ford. He walked down the asphalt to where he knew the bathrooms were, with the outdoor showers Jennifer used to wash Rebecca's feet after they'd left the beach. The shower to his left, he looked up at the dunes and the trail that would take him out to the beach. He pulled the Glock-19 out of its holster and headed toward the sound of the surf, the big pistol at his side. It felt familiar in his hand.

As he struggled in his dress shoes through the sand he heard his wife's voice, and saw she was walking with him. He stopped. I'm going mad. He looked down at the pistol.

"It's the right thing, Michael," Jennifer said. "Come on — I'll help you. With the water. Don't be afraid. It's just the ocean," his wife said. "We loved the ocean, you and I."

He was walking, the sand white grey, the grass on the dunes turning teal colored in the wind, the gusts strong. He got to the pedestrian bridge over a wetland behind the beach. He felt it then, all of it, crashing through his defenses, the fear of all of it. He looked for his wife, but she'd disappeared. He looked ahead toward the top of the dune and Jennifer was waving to him.

I can't, he thought.

He was frozen. He turned and looked at the water on the wet land, almost black, its surface rippled by strong winds. Ducks were harboring in the water, their heads tucked down. It was a kind of lake, ducks and grass and wind all on its grey surface.

He began to walk again, realizing he had to hurry. He started to jog up the last hill, the sand giving way under him as he climbed the dune. He could hear the ocean clearly, loud and unmistakable. It was the sound he had been so afraid of. It was a raw unforgiving sound of the universe moving through all time and all space.

He sank to his knees just at the crest, as if he'd been hit, almost dropping his weapon. On all fours he looked up. I can't.

"Yes, you can." He heard Jennifer's voice. She helped him get up and led him to the top of the dune. And then he saw it. The enemy full face, daring him. The Pacific Ocean staring at him, crashing against the sand, its voice a blue-white roar.

"You're all right now, Michael," Jennifer said. "It's all right. I love you."

He looked to his side and Jennifer was standing next to him. She was dressed as she'd been the day of the accident. Then she was gone. He looked for her but saw instead a fire start far down on the beach, smoke pulled from it—a thin trail of grey black spinning up into the darker sky.

He began to run down the dune and toward the fire.

He'd decided to run on the strip of wet sand where the surf

broke, the waves washing over his shoes, his pistol at his side. The beach was foggy. The fog, having pushed down from Point Arena, covered Point Reyes so that the famous white lighthouse at the tip of the point was hidden, the whole of Point Reyes peninsula draped in grey like a heavy soldier's coat.

Das had taken her up the beach to a place where the cliffs were broken up, making little indents in the sand stone. But he could see the smoke from the nascent fire; it sat on the beach drifting toward the water in bursts like the tail of a kite. He tried not to look at the water, but he could hear it over his labored breath.

He turned once to his left and saw a wave crest, its white foam outline plain and stark as it collapsed onto the wet bird-strewn sand. He heard his wife's scream as she was taken by the shark. He fell down, unable to get up, trembling with fear. He saw his pistol, black on the sand where it had fallen, the surf washing white foamy water over it.

He sat his knees in the surf, the ocean rushing around him. He had been so terrified by what he'd heard while he swam towards Rebecca his arms numb. And since that moment, he'd been afraid that he would hear it again. Now he realized he'd been using up every ounce of his strength to suppress those last moments with his wife, but he couldn't anymore. The strain of it had finally broken him open and left him like this: just a thing stranded on the edge of the surf, exposed to all that horror again.

It was the feel of the salt water rolling over him — the taste of the ocean in his mouth — the way it had been that day that finally broke him down.

***

"I'll go," he'd managed to say to Jennifer. She'd let go of his hand. He started to swim, his life jacket making it almost impossible. He remembered that moment so clearly, the release of her hand, and immediately they started to move apart, the ocean tearing at them like bits of nothing, like so much flotsam from the boat that surrounded them. A wave rolled over his face, and when he looked, Jennifer had disappeared behind the inflating life raft.

He heard himself screaming as he'd screamed that day his wife was ripped away from him. His mouth filled with water and dregs of sand from the breaking surf. He screamed and stood up and looked out toward the north and saw that the smoke from the fire had built a kind of black line over the surf break, thin and pleading.

It hadn't been the water he was afraid of all this time. It was seeing Jennifer taken. He'd done everything in his power to not re-live that moment. It was as if he too were gone now. A great chunk of him went out to sea and he let it go without even trying. The fear had died, finally, disappearing. Gone forever.

He looked at the sliding water around him for his weapon. The surf rushed away, leaving bits of foam caught out quivering in the wind.

"You have to go," he heard Jennifer's voice. "You have to go now, Michael. Go!"

He turned and saw his wife. She was in shorts and wearing the backpack she'd worn when they'd been in Asia, years before, after they'd first met. He'd thought that there was one person in the world who could trip the lock and open him up to find what he'd been before the war, and he'd found her. She'd brought him back to life made him fully human again.

"Go," she said.

"I can't."

"You have to, Michael. She needs you."

"I can't. Didn't I die, too? That day? This is all a dream, isn't it?" He was transported to Angkor Wat again, standing in a long dark stone hallway littered with carvings and history. It had felt ancient-alive, full of the marrow of history. The carvings were grey-green, some marked with the scars of modern war.

"Jen!" He'd called her name because he'd lost sight of her, and she'd come out around a corner, laughing.

"I'm here, silly." It had started to rain over the Angkor Wat ruins, a tremendous rain shower, a magnificent downpour. Cleansing, he'd thought. They'd held each other and looked out at the magical rain beating against the temples, the sky beautifully mottled.

"Did I die, Jen?"

He watched her walk into the ocean. She picked up his weapon and threw it back toward him. It lay on the sand at his feet. He could smell the smoke from up the beach, acrid. He bent down and picked up his pistol. He looked out at the ocean. It was flat, fog-covered, cruel, unfeeling, moot. He looked out at it, then turned and ran up the beach, his shoes sodden. His eyes stung from the salt water.

Asha was climbing a huge pile of bleached drift wood logs that had collected for years in the snag of the cliff. The logs came from all over Asia on their trip to Limantour. The Colonel had doused one end of the enormous pile with gasoline and was videoing the fire for Nirad to watch. Asha climbed toward the crude pyre's top spot, the smoke sometimes obscuring her progress. The top was a tangle of great, upturned, bleached-by-the-sun logs, pushed around by the ocean until they'd been left here after one terrible storm after another. A haphazardly built Storm Temple.

It was a place he recognized. His daughter had climbed the huge tangle of driftwood, and they'd often come and taken small pieces from the pile for their campfires. It was where the sandstone cliff had collapsed in places, leaving a colorful, almost new looking gold cliff face, perfect. Raw.

The Colonel was holding his cell phone out in front of him, the jerry can beside him. He turned and looked at O'Higgins.

He ran by Das, ignoring him, and started to climb the pyre. He could hear the fire's ripping sound as it darted over and between the logs, smelling of gasoline. He turned and saw the Colonel lower his phone and reach for something. It was a look he recognized. He raised his Glock and fired. He emptied his pistol, the shots hammering the big man in the face. He turned and scrambled up the pyre toward Asha, the burning logs rolling dangerously underfoot, the heat terrible by the time he reached her.

***

His brother's house on the mesa in Bolinas had a view of Duxbury Reef. It was a two-story shingled Craftsman and very old, its wet shingles stuck out in the rain. It was empty when they walked in. It had started to rain as hard as he'd ever seen it as they made their way down Highway One turning right off the road from Limantour. They had not spoken from the moment he'd fired his weapon.

"It's my brother's place. He works in San Francisco. But he has a girlfriend … He'll stay there with her," O'Higgins said.

"Why, Michael? Why?" It was the first thing Asha said to him since he'd shot the Colonel dead.

"We'll have something to drink," he said. "You're wet."

She slapped him across the face. Her boots were still ash-covered, smeared dark from the flaming pyre he'd pulled her off. He just stared down at her boots, the horrible sight of her sitting on the pyre. The sound of the crashing surf, the look on her face, the resignation and the fear on it, too. Das holding a camera, recording it all.

"You're safe here," was all he said. They were both wet from the walk up to the house in the rain, the house fenced on one side by old cypress trees.

"Do you think I would be grateful? Is that what you thought?" she said angrily.

"I don't know what I thought," he said. "I'm in love with you. That's it. That's what I know. That's what I think."

"You're a bloody fool! You can't fix this! Don't you understand? He owns India. It's his to do with as he likes. Did you think you can stop that? I need to call him and explain. I'm going to tell him it's your fault! I'm going to tell him you shot Das —" She turned and walked into the living room with a big picture window. Outside was Duxbury Reef, the ocean sliding violently around its black rocks.

"I wasn't afraid," she said, moving toward the window, realizing what she was seeing.

"You're wet," he said stupidly.

"I wasn't afraid of dying. I thought I would be. I thought I couldn't do it, sati. When I saw the Colonel dousing the wood with gasoline — I just thought of my mother waiting for the girls. There's a big room with a view of the street at my parents' house. I thought of that room with my mother and her piano waiting for the girls. It was as if I was there with her, waiting for them. Why did you stop it?"

He walked into the kitchen. Dishes were in the sink, a laptop on the kitchen table. His brother, older than him, was a strange person in so many ways. He made big money as a brain surgeon, but gave most of it away. He lived here sometimes by himself, sometimes with a woman he'd met recently, another doctor, a young Chilean just out of medical school, half his age. They seemed to fight and break up and then get back together again, a circle of pain and love.

He turned the burner on and put on some hot water. His suit coat was soaked and heavy. He could smell the gasoline and wood smoke on his clothes.

It had been his brother who had stayed away from platitudes. The first time his brother had walked into their house after the accident he had not spoken a word, but had taken Michael's blood pressure and examined him, as he'd refused to go to the hospital despite a bad cut on his hand.

"You look like shit," his brother had said finally. At the time, and for days afterward, he'd not spoken more than a few words to anyone.

"I'm taking Rebecca to Mother's," his brother told him. "She's okay, physically."

"All right," Michael had said.

"It's a bad cut, but it will heal," his brother said. He'd cried in front of his brother then, like a little boy that had lost something. His crying had shocked his brother, who continued to stitch up his hand not saying anything.

"Where's Rebecca?" his brother asked.

"Her room."

"Do you want Mother to come? Stay with you."

"No. No one."

"All right," his brother said. "Do you want to come out to the beach? Maybe you two shouldn't be here right now."

"No. Take Rebecca to Mom's," he said. "Will you take care of her — if something, if something happens to me?"

"Okay."

He'd expected his brother to say something else, something ignorant, but he didn't. He'd understood, perhaps, that some pain is just too much to take. Perhaps only a scientist would understand that kind of pain, he thought, looking at the stove-ring's blue flame.

O'Higgins heard the kettle begin to whistle. He took his wet jacket off, laid it on a chair, then pulled the empty pistol from its holster. He set it on the counter and started to make tea.

Asha came into the kitchen. "Michael — I — I don't know what to do now," she said. She ran to him and threw her arms around him, crying. "I didn't want to die. Thank you."

CHAPTER 24

Michael watched Asha end the call, then lay her phone on her lap.

"Nirad wants to meet you. At our home, on Broadway," she said.

"Okay. You should turn your phone off, or they'll use it to trace you." He'd made her turn it off the moment she'd gotten back in the car at the beach. But he'd agreed to let her call Nirad.

"The girls? Can you get them back, Michael?"

"I don't know. Maybe," he said.

"Please. Try," Asha said.

She'd pulled an old purple Mexican blanket over her legs. His brother, Andrew, had traveled throughout Mexico, hitchhiking, after he'd gotten out of medical school. He'd sent back gifts, small things in the mail to everyone in the family. He'd been gone a year, walking away without having told anyone he was going. His brother was a brilliant neurosurgeon now, with a big practice in the city.

They'd spent the night at his brother's place in Bolinas. Michael called him at his office in San Francisco and asked him to stay away. It wasn't a problem, his brother said.

He'd wanted to be alone with Asha. It was selfish. He would have to go explain what had happened at the beach to the Marin

County Sheriff's Department. The body of an unidentified man had been found shot dead, people on horseback had discovered it on Limantour Beach. It was on the news.

"Okay. I'll try."

"Aren't you afraid of him? Nirad?"

"No. Should I be?" He smiled at her.

They'd slept in his brother's bed. The feel of her in the night, her touch-presence was extraordinary and wonderful. Making love to her was like sailing, before the accident, when he'd first started to learn and realized what it was like to be close to nature like that, hand-and-hand, and part of it: boat-man-water. That's what it was like making love to her, he thought, looking at her.

"It's strange that I saw Duxbury Reef like this," she said. She turned and looked out the window. His brother's house had been built above the reef on the Bolinas Mesa, with a perfect view of it. "It looks so cruel in real life — the reef — not like the painting. Here, it's cruel-looking."

She was wearing her black pants and a t-shirt they'd found in his brother's chest of drawers. Half the pulls off the chest of drawers were broken off. The chest was old, from a secondhand shop by the looks of it. His brother, a hippie, was brilliant but eccentric.

A poster of a ski jumper hung on the living room wall, the skier full on in the air, mid-jump. His brother was someone he didn't really know, Michael realized. But he loved him. Loved him for staying away. Loved him for knowing when not to talk or ask questions. Loved him for being a hippie surgeon who would disappear into Mexico and come back sunburnt and so alive and happy.

"You'll have to stay here. I've told my brother. I called from the landline. It will be safe. They won't know where you are. I'll come back for you in a day or two. Keep your phone off. Promise me," he said.

"All right. Can I call my mother from here?"

"No. Better if you don't. They'll expect you to call her."

"Will you go see him then? Nirad?"

"Yes."

"I love you," she said. "Please come back to me. I'm alone now."

He nodded and took a coat out of the hall closet. His brother was a big man too, but didn't seem like it, he thought, slipping on the coat that smelled of the beach. He handed her his backup revolver, the one he'd bought in Yuma, and showed her quickly how to use it if she had to.

He realized he was out of ammunition as he walked away from the house on the muddy dirt road leading down to where he'd left the Ford. He stopped at a gun shop in Petaluma, an old-school mom and pop place, and bought a box of nine millimeter ammo for the Glock. He called the Marin County Sheriff's Department from the car. Identifying himself as police, he explained that he'd shot a man in self-defense on Limantour Beach the day before, in the course of an ongoing investigation. Then he hung up.

***

They were sitting in Marvin's car in front of the Chaundhry family mansion on Broadway.

"What happened to your damn eyebrows?" Marvin asked him.

"They got singed," O'Higgins said.

"Did you shoot that asshole, Das?"

"Yes," O'Higgins said.

"Where's Asha?"

"At my brother's place," O'Higgins said.

"The Marin County Sheriff's office is looking for you," Marvin said.

"I know."

"Where's Rebecca?"

"She's at home. She's okay."

"Do you want me to go in there with you?"

"No. Call the cops, tell them I'm here?"

"You sure?" Marvin said.

"Yeah," O'Higgins said.

"Did you — you know?"

"It was a fair fight," O'Higgins said. "He was armed."

"Are you sure you want to talk to him? Nirad?"

"Yes," O'Higgins said.

"Why? He's no threat now."

"Because. I'm going to arrest him for the murders."

"You can't. You don't have any proof, Mike."

"Yes I do. It's in there somewhere. I know it. The murder weapon," O'Higgins said, turning to look at the house.

"It's too late, amigo. He's still holding all the cards. The DA is charging Robert Thomas. They've arrested him again. They found incriminating things from the house at his gallery. He's some kind of serial killer they think. Thomas," Marvin said.

"He didn't do it, Marvin. Not this time. I want you to leave. The police will come and pick me up for shooting the Colonel. You don't want to be here, Marvin."

"Mike —"

"Marvin, it's okay. I did it to myself. Right?"

"Stubborn Irish fuck," Marvin said.

"I'll need a lawyer, I guess," O'Higgins said.

He walked up the steps to the mansion. It was the first day in April. The sky was cold and blue and clear, all new feeling as if the world were starting over again. The fog would move down from the Marin Headlands and stop bothering the sailboats around the Golden Gate. All through April and into June it would stay clear, and sailors would be able to see the Farallon Islands to the west.

Tourists on the Golden Gate Bridge would see a place they'd dreamt about. Families would have strangers take photos of them that they would look at fondly years later. From Iceland to Egypt, these photos of excited family faces on Golden Gate existed in drawers and scrapbooks.

O'Higgins glanced out toward the bay, punched in the code to the Chaundhry mansion's front door and walked in.

"I'll pay you," Nirad said.

Chaundhry was standing alone in the living room. He put down his cell phone. He'd been speaking to someone. O'Higgins watched Marvin get in his car and pull off down the street. He imagined Rebecca with Marvin's daughters, and he smiled. He sensed that the world was changing when he saw the girls together, beyond the awful prejudices generations had grown up with.

Nirad turned and faced him, leaning on his cane.

"You killed the girl because she was pregnant. I understand that. But why Rishi? He was your son. You loved him — I saw the photos of the two of you, in the office. You and him. He kept them, so it must be true. He loved you," O'Higgins said.

"It was true," Nirad said. "He did. I did. I loved him too."

Nirad put his phone down. He leaned heavily on his cane

while he pocketed the phone. It was the cane he'd seen at the lawyer's office leaning against the conference table. It had a white ivory head of an elephant on the end of it.

"But you killed him. I don't get it. Why? That's what I want to know. I want to know what someone like you tells themselves."

"I came to offer you money to give me the photos of the girl and me. You took the phone back from Das. You still have her phone," Nirad said.

"How much?" O'Higgins said.

"How much do you want?" Chaundhry said.

"It's all about money, then?"

"Yes. Most of the time, yes. I'm afraid it is. My grandfather was a farmer. One bad crop, one late payment to the money lender and we would starve — I learnt what money meant then. We lost the farm and were forced to move to the city. Do you know what that's like in India, to be destitute? How much, Detective?"

"You tell me why you killed Rishi first."

"He was hysterical. He threatened that he would tell the press what I'd done."

"Why?"

"Because — the girl had gone to him, unfortunately."

"When you walked in that afternoon, Rishi knew about what you'd been doing to the girl?"

"Yes."

"Bharti Kumar knew she was pregnant?" O'Higgins said.

"Yes. I should have been more careful, but sometimes I can't control myself. It's a problem I've lived with my whole life. A bad temper. Impulsiveness."

"Careful?"

"Yes. How much, Detective? For the phone," Nirad said.

“And what happened when you got here? I want to know,” O’Higgins said.

“I told Rishi it was none of his affair.”

“You mean he wanted you to stop it.”

“We both lost our tempers, I suppose,” Nirad said. “But Asha thought Rishi was the guilty party.”

“Now you’re lying,” O’Higgins said.

“Asha killed them. I couldn’t stop her. I’m an old man,” Nirad said.

“You’re lying.”

“I want those photos. Give me Bharti’s phone,” Nirad said.

“Fuck you,” O’Higgins said.

“How much, Detective? Ten million. Is that enough?”

“Asha was at the market when you got home,” O’Higgins said. “That’s why you had to bribe the Gilberts, to make the timeline work. You killed them both, and then you walked across the street and picked up the girls and took them to the Consulate.”

“You’re in love with Asha, is that it? You’ll need money. She’s a spoilt girl. She won’t love you if she can’t have all of this.” He gestured around the room with the cane. “She’s used to it, you see. To having money, to the private planes, and the mansions around the world. She’ll leave you, Detective. What are you? Just a policeman. Twenty million for the phone?”

“Not enough,” O’Higgins said.

“What is it you want?” Nirad said.

“The truth. I want you to tell me what really happened. Tell me that, and I’ll give you the phone.”

“A full confession? There is no confession, because I didn’t do it.”

O’Higgins took out his phone. “I’m going to call someone,

and when I tell them, they'll send an email to the Times of India. It's all there, the photos. Just the best ones. You're an email away from being ruined. Is that what you want?"

He started to punch Madrone's cell phone number into his phone. "Yeah, it's me," O'Higgins said.

"Wait!" Nirad said.

"Hold it," O'Higgins spoke into the phone.

"How do I know — how do I know you'll give me what I want?" Nirad asked.

"You don't, asshole," O'Higgins said.

"Thirty million?" Nirad said, walking close to him.

"Send it," O'Higgins said into the phone.

"It's gone," Madrone said. "The file. Something's happened to it. The file is gone."

O'Higgins ended the call and put his phone down.

"We knew about what you planned. The Americans are very interested in me becoming Prime Minister," Nirad said. "They know about your friend, and they know your partner went to the Gilberts. Those photos are gone. All that is left is on that phone." Nirad stepped closer, so that he was close enough for O'Higgins to see the spit accumulating on the corners of the old man's mouth.

"You want to know what happened, that afternoon?" Nirad said.

O'Higgins realized that he'd been beaten. The evidence was gone. Probably from every place the photos had been sent. Kumar's phone was blank. Kumar's iCloud account had disappeared. Nirad Chaundhry was safe. The bluff was over. He'd won.

"You're a fool," Chaundhry said. He pulled at his cane, furious. O'Higgins saw a blade emerge as Nirad lunged at him with it, screaming, wild-eyed and murderous. The blade caught him in his side. The old man shoved it into him, running him through, a queer look of glee on his face. O'Higgins could feel the hilt touch his stomach, his gut punctured.

"I killed them both," Nirad said, his eyes bright with hate. "It's how the world works." He pressed the hilt into O'Higgins, his hand bloody. Nirad's face strained, his neck thick with hate and blood-engorged.

A gunshot fired. Nirad's face, looking at him, so terrifying, changed, its expression going soft.

Asha held the barrel of the gun against Nirad's side. O'Higgins reached down and drew the sword from his abdomen. He turned and saw Asha standing, the backup .38 from Yuma he'd left her in her hand. Neel was standing behind her. Both were watching Nirad, teetering as if they were watching some kind of immortal die.

Nirad was trying to stay upright, but buckled and fell onto his knees. He looked up at Asha in disbelief.

"Vishnu for protection," Nirad said. He tried to get to his phone, despite his wound. Neel stopped him, walking up and standing on the phone, crushing it, keeping Nirad from calling an ambulance until he bled out. The three of them watched him die.

Later, Asha came to visit O'Higgins in the hospital. She explained what Nirad had been saying as he was dying. It was a line in a famous Indian poem, Asha said as she pulled the curtains open, letting in the sunshine. It was the second day of April. He'd slept without dreaming. She walked from the window toward his hospital bed and quoted:

"Brahma for creation

Vishnu for protection
And Siva for termination.
Is there any gods made out of love?".

CHAPTER 25

He came to see Robert Thomas, who had confessed to several unsolved murders including his stepfather back in the 80s, before they moved him from the San Francisco County jail to San Quentin. Thomas had his own cell. The county jail smelled of cooped-up human beings, an amalgam of hapless young men's fears. Or was it just the stink of the vicious, O'Higgins wondered, being led down the cell block where he'd been countless times before. All of them, guilty and innocent, wanted to believe that someone, somewhere would intervene on their behalf. Hope is the last to die.

"How is Asha? She writes me, you know. Long letters. I have them all here. I re-read them. She writes wonderfully. All about India. It's like being there, reading her letters," Thomas said. "I always meant to go."

"She's fine," O'Higgins said.

"The girls," Thomas said. "She got them back. Thank God."

"Yes. She's with them. At her mother's."

"Good. Good," Thomas said.

The two men looked at each other. They'd shared something profound, and knew it.

"Why are you doing this?" O'Higgins said finally.

Robert Thomas had confessed and been found guilty of the

murders of Bharti Kumar and Rishi Chaundhry, and was sentenced to death by lethal injection. The case had faded from the headlines, in part because the U.S. State Department and various intelligence agencies worked to keep the trial out of the newspapers.

"Confessing, you mean?" Thomas said.

"To something you didn't do," O'Higgins said. "Yes."

"Not sure, exactly," Thomas said. "Guilt. I wanted to protect Asha. It was obvious what was going to happen if I didn't. And some men came here and said they'd make sure she got her children back if I said I'd done it. That I'd found his cane in the foyer. That I snuck in and killed them."

"I don't understand. The photos they had weren't enough to convict you," O'Higgins said. "We had the murder weapon. You weren't connected to it, Nirad was. It was his cane-sword. There were photos of him with it everywhere."

"I had been there, you know — stalking her. I'd stalked other women. I had a problem with that," Thomas said. "But Asha was different. I couldn't get her out of my mind once she walked into the store. It wasn't just the sexual attraction, that was the thing. It was something else."

He looked at O'Higgins. Thomas had been diminished by the jailhouse jumpsuit and the bad food and the fear of dying in a room with people watching him go. But for a moment he was back there, in the store, the day Asha had walked in off the street by chance. O'Higgins understood what he was saying about her, about her presence, about her power over them.

"I've nothing but time," Thomas said. "In Hinduism there's something called a Bodhisattva, I've read. A holy being, I guess they are. Is she one — Asha?"

"Maybe," O'Higgins said. "I don't know. Maybe."

"I read you were exonerated," Thomas said. "For the shooting on the beach."

"Line of duty," O'Higgins said. "The feds cleaned it up. I was in their way. Nirad's wife is going to be Prime Minister of India. It's all the same to them. I just have to keep my mouth shut."

"I want to — I was going to write you. I want to give you something. Something from the store. They're selling everything soon. But I made arrangements with the lawyers," Thomas said. "It's a painting, a painting of Tomales Bay."

"Okay. Thank you. I still don't understand," O'Higgins said. "Why?"

"I've done bad things. Doesn't matter now, I suppose, but I was changed. She — did something. I didn't want to do those things anymore. I love her. Asha. That's why. I can't quite understand it all myself. I wish I did. I just know I love her.

"Would you come?" Thomas asked. "When they — you know. Would you be there? They say you can't see who is watching. But if you were there — I would like that. I don't have any family left."

"Sure," O'Higgins said. "I promise. I'll be there."

***

51 Altamont Rd.
Mumbai
India

Dear Michael,

I'm so glad you were able to go — when Robert was executed. He said he'd asked you to go. He said he didn't want me there, or I would have gone. I would have done anything he asked.

He said he left you the painting of Tomales Bay. I'm so glad you have it. It's a remarkable painting. I remember so well the day I first saw it. I was standing on Geary Street and it was in his window.

I hope you keep it, and that I can come to see it. May I? I would like that very much. If you want me to.

The girls are fine, and call you uncle Ganesh.

Love,

Asha

O'Higgins put down the letter. Like Robert Thomas's, it came in wonderful old-school air mail envelopes, blue and red, sometimes with stamps depicting one of the Indian gods. He folded up the letter carefully, slipped it back into its envelope and walked to the kitchen window, holding it. The crows were back in the eucalyptus trees. It was summer again in San Rafael.

* * *

That morning of the execution, the entire morning before they came for him, he wasn't afraid. Robert Thomas was not in his cell at all, not really. He was looking at the wall of paintings in his gallery on Geary Street. He went to all the places in California again, walking slowly by each one, the way he had some mornings before he opened for the day.

Even when they finally injected him, he wasn't really there. He had turned and looked, once last time, at Asha Chaundhry as she walked through the door.

"It's a Piazzoni," Robert said, smiling at the young Indian woman. "My name is Robert — Robert Thomas."

And then he was gone.

Acknowledgments

I am very much indebted to those who have helped me understand the world of the two homicide detectives portrayed in this work. Many people in law enforcement have generously given me help in understanding how things work. Anything in this novel that is on-point about police work is certainly due to their generosity.

I especially want to thank Detective Michael Rodriguez of the LA County Sheriff's Department's Homicide Bureau, without whose assistance this novel would simply never have been written.

Det. Rodriguez made time for this novelist and my countless questions. Without his help I would not have had the confidence to take on this kind of book. It was Det. Rodriguez, too, who suggested I visit the department's famous Murder School, which LASD runs for new homicide detectives. That opportunity was the chance of a lifetime. Good fiction needs to be inspired fiction, and I can honestly say I left my visit to the school inspired and determined to get things right. I only hope I did.

I must also give a special thanks to Detective Richard Tomlin of LASD for taking me aside during lunch at the Murder School. In many ways Last Ferry Home started there over lunch with Detective Tomlin who had, I learned that afternoon, worked the Phil Spector case. His insights—given in a wonderfully cinematic way—concerning that case, and the extra pressures a homicide detective faces in high-profile murder cases, really brought his world to life for me. That conversation also, I think, infused this novel with something undefinable— perhaps just the spirit of a great and compassionate homicide detective.

Criminalists, the scientists who patrol homicide's always complex crime scene, are much more interesting, I think, than the characters we see portrayed on TV shows. TV misses something important about them as people and as front-line troops. They are not only highly intelligent and highly educated men and women—some have expertise in many related fields, from cell-phone cloning to blood cast-off patterns—but they are truly the murderer's bête noire.

So, to the Criminalists who helped guide me and took my calls: Tiffany F. Shew, Senior Criminalist LASD-SSB Biology/ DNA Section, Criminalist Christy Henry, and Criminalist Cordelia Willis—thank you so much!

About the Author

Kent Harrington is the author of numerous acclaimed novels, including *The Good Physician*, which was named as one of the best novels of the last ten years by *Booklist, Dark Ride, Dia de los Muertos*, and *The American Boys.* Of *Dark Ride*, Michael Connelly said, "It reads like Jim Thompson interpreted by Quentin Tarentino."

Visit him at http://www.kentharrington.com.